AN UNQUIET PLACE

An Unquiet Place

CLARE HOUSTON

PENGUIN BOOKS

For the real author, the miracle maker, the only one who can bring something out of nothing. That is what he has done with me.

Published in 2018 by Penguin Random House South Africa (Pty) Ltd
Company Reg No 1953/000441/07
The Estuaries No 4, Oxbow Crescent, Century Avenue, Century City, 7441, South Africa
PO Box 1144, Cape Town, 8000, South Africa
www.penguinrandomhouse.co.za

First edition, first printing 2018
1 3 5 7 9 8 6 4 2

ISBN 978-1-4152-0962-2 (Print)
ISBN 978-1-4152-1024-6 (ePub)

Cover design by Riaan Willemse
Author photograph by Shane Doyle
Text design by Fahiema Hallam
Set in Adobe Garamond Pro
Printed and bound in South Africa by Novus Print, a Novus Holdings company

MIX
Paper from
responsible sources
FSC
www.fsc.org
FSC® C022948

Penguin Random House is committed to a sustainable future for our business, our readers and our planet. This book is made from Forest Stewardship Council® certified paper.

CHAPTER ONE

High on the plateau, evening crept across the sky. Swallows pitched and swung through the air, and a small breeze lifted the grasses, sending a ripple across the surface of the reservoir. The breeze shivered through the grey leaves of the old gums, and gently picked up the skirts of a woman carrying buckets across the flat ground. A fabric kappie hid her hair, its floppy brim obscuring her face. Her tattered skirts brushed the tops of buttoned boots, their soles gaping with each step. The tin buckets were heavy. The handles cut into her blistered hands, causing her to wince as she walked, her bony shoulders taking the strain.

On the slope below the plateau, Alistair's herd of blesbok looked up from their grazing and the male snorted a warning. The woman placed her buckets on the ground, side by side. Bending low, as if ducking through a low door, she disappeared.

CHAPTER TWO

'What do you want, Hannah? It's nearly midnight.'
        'I need the paperwork for my car. You still have it.'
'So? I can carry on licensing it for you. My secretary does it.'
'No, I want to do it.'
'Why? You're useless at admin.'
'Todd, it's my car. I'm leaving Cape Town and I don't want you to be involved any more.'
'Jeez, Hannah, I was trying to be helpful. Fine. I'll get Monique to run it over in the morning.'
'No. I don't want to see her. I'll give you my new address.'
'What new address? Where are you going?'
'I'm moving to Leliehoek in the Free State.'
'Where?' She could hear his frustrated sigh. 'Grow up, Hannah. Don't sulk because Monique and I are now together. You left me, re-member?'
'Believe it or not, this isn't about you. I've got a new job.' His silence stretched for a moment before she filled it. 'It's in a bookstore. I need a break from … everything.'
'I suppose you're going to dump Patches on me before you go to Plaas Jaaphoek or wherever it is.'
'No, Todd. She's my cat. She and I are both going to have a new start.'
'Seriously, Hannah. You're really moving to the bundu? You? I don't buy it. You're just doing what you always do. Giving up and running away. I won't hold my breath – you'll be back.'
'You're such a bastard.'

'Say what you like, Hannah. I know you. You won't stick at this. You never engage. Never persist. You'll bail at the first hurdle.'

'Oh, piss off, Todd, and leave me alone!'

'You called me.'

Hannah swiped the call to an end, furious with herself. Why hadn't she emailed him rather? Kept it impersonal.

Rocking back in her chair, she stared at the old-fashioned ceiling of her room. She had grown up in the ramshackle Victorian house in Kenilworth, just above the railway line. Her parents lectured in the anthropology and classics departments at the university, treating the house much as they did Hannah. Spurts of attention every now and then, usually when something went wrong. Cupboard doors were replaced one by one as they came off their hinges, and flooring was replaced room by room as needed, the result a hodgepodge of styles and colour which Maud and Stephen Harrison rather liked.

Piles of books inhabited every room, stashed behind couches or teetering on small tables. Hannah found the clutter overwhelming. When she had left Todd, she had walked away from rails of dressy outfits and work suits. An enormous shoe rack left untouched, except for her running shoes and a pair of blue plastic flip-flops. She didn't know or care what Todd had done with all her stuff. She guessed the housekeeper had bundled it into black bags and had it delivered to the nearest SPCA shop. Monique would balk at even handling second-hand clothes, let alone wearing them. Hannah had seen a few pictures of them in the Sunday newspapers, usually on the society pages, and couldn't help a small, malicious smile at the printing which had distorted their features so their eyes hovered to the left of their faces.

She didn't miss that life for a second, and just felt enormous relief that she no longer had to force herself into the ghastly miasma of false faces and breathless small talk. She had gone along with the bulldozing flow of Todd's charisma from the moment they had met on Jammie steps all those years ago. A break between under-grad lectures, a patch of sun on an otherwise chilly Cape autumn day, and an introduction by someone in her English class were all it took to put her on a fast-moving track that had pulled Hannah along for so many years. The biggest betrayal was that their relationship had been instigated and driven by him, and then he had dropped her. Like a pair of old shoes. Shaped and moulded to fit his feet and then binned when he'd decided they were no longer useful. It bit her still.

Hannah had sworn she would take control of her life at last. That said, she had moved back in with her parents, registered for a PhD, and struggled every moment to wade through something she wasn't interested in. Coming back home after leaving Todd was like immersing herself in a familiar, suffocating pool.

Her room hadn't changed at all since school. Her blazer still hung in the cupboard and seeing it today, as she emptied her few clothes into a suitcase, brought a mix of fondness and leaking sadness at the memory of her young self. Boldly pretty and so confident she would make a success of her future. Honours braids and badges had set her up believing that the world was completely hers for the taking; that a career and a man and a family would fall into place as if owed to her. Now, at thirty, all she had to her name was a half-finished thesis that not even she wanted to read.

Hannah climbed into her childhood bed and pulled the quilt up to her ear. She closed her eyes, crossing her arms over her chest and curling up like a child. Her back was to the desk lamp, which cast a soft yellow glow across the room. It didn't matter how many years passed. The dark still frightened her. Sometimes she wondered if she hadn't stayed with Todd just so she wouldn't be alone at night.

The shrill alarm came far too quickly. Hannah stumbled from her bed. She pulled on her jeans, T-shirt, and a fleecy top, twisting her hair into a ponytail. Padding in her socked feet down the old staircase, she sat on the bottom step and pulled on her running shoes. Patchy followed her into the kitchen and Hannah quickly grabbed her, pushing her into the cat box. Patchy's indignant expression made Hannah smile. 'Patchy, you and I are going on an adventure.' On the kitchen table was a bowl with ProNutro already poured, the sugar bowl set alongside it. Hannah peeped into an ice-cream tub next to her place and grinned at the neatly wrapped sandwiches and chocolate brownie that were packed inside. A thermos stood alongside the tub, and Hannah knew that inside would be sweet milky coffee. Nellie's thoughtfulness brought a lump to Hannah's throat. Nellie had worked for the Harrisons for as long as Hannah could remember. A solid presence at Hannah's back, rather like that feeling when she woke in the night and lay facing the shadows in the room, but knowing that the wall was behind her – no attack could come from there.

She gulped down her breakfast, picked up Patchy, and let herself out, pulling the door and hearing the Yale lock click into place. It seemed to signal a life closing behind her and, as she reversed her Mazda pickup out of the garage, she felt like she was heading into no man's land. One door closed, and nothing yet open before her.

The highways around Cape Town were never empty, and it was four am by the time Hannah cleared the outskirts of the city, heading up the N1 towards Paarl. The sun began to rise as she passed through the Hex River Valley, the sky lighting pink over black, ragged mountains. She passed the stony town of Laingsburg, her little Mazda purring as they cruised along, the landscape opening up into the spectacular expanse of the Karoo. Miles and miles of semi-desert, coloured in greys and oranges. Small sparse bushes dotted the ground and, in the distance, rose-blue mountains.

The road stretched before and behind her in an absolutely straight blue ribbon to the horizon, the November sun glaring bright off the now silver-and-green landscape. Crossing the Orange River, the longest in South Africa, was a milestone in Hannah's day. It marked her entry into the Free State, taking her well over the halfway mark. The landscape shifted after Bloemfontein to vast fields which stretched flat to the horizon. She passed kilometres of maize, wheat, and sunflowers. The golden light was softer and more forgiving than the bright white light of the Cape. She smiled to herself, fancying that maybe life here could also be so.

At a small town called Winburg, she turned off onto the N5. As she passed the dusty-looking town, she caught a glimpse of tall concrete needle-like structures set back against the hillside. She had heard of the second Voortrekker Monument, dedicated to those fierce, determined pioneers who had crossed the rough country by ox wagon. Their history was much contested now. The apartheid government had turned the Voortrekkers into an idealised mythology and now the pendulum had swung, with their history removed from school curricula and their monuments defaced. Hannah wondered as she drove, *What if somewhere in the middle, they were ordinary farmers looking for a quiet place to settle?* She smiled at the thought of how wild that would make her mother. Her academic mother, who, despite – or perhaps because of – her Afrikaans roots, would now make a strong case against the Afrikaner history having any place in a new South Africa.

When Hannah saw the first sign to Leliehoek, she gave a shout of triumph, 'We did it, Patch! A freaking long way in one day and we did it.' At half past five in the afternoon, she turned off the main road into the small town. A tall stone Dutch Reformed church stood on the corner, appearing too large for the scale of the little town. The light had faded, dimming the stretch of grass on the town square to blue-green. On the next corner, old trees shadowed a small stone Anglican church. The shops around the square were quaint. A gallery nestled alongside a cafe and a gift shop, and on the opposite corner Hannah could see a bistro-style restaurant. Next door was an attractive old house, newly painted white with a narrow stoep running along two sides. A metal sign hung on one of the stoep's wooden pillars, 'Leliehoek Books'.

Hannah parked alongside the house. As she was rummaging for her bag in the debris of the passenger footwell, a short man with dark curly hair and thick black-framed spectacles opened the garden gate at the back of the house. He stood on the pavement with his hands in his back pockets, grinning at Hannah.

'You are so welcome, Hannah Harrison,' he said. 'I told Chris that we must wait – and here you are!'

Giving up on her bag, Hannah unfolded her long, stiff legs from the car and was engulfed in a hug, just managing to squeak, 'Hi, Tim,' before the breath was squeezed out of her.

'You must be so tired from that drive, goodness me … Let's get you inside. Chris is champing at the bit and the car is all packed. Our flight to Oz leaves on Sunday and we're spending our last day with friends in Joburg. I can't believe we're actually leaving. I know Chris needs to explore this. I know he does. He's given up so much for me, you know, agreeing to live in the backwoods and working from home. Now's his chance to try something new.'

Hannah nodded, her scrambled brain only just keeping up with the continuous stream of chatter. 'How long will you stay in Australia?'

'For the foreseeable future. We need to give it a proper shot, you know? Although I just couldn't bring myself to sell this place. Not until we know for sure that it will work out over there. I need some security, and we worked so hard on it.'

Tim steered her up the garden path. A tall, distinguished-looking man opened the French door with a smile.

'I'm Chris. Come in,' he said.

She stepped into a spacious kitchen, decorated in country style. It was furnished with free-standing antique pieces. A dresser with glass-fronted doors held a collection of pretty, mismatched china, and a square kitchen table and chairs stood in the middle of the room. Set below a window was a rectangular porcelain sink, plumbed into a concrete plinth with an old-fashioned copper tap and spout.

'This is gorgeous,' Hannah said.

'We just love it!' said Tim. '*Country Life* did a feature last year – you might have seen it? We're auction addicts, so we've picked up bits and pieces over the years, and it's all just come together so beautifully.'

'Let's show Hannah the rest of the house,' said Chris, 'and then we really must be getting on the road.' He ushered Hannah into the passage. To the right was a small bathroom.

'That bath is the pride of the house,' said Tim, peeking over Hannah's shoulder. 'We found it in the compost heap. Can you believe it? Look at those clawed feet.'

Hannah smiled back at him. 'We have two at home, but my parents' bathrooms haven't been updated since … well, ever really.'

'Ooh, authentic,' said Tim.

'More like neglected,' said Hannah, grinning.

'And this,' Tim continued his tour, 'is our tiny lounge–study. You know, in summer we live on the deck outside, so it's really only in winter or on rainy weekends that we sit here. And we do use the fireplace,' he said, gesturing at a small Victorian stove. 'It's heaven on a freezing night – warms up the whole house actually.'

'There's Wi-Fi throughout the house and garden – I use it for work,' said Chris from the doorway. Another French door, like the one in the kitchen, led out onto the wooden deck with a wrought-iron table and chairs.

The garden, in the soft early evening, was lovely. It had been carefully planted to look wild, with roses rambling amid meadow grasses and herbs. Clumps of aloes broke the softness with their thick structured leaves. Hannah could see the hand of a clever gardener.

'It's beautiful,' said Hannah.

'It's Chris's work,' said Tim. 'I just follow instructions and do the manual labour.'

Hannah turned back inside and found the last room in the house. The bedroom window looked onto a narrow strip of garden that bounded the property. A tall hedge marked the fence line, and between this and the house was a grove of small trees, planted close together, groundcover spread at their feet.

'Those trees are just alive with birds in the mornings,' said Tim, 'gorgeous to wake up to.' Chris rolled his eyes at Hannah, who smiled. Cotton rugs were spread on the wooden floor and, like the other rooms, simple antique furniture was used to create a neutral, fresh look.

'And lastly, the shop,' said Tim. 'I told you that Barbara would be in tomorrow to really give you the rundown. She's lovely. Organised but not bossy, which is the exact opposite of me, so we made a great team.'

A door blocked the passage. Tim opened it and led the way into the other half of the house. Hannah breathed deeply, the woody scent of old books floating on the air.

'These two rooms must've been the front living rooms of the old house – they work perfectly for the shop,' said Tim, standing aside to let Hannah pass. 'This room on the right is where we keep our second-hand stock.'

Polished wooden floorboards warmed the feel of the room, echoing comfortingly as Hannah entered. White-painted bookshelves reached from floor to ceiling around the room. Books filled the shelves, stacked with their spines facing out. Hannah ran her finger along their edges, leather and gilt alongside faded fabric and cracked paperback.

A Victorian tiled fireplace stood at one end of the room with a battered leather couch and a velvet-upholstered wing-back chair facing the fireplace. An antique table and chairs stood in the centre of the room. It had the feel of an old-fashioned English reading room, and Hannah smiled at the thought of spending her days there.

'Working here might be a problem,' she said, quickly adding as Tim turned to her with frown, 'I mean, with all these books and this room. So distracting.'

Tim smiled. 'You'll see, the shop gets busy. There won't be a lot of time.'

'People sit here and read, especially in winter when Tim lights the fire,' said Chris.

'Our new stock and the till are over here,' said Tim, leading the way across the passage. This room too was filled with white-painted bookshelves, but they displayed glossy books, covers facing out.

Hannah crossed to the desk where a new computer presided over the shelves below, stacked with ledgers. Chris caught her frown. 'Honey, you could do this in your sleep. It's just running the shop and managing stock, and we have Barbara to help you. You could do it easily without her, but she's retired and loves the company. She makes enough pocket money to take her to Joburg to see her daughter.'

Tim chipped in, 'She'll show you the computer system. It's pretty up to date but not difficult to use – even I manage it.'

Tim and Chris walked Hannah back through to the kitchen.

'Mind the doorstop,' said Chris, pointing to an old Victorian iron holding the door open. 'That thing has taken at least two of my toenails!'

'But it's too cute to abandon,' said Tim. 'It's the real thing, you know. I love the idea of little irons lined up on the woodstove to heat. So romantic.'

'Unless you actually have to iron with them, I'd imagine,' said Hannah.

'Exactly.' said Chris, laughing.

They stood with her on the deck outside the kitchen.

'We so love this place.' Tim's eyes glittered with tears. 'Selling it would have broken my heart. You know, I advertised for a manager for six months without a single response. And then you called out of the blue! It's providence or fate or something ...' Tim turned to Hannah, anxiety pulling his brows into a frown as leaving became real. 'I feel like we've dumped this on you. Will you be okay?'

'I think so,' said Hannah, forcing a confident smile. 'I'll give it my best shot anyway.'

'She's going to be brilliant,' said Chris with his hand on Tim's shoulder. He looked across at her and winked. 'There are a dozen people in this town who'll be knocking on your door tomorrow to help you. And, as of Tuesday next week, we'll be online to field any questions you have. I left a file in the kitchen with basic information. Emergency numbers, refuse collection days – useful stuff.'

Hannah smiled at him, feeling marginally encouraged by his faith in her.

'And anyway,' he said, 'you're a bright girl, you'll figure it out.'

Their white BMW SUV was parked in the street, jackets and a laptop on the back seat.

'Bye, gorgeous girl,' said Chris, hugging Hannah warmly.

They drove away, leaving Hannah staring after them, feeling as though she had been run over by a train.

From deep inside her own car, she heard a mournful yowl.

'Oh, Patchy!'

When the cat was safely, if grumpily, shut in the bathroom, Hannah set about unpacking her car.

At last, she turned on the kettle and began opening all the old-fashioned canisters on the counter. Tim and Chris seemed to have collected every possible flavour of herbal tea. Eventually, the biggest mug she could find was steaming on the counter, the scent of Five Roses drifting in the warm evening air. The men had stocked their retro-style fridge for her, and it burgeoned with produce and expensive-looking deli packages.

She moved to the edge of the deck leading to the garden and sat on the top step, hunching over her knees and sipping her tea. She breathed deeply and hung her head back, looking up at the now pale sky. Swallows and swifts were wheeling about in the last light and, as the garden dimmed, a bat dropped out of the eaves behind her and disappeared into the evening. Hannah was bone-tired from her day's driving, but underneath that was a pump of anticipation. It had been many years since she had not known what tomorrow held for her. Nobody had given her permission to be here; in fact, her parents didn't even know where she was. She felt a trickle of rebellion and, laying her cheek on her knees, found herself smiling.

CHAPTER THREE

A knock at his kitchen door broke Alistair Barlow's concentration. He sighed, pushing his chair back from his desk as he heard his mother call hello. Her footsteps thumped briskly on the wooden floors as she came down the passage towards his study. Sarah Barlow stopped in the doorway, looking at her son. Spreadsheets were open on his computer screen and his desk was piled with paperwork. His hair was tousled into a crest where he had pushed it back repeatedly. He knew he looked tired.

'What, Mum?' he said, resigned to her intrusion.

She ignored his question. 'What are you busy with?'

He pushed his hair back again and glanced at the screen. 'Game sales mainly. I'm trying to keep on top of admin so that the farm audit in February isn't a panic like last year.'

'You've got a lot on your plate, Alistair. You know how much better your father is now that he doesn't have to worry about all this desk work? It was never his strong point. I'm just sorry it takes up so much of your life at the moment. I'd love for you to get some time to do other things, see some people …'

'What were you wanting, Mum?' said Alistair, hoping to divert her attention away from his social life.

'I'm heading into Leliehoek and was wondering if you needed anything?'

'No, I've got everything I need,' he said shortly.

'No, you don't. Your kitchen is practically empty.'

'How would you know that, Mum? Been going through my cupboards again?'

'No, of course not, but I did check in the fridge. You're down to half a litre of milk and a beer.'

'Sounds like enough to me,' said Alistair deliberately, knowing this would rile his mother.

'Alistair Barlow!' said Sarah, rising – as she always did – to the bait. 'I stand by. I watch you limp along with your life without so much as a comment. I love you. I don't think you realise how hard it is for me to see you like this.'

'Like what, Mum?' Alistair sighed and leant back in his chair.

'You're becoming a recluse. You never go out. You never see any of your old friends. You've lost interest in all the things you used to love doing. We're worried about you. I mean, your sisters and I are. Your father takes your side. He says you need time, but it's been eight years, Alistair! Isn't that enough?'

Alistair's eyes hardened. Pushed beyond his usual resignation, his voice turned cold and he said slowly, 'Do not, for one second, think that I don't know exactly how long it has been.'

Sarah stepped into the room towards him, her face filled with concern.

Alistair turned from her to his computer, and said, 'I live with what I did every single day.'

'You did nothing, Alistair. For heaven's sake! What's it going to take for you to let go of this crazy guilt?'

'Please just go, Mum. I'm not up to going around and around this with you today.'

'Alistair, I'm your mother. I can't help loving you.'

'Is it loving or suffocating, Mum?' he said sharply.

He heard her intake of breath and he winced inside. There was no satisfaction in hearing her footsteps retreat down the passage and the front door slam shut behind her.

In the kitchen, he moved the kettle onto the gas hob. Leaning back against the counter, he scrubbed his face with his hands, willing his head to clear. He opened the fridge for milk and saw, stacked in a neat pile, five plastic ice-cream containers. Each was neatly labelled in his mother's handwriting. Chicken curry, bolognaise, oxtail stew, cottage pie, sweet-and-sour chicken.

'Dammit!' he said, as guilt rose.

Back in his office, his coffee stood untouched, the surface wrinkling into a cold skin. The view from the window looked across the farmyard to the old stables where ploughs and water tank trailers now lined up with two tractors. His thoughts saw a different view, though. Eight years ago, horses had dominated the yard. The ring of hooves, soft snorts and grumbles, and that sweet, dank smell were as much part of the house as the stones themselves.

Alistair sighed, pulling himself back to the present, and trying to see through the past to the work open in front of him. He laid his head down on the desk instead, his cheek pressed to the old wood. His gaze came to rest on a carved frame. The glass in the frame caught the sun, and he shifted it slightly. His smooth face was grinning down at Marilie, one arm pulling her towards him. Her wedding gown trailed in the dust of the farm road, but her eyes and smile were serene as she looked directly through the camera to the present. Alistair grabbed the frame and, opening the bottom drawer of his desk, stuffed the picture beneath a pile of scrap paper. Enough. He pushed himself out of his chair and headed out the house, sliding his keys off the hallstand at the back door.

The dogs sped around the side of the house like a tornado at his whistle. The diesel engine of his Toyota Hilux roared to life, and the dogs went mad at his door, jumping and play-biting at one another. Once out the yard, he turned off onto a track that would take him to the higher pastures of the farm.

As he drove, he noted the small herd of blesbok grazing on the hillside and counted four calves. He had lost a few last year to predators. Jackals had obviously been at the carcasses but he had wondered, and secretly hoped, that a leopard might've been responsible. He had looked for tracks, but knew that leopards living wild in the ravines and pockets of forest would never be seen.

Alistair was passionate about rehabilitating the land. He'd researched shifting farming practice to imitate the natural grazing patterns of the old herds that used to move through the Free State in their thousands. Years of eliminating the use of insecticides and other poisons had made a visible difference in the landscape. Veld flowers and bulbs had appeared this past spring like had never been seen in his family's memory. The hillsides had been a pink wash of Watsonias, the cooler folds of land filled with the flash of white arum lilies.

Hunting and trapping were forbidden on the farm, and they were seeing the results. Animals that had not been seen on the farm for generations were returning, and with them came the ecological knock-on of plants and insects and birds.

He had had many arguments with his father in the beginning but, slowly, as Alistair was given more leeway with the farm, his father had seen the changes and relented. Now, as his dad withdrew from the active running of the farm, Alistair saw him enjoying the farm more than ever. He walked every day with his binoculars, came home excited he had seen something new.

Thinking about his parents snagged something in Alistair. He and his sisters had grown up secure and much loved. Their childhood had been idyllic, dreamlike even, he thought now. It had done absolutely nothing to prepare Alistair for the brutality that life was to throw him.

The dogs caught up with the pickup and overtook Alistair as he slowed to handle the uneven, rolling track. Hugging the side of the hill, the track wound steeply to meet a wire fence gate at the top. Alistair left the engine idling as he unhooked the loop which pulled the wire-and-pole gate taut. He dragged the gate across and dropped it on the grass. The Toyota crested a rise, and a wide plateau opened up in front of him. A steel wind pump towered over a round concrete reservoir. Leaving his door open, Alistair crossed to it and stood up on his toes to peer into the dam. The end of a black rubber pipe jutted out into the reservoir, dripping into the deep green water. As Alistair sank back onto his heels, his boots squelched into mud. A concrete trough lay to one side, filled from the reservoir by a pipe with a shut-off valve controlling flow. Today, the water in the trough overflowed, leaking down and pooling on the ground. Alistair squatted, reaching into the water to examine the valve. The surface had been warmed by the day's sun but, below the surface, his arm slid into smooth cool water. The orange plastic float controlling the water flow looked cracked. Kobie would have to come up with some tools and repair it.

Alistair stood, wiping wet hands on the back of his jeans. The sun was low in the sky now, and the light bent the wind pump's long shadow to the east. It was silent. No wind stirred in the line of eucalyptus trees and there were no animals about – there never were. The water was good, and so Alistair and his father kept the water trough filled, but it had a desolate feel, this part of the farm. It was stony, the vegetation growing in sparse patches rather than the thick cover of grass which grew elsewhere.

He hadn't liked this place as a child, and still found it strangely unsettling, creepy even. It was only as an adult, when he could override the irrationality of his deeper feelings, that he came up here. In fact, like today, he came as an obstinate show he could override emotion with logic; that the deeper currents could be pushed back by will.

He turned back to his vehicle to find all three dogs sitting in the cab, watching him. The dogs' tongues lolled out the sides of their mouths, their tails thumping the plastic upholstery. 'Out! Lee, Jackson, out!' The black and cream Labradors jumped out the car, leaving the biggest dog of them all, the Rhodesian ridgeback, sitting in the cab. He sat resolutely looking out the front windscreen. 'Grant! Out, you mopey mutt!' said Alistair, leaning on the open door.

The dogs trotted behind the Toyota, their exuberance exercised out of them for the day. Back on the gravel road, Alistair gunned the engine and the Toyota leapt forwards. Grant, with his long loping stride, gave a last push of energy and came bulleting past the cab. No doubt he would already be grinning on the step when the truck pulled into the yard. Alistair smiled for the first time that day.

CHAPTER FOUR

Hannah surfaced through kilometres of sleep, pulled by desperate yowls coming from the bathroom. Grey light seeped from beneath her curtains. She stretched to turn off the bedside light, surprised at how deeply she had slept. Usually, she lay awake for ages, needing the light to keep the darkness at bay. But now she had no memory of anything after climbing into bed and pulling the quilt up. It was a first.

In just her sleep shorts and T-shirt, she carried Patch out into the garden. Her bare feet sank into the wet grass, the dew chilling her toes. She watched as the cat, with wild wide eyes, slunk slowly across the lawn into a flowerbed, looking for a toilet spot. Hannah averted her eyes, feeling ridiculous as she did so. A few minutes later, Hannah scooped up the cat and retreated into the kitchen. 'Patch, a week inside for you, I think. Just until it feels like home.'

Hannah's stomach growled, last night's toast long forgotten. She found a glass canister of muesli which looked homemade, rich with nuts, and topped it with thick Greek yoghurt. Her pantry would no doubt retreat to ordinary once she had finished Tim and Chris's supplies.

Out of the shower, she rubbed her wet hair with a towel and ran a brush through it, wincing at the snagging long tangles. Todd had insisted it always be ironed into sleek brown waves to the middle of her back. Said it was her best feature. She had slashed it short in defiance and rage when she'd left him. It had grown out a bit, now brushing her shoulders, long enough to pull into a ponytail to keep it out of her face. She didn't own a hairdryer any longer, and simply pulled a hair elastic onto her wrist for later. A glance in the mirror had her grimacing at the unmade-up face reflected back at her. Maybe jeans and a t-shirt were too casual for a store manager. Maybe she should get some proper shoes.

She took a breath, pulled her shoulders back, and stepped into the passage, unlocking the interleading door. As she drew the door closed behind her, the Yale lock on the shop's front door clicked back. A Doc Martens boot pushed the door open, and there stood a woman with spiky white hair, balancing a quilted bag and two take-away coffee cups. They stood for a moment, staring at each other, before the woman said, 'You must be Hannah.'

'And you would be Barbara?'

'I would, yes. Take these, will you?' Hannah grabbed the cups and followed Barbara to the desk, watching her stow the embroidered bag in a drawer. Though Barbara's mouth did not smile, her eyes crinkled as she said, 'Tim is a nut, but even I was surprised that he would dump this shop on you and disappear.'

'I'm not sure who is more of a nut, him or me,' said Hannah.

'Indeed,' said Barbara, humour evident on her face as she looked Hannah up and down. 'Let's just say that being … unusual … is an advantage in this town. It's a small place and people will make it their business to know all of yours. Being on the quirky side means they'll write you off as eccentric and not delve too deeply into your life. Believe me, I know this.'

Hannah took in Barbara's dangly guinea-fowl earrings and black waistcoat, embroidered with little mirrors, and believed her.

'Right, let's get this show on the road. You stand here,' said Barbara as she ushered Hannah in behind the desk to the computer. 'I always say the easiest way to learn a new system is to do it.'

She had Hannah practise all the applications on the computer, learning to record sales, register stock, and find books using the store's software. She then showed Hannah the cataloguing system, which ordered the shelves, so that she could go directly to the right shelf for any particular book. They spent a good two hours working through every aspect of the shop's systems.

'As you have to do things, you'll figure it out and then get more comfortable with it,' Barbara said. 'And people here already know all about you, so they'll cut you slack if you make mistakes.'

Hannah looked up sharply. 'What do you mean, they know all about me?'

'Part of Tim's charm was his willingness to chat to customers. They will all be in on Monday to see you for themselves.' Barbara grinned at Hannah's discomfort. 'Don't look so worried. They're harmless. Mostly.'

'Great,' muttered Hannah.

Still grinning, Barbara hauled a large cardboard box from under the desk. 'We're not open today – Tim felt you should have a day to adjust. I thought we could go through this box of second-hand stuff. It's been sitting here for ages, but what with Tim and Chris's getting ready to go and my manning the shop, we simply haven't had the time.'

'What should I look for?' said Hannah, opening the cardboard flaps. The dry smell of dusty books hit her, half fish moth and half fraying leather. She sneezed.

'It's your shop now. You decide. It came from a deceased estate in Bethlehem. Someone thought we might be interested. See if you are.' She left Hannah dragging the box into the reading room, and disappeared into the apartment to find something to eat.

Hannah heaved the box onto the table and began sifting through the books. Most were written in Afrikaans, in variable condition. Some were held together only by a few binding threads. Looking through their introductory pages, some interspersed with tissue paper leaves, Hannah saw that many were first editions published in the 1950s. When Barbara came back with the two cups of tea and a little plate of biscotti, Hannah took hers to the computer and began to google Africana book values. She eventually happened onto an auction site, where she investigated how to sell rare books.

'Barbara, was Tim selling any stock online?' called Hannah.

'Heavens no. He hates computers, could barely bring himself to ring up a sale.'

'It might be worth exploring though. From what I can see here, books that would never see the light of day on a shelf can be viewed by anyone internationally. I must explore how to register as a dealer and see if it would be worthwhile for us.'

'You see?' Barbara's face appeared round the door, grinning at Hannah over the rim of her cup. 'Your first day and you've found a market we would never have dreamt of. Good for you.'

Hannah smiled back. 'We'll see. Don't get your hopes up.'

She separated the old books into piles of valuable-looking editions and more generic copies. When she reached the bottom of the box, she saw, lying flat against the base, a hard-covered ledger. The spine was deep maroon, as were the corners, and the cover, a dark royal blue. She lifted it out. The pages were ruled with lines and red ink columns were printed to the right of each page. The pages, however, were filled with writing – tiny writing that spidered from edge to edge, making the ledger printing redundant. It was in Afrikaans. Hannah's gaze flicked to the top of the first page, which began with the words:

> This is the account of Rachel Badenhorst, aged twelve years, of Silwerfontein, Orange Free State, 1899.

Hannah's mind ran through what she knew of that period in South Africa's history. It had to have been written at the time of the South African War when Britain wrested control from the Boer republics. She sank into a chair and began reading, carefully turning each delicate, browned page. She had to adjust to the language. A friend who had been with her in the languages department at university had called this deep Afrikaans, rarely seen now outside of universities and older literature.

> 10 November 1899, Silwerfontein, Orange Free State
> Dear Wolf,
> Oupa Jakob has given me this ledger, and I will write an account of life on the farm for you. When you return, you can read it and know that everything here has remained just the same.

It has been a month since you and Pa left. A whole month. Time has slowed to a crawl and, although Ma is trying to fill the time with extra tasks, I find myself with too much time to think. I think Ma feels the same as I do because she is working harder than I have ever seen. She calls it spring cleaning, but no spring has seen the house this clean. We have washed every curtain and window. The walls have been scrubbed inside and out, and when it is too hot to work in the sun, she hauls out linen from the chest to mend. You know how determined she can be. Even Oupa Jakob has not been able to stop her. It's as if she wants to exhaust herself so she can collapse on her bed at night and sleep without dreaming. We all say the right things: that you and Pa will be home for Christmas, that the British are no match for our strong, passionate men, but then there is a silent, low twisting pain that sits in me. What if we're wrong? So we do what Ma says. Even Kristina is listening, so you know how serious Ma must be!

Streams of burghers are moving through the valley on their way to Harrismith and the Natal border. Ma says we must stay close to the house. Ma says they may be burghers, but they are still men, and a decent household of women should rather keep their distance. Kristina and I climbed the ridge, though, and watched the lines of men and horses from up there. Sitting in the shade of a rock with a picnic basket felt like we were watching a parade. The men are in good spirits, talking and laughing together. It must be so with you too.

I am looking after Spikkels. She is well, but I can see that she misses you and Lofdal. Paul takes her out to ride, but he has to exercise Sokkies and Feetjie too, so she doesn't get as good a gallop as when you are here. Oupa Jakob says we have to keep all the animals close to the house now. He says there will be days coming when all the wrong sorts of people will be wandering the veld. Now we must look to our boundaries.

I pray for you every night, Wolf. You and Pa.
Rachel

As Hannah read, she smiled at the pictures conjured by Rachel's voice – the strong, formidable Ma who would do anything to keep her family together. Life on the farm where horses became family members. Hannah wondered about Wolf, this clearly adored brother who rode off to war with his father. People pushed to the limit of their endurance and strength. Hannah settled back into the chair and continued reading …

22 December 1899, Silwerfontein, Orange Free State

Dear Wolf,

It's been two months since the war broke out and the end is not yet in sight! I wish we knew where you were. We hear the reports from Ladysmith and Mafeking, but we don't know if you and Pa were part of either. Freddie Basson came home to his mother last week. He was shot in the leg but is doing fine. Ma says he will have an ugly scar. Just think how Freddie will love showing it off! He told Ma he was with you and Pa until he was sent home. It's very wrong of me, but something in me wishes you could come home too. With just a small wound, mind!

December has not been a good month for our Free State. The stories (which I'm sure you hear too) coming from the western border speak of Khakis overrunning the battlefields. People are starting to wonder if it is indeed possible to stand against the might of the British. This is new talk and it frightens me.

It is Christmas this week, but what a different one it will be! I wonder if we will even gather for church like we always do. It feels like we have been stuck on the farm forever.

Obviously, Tannie Elsie and the children will not be coming from Pretoria, and we will miss the games and the chaos they bring.

Other men in the district seem to visit their families often. Oom Steyn came home to help plant their fields and his sons seem to return home every second week for horses or food. Why aren't you coming home like they are? Ma says they are abandoning their duties and we should be proud of you and Pa, so committed to the Boer cause. But still, she is packing parcels for you in the hope you and Pa make it home for Christmas.

Things on the farm are quiet. I have started lessons again with Oupa Jakob. He tries so hard to force Kristina to sit with us, but she is only interested in running free. At nine o'clock, when we sit at the table on the stoep, Kristina is nowhere to be found. She emerges at lunchtime with twigs in her hair, as if she has been hiding in the bushes until lessons are over!

Paul is miserable company. He hates being the only boy in the household. He resents having to manage his work without you, and complains you are having all the fun. He wants more than anything to be in the veld with you and Pa. If he were not only ten, I would worry he'd run away to find you. Oupa Jakob tries to distract him with interesting lessons, but he is like you. Why sit at a table doing sums and writing when the sun is shining, there are horses to ride, and the veld to explore? It would seem I am the only one who likes lessons. In fact, the time with Oupa Jakob flies by and, before we know it, Ma is frowning at the door and I must pack away quickly and help her with the midday meal.

Lizzie is growing so fast. You will see a big change in her when you come home! She is losing her fat knees and wrists which I love so much. She reminds me of you more and more. None of the wild joy of Kristina, but she is full of happy contentment. She is quiet as she plays, but I can see her following every conversation with her clever blue eyes so like yours. She knows what she wants, but is too good natured to fight about it and, in the end, we all give in to her anyway. If she were in charge of this war, both sides would part smiling, convinced they had each received the better deal.

There, Ma is calling me. There are chickens to pluck. Life is not the same here without you, Wolf. The brightness has disappeared.

Rachel

Barbara's voice called from the next room, drawing Hannah from the ledger. 'Sweet cat, by the way – she was begging to go outside so I let her out into the garden.'

'What?' Hannah leapt from behind the desk, sprinting down the passage and out the kitchen door to the deck. 'Patchy?' Her heart skipped in panic. She looked around desperately and, out the corner of her eye, spied the gleam of white curled on the cushion of an outdoor chair. There lay Patch, warm in the sun, squinting at Hannah. Hannah ran her hand down the sleek, sun-warmed coat. 'Comfortable enough? You think you can manage this new life?' The rattling purr was answer enough.

Barbara innocently dunked her biscotti into her tea. 'I hope you can bake like Tim. These cherry biscotti are better than anything one can buy.'

'No luck, I'm afraid,' said Hannah, helping herself to one and accepting the change of subject. 'I blew up my mother's microwave warming a mince pie once. The force and temperature of that fruit mince pitted the interior and almost blew the door off its hinges.'

Barbara choked on her biscotti, and Hannah took her cup back to the reading room, saying over her shoulder, 'I haven't attempted anything since.' She grinned to herself at the spluttering laughter which came from the other room.

CHAPTER FIVE

Kobie turned the key and the scrambler engine died with a sputter. The silence dropped, heavy and cold around him, ringing in his ears. The sun had disappeared an hour ago, leaving the sky an insipid grey. He glanced up, expecting to see summer swallows swinging from the air to dive low over the grass, but the plateau was empty. It was perfectly still, a blueish light casting the grasses in silver. A light shiver ran up his spine, and the skin on the back of his neck rose. He had been coming up here for sixty years and had never felt at ease.

He swung his leg off the bike, old knees creaking as he walked across to the water trough. The orange plastic float was indeed split, and water ran continuously from the reservoir, brimming over the rough concrete edges and turning the dust surrounds into thick mud. Animals stayed away from this place, but Mr Alistair wanted the trough kept in use, especially now in summer when the daytime temperatures reached the mid-thirties. Kobie squatted, submerging his arm in the icy water to close the valve. He drew a breath at the sting of the cold, frowning at the incongruence. Concentrating hard on unscrewing the brass arm, he didn't immediately register the mud he was standing in. It was trampled, as if many feet had walked in and out. He straightened and stared. Much like a herd of cattle would do to the surrounds of a water hole, this mud was pocked with footprints. Footprints, not hoofprints. Bare feet and boots had ploughed up the mud, some leaving small prints deeply pressed. Small, careful feet, carrying heavy weights.

Kobie quickly finished removing the float and retreated to his motorbike, disturbed. Nobody came up here but him. Maybe Mr Alistair every now and then in his pickup, but certainly not crowds of people or children. He kicked the bike's engine to life and, as he turned his back on the plateau, a faint, thin crying reached across the cold air. Over the shudder of the engine, it needled his skin into a crawl.

25 March 1900, Silwerfontein, Orange Free State

Dear Wolf,

Bloemfontein has fallen, and we hear reports of the Khakis moving south. I never dreamt the Free State would be breached, nor that the outcome of this awful war would be in doubt. We are most shaken by this news.

On the farm, things seem to remain the same. I feel like I'm repeating myself about lessons and horses and work. I apologise if the entries have become short, but it is truly a reflection of our wartime life here. We may not leave the homestead unaccompanied, and there is no one to accompany us. So here we are.

April 1900

We keep hearing news of our wonderful Commander-in-Chief, General De Wet. Have you met him? His victories give us hope that we might prevail against the Khaki storm.

Lizzie asks about you every day: 'Tell me stories about Wolf, Rachel. Tell me about when you were little.' I'm afraid I told her about your stealing Pa's peach brandy and it nearly blowing the top of your head off! If Ma overheard, she hasn't said anything, but I think you're safe from a scolding. She would give anything to see you. As would I.

Late May 1900

We have lost Winburg and Kroonstad this month. How much closer can they come? We have heard that Roberts has 'annexed' the Orange Free State for the Queen, and changed its name to Orange River Colony. Ha! As if he has control of the whole republic because he has a few towns occupied! It is so obvious he doesn't understand us. We have our farms and the veld under our feet still. President Steyn's government is now mobile, but his lead is still the one we follow. I take comfort knowing that you and Pa are on your horses, riding where the British cannot march, invisible because they don't know where to look.

June 1900

We received word from Tannie Elsie this week. She is disheartened but not broken by the British occupation of Johannesburg and Pretoria. The Transvaal government and President Kruger left the city in good time, so people can take comfort that all is not lost, though their capital has been. She remains in her house for the moment. She has the shop to run, and no doubt will continue to do well. The Khakis are likely to enjoy her tobacco and cigarettes as much as the burghers did!

August 1900

The war has come to our doorstep. First Bethlehem fell, and then we began to see burghers – hundreds and hundreds of them – coming over the hills and down the roads. And you were amongst them! I cannot describe our joy when you and Pa rode through the gate. I know it wasn't for long, and that you needed to get into position on the Nek, but that single day was most precious to me. I'm sorry Lizzie was scared of you; I tried to tell her it was you and Pa, but you both looked so different. So hard and tall and thin. And too serious to match her memories of you.

The past month has been nightmarish. When you left, we had to steel ourselves not to weep openly, though I wanted to more than anything. Ma said it would upset you and you would need to focus and be in control. This leaving was the worst. Especially with what followed.

We guessed you would be guarding Naauwpoort Nek to stop the Khakis breaking through into the Basin. We have always felt so safe here in our valley, surrounded by mountains. Now the war had come to our boundary. We knew you were up there on the hillside protecting us. But then the bombardment on Naauwpoort Nek began and we could hear the guns from the house. I have never heard the like, and hope I never will again. Like staccato thunder, those guns boomed, and all we could do was sit in the house and pray for your safety. At two o'clock it became quiet and we continued to sit, not knowing who had won or who was dead.

When Pa came riding through the gate alone, I saw Ma's knees buckle, though she held the doorframe for support. He scaled the steps in one stride and pulled her into his arms. I had never seen them display affection, but this was a different day. He whispered fiercely into her neck and then looked over her weeping shoulder to where I was standing, hoping I looked stronger than I felt. 'He's fine, Rachel. He's fine,' were the sweetest words in my ears. Pa had come to say goodbye before you both left quickly for the Golden Gate Pass. He said he planned to escape the Basin. All the passes had fallen, and everyone left was trapped. He said he had lost faith in General Prinsloo and was going to make a run for it. He didn't know where you and he were going, but he hoped to join General De Wet. He grasped Ma's arms, holding her firm, his eyes worried, and said, 'Aletta, hulle kom.'

5 November 1900, Silwerfontein, Orange Free State (my small defiance)

Dear Wolf,

Life has changed dramatically in the district. We are all on edge. There has been much British movement through the valley since General Prinsloo's surrender at Brandwater Basin. We have been told we have to inform the British authorities of any 'enemy' presence on our farms. If we don't, they will assume we are supporting the commandos and we will be punished. Already, the Van Rooyens' farmhouse has been burnt down. Tannie Grietjie and her children are hiding in a cave in the cliffs.

We are seeing more and more Boer families on the road, women with their children packed into wagons heading for who knows where. There is nowhere to go, and they can only wander the veld, hoping to return to their homes eventually. Ma says they're crazy. It's dangerous in the veld now. Soldiers are everywhere, and the commandos have to move fast. Even if they wanted to, they could not let their families travel with them. There are rumours the British are making camps for the refugees where they can be fed. Ma says it's a trick, that they'll be kept prisoner there.

Silwerfontein has been lucky so far. They have left us alone. We've had the odd soldier looking for food, but they have been no threat, and Ma packs them a parcel of bread and tells them she thinks our menfolk have been taken prisoner already. That you and Pa are probably in Cape Town. They nod apologetically, grateful for her kindness. She watches them ride away with her fingers crossed behind her back.

The vegetable garden has done well this season, and our pantry is full. We are careful, keeping the animals close. Maybe we'll be able to ride out the war like this. Quiet and circumspect.

I miss you, Wolf, but I don't want you to come home. It is too risky – for you and for us.

February 1901, Silwerfontein, Orange Free State

Dear Wolf,

I've hidden in the fort we made in the hedge. Ma is looking for me to start the week's washing. Kristina is looking for me to walk with her to the orchard. I just need a little time to write to you without being disturbed. You'll be able to imagine the scene exactly. It's a hot day (it's why Ma wants to get the washing done and hung out) and my hideout here in the shade is delicious.

The farm continues as usual. Not much to report, except Oupa Jakob returned from the neighbours worried. Oom Steyn said more farms are being burnt. He said the British aren't even waiting for an argument or proof that we are 'colluding' with the commandos. That they are just burning indiscriminately now. Ma said that Oom Steyn has always been full of gloom and we can't believe everything he says. Anyway, I think that th

The sentence ended abruptly. Underneath, a heavy double line had been drawn across the page. Below the line, Rachel continued in pencil. The writing became much harder to read, scrawled and more desperate.

March 1901, Goshen, Orange River Colony
(Have I given up on our 'free' state already?)

Dear Wolf,

Oupa Jakob always told us that reading and writing would be more valuable than shooting, riding, or making a fire. Everyone used to shake their heads at him. How could it possibly be true when you lived in the veld where those skills would keep you alive? Most people only have the family Bible and most cannot read it anyway. I never understood what he meant until now. Now this ledger is most precious to me.

I think of Oupa Jakob every time I take it from my blanket. I think of the lessons on the stoep at home, squeezed between our chores. Oupa Jakob's insistence on the lesson time every day, even though Ma wanted us to help more. Especially me. I can feel that sideways guilt of knowing I should be stirring the washing rather than sitting there with you. You, peeking at my slate, copying my answers. Me, keeping my arm clear to give you a good view. I loved every moment of sitting next to you.

I tried to work harder, faster, to make up the time for Ma. I heard her tell Ouma Anna it would be trouble teaching me to read. That Oupa was spoiling me for work – what good could come of giving me ideas? But he loved me. He said I was clever and quick. And he was the head of the family. Who could cross him? I can see him cajoling Kristina to sit with us too, but she danced away from him, laughing and tossing her curly hair. Even Oupa's stern look behind those bushy eyebrows wasn't enough for Kristina. Six years old and she had all of our hearts on a string, didn't she?

I want to write and write about our family, as if I could write them into life, to stand in front of me like before. I fear so much that I will forget their faces. I thought, if we were compliant and quiet and careful, then the British wouldn't bother us. I had no idea what was coming.

Groups of soldiers began coming to the house more. What happens when men are in a group? How does an ordinary man on his own turn ugly in a group? They became more demanding, not satisfied with a simple parcel of food. They wanted information. They wanted liquor. They wanted anything valuable in the house. They shouted and demanded. Ma started to hide the little girls when she saw riders approach. They called us undesirables because you and Pa are on commando fighting. They said that if you surrendered, we would be looked after. We must tell our menfolk to give up, they said. Ha! If only they knew Ma like I do. I saw her eyes harden, the signal to get out of her way. Her lips, compressed and silent, but I knew how angry she was.

I was in the fort in the hedge, hiding from Ma, when the British came to the house for the last time. I heard their shouts and stamping horses. I kept hiding. I am a coward. I just couldn't come out. I wanted to, but I couldn't, Wolf. I could see Ma and the girls running, grabbing what they could, coming out the house with blankets, pots, and what warm clothes they could find.

The soldiers took all the food. Even the jars of konfyt we'd worked so hard at last year were loaded into their carts. Two Boer men herded all the cattle together and drove them away, their shame sneering like dogs, tails between their legs.

Then the worst – the soldiers went into the kraals and shot everything – the pigs and goats, the chickens. Wolf, they shot Lofdal. He and Sokkies came to the fence to greet them, and they just lifted their rifles and fired. And when the horses tried to get up, they shot them again and again. They chased the dogs into the stable and shot them till they were quiet. Kristina's dogs. Like a nightmare, those shots ringing off the stone kraal walls and Kristina screaming.

Little Lizzie had her head buried in Ma's skirt, and Ma just stood with her eyes distant and cold and hard as stone. Ma and the little girls were loaded onto our wagon.

Oupa Jakob stood in the yard, turning in a slow circle, looking for me. I knew he couldn't call me, didn't want to give me away, but his eyes were desperate, searching, searching. He looked like a crazy old fool, turning around and around. I couldn't stop the tears or the sobs which seemed to come from so deep, my stomach hurt. Then I heard his voice. He was too far away for me to see his lips move, but I heard it as clearly as if he were crouching next to me in the bush, a whisper, 'You're strong and clever, Rachel. Think on your feet and make yourself useful, make yourself indispensable.' To this day I don't know how I heard him whisper.

The soldiers bundled him into the wagon, another old man crazed with grief. Kristina was quiet now and sitting on Oupa's lap with his long arms wrapped around her. I remember her big eyes, shocked and staring. Lizzie clung to Ma, her face hidden from me. And me, trying so hard to be brave for Oupa, but I could feel my eyes stinging and my mouth twitching like it wasn't mine. I watched them drive away from me – and that was the last time I saw them.

The soldiers were finishing up now, and they set fire to the house. They smashed our lamps against the walls, the oil running down the white-washed walls, its stringent reek reaching my nostrils across the yard. A soldier had been slouching against a wagon and now he took one last deep pull at his cigarette before tossing it into the paraffin. Blue flames flared tall, stretching for the roof. I squeezed my eyes shut for a moment, waiting for the thatch to catch, and suddenly it was a snapping, cracking roar. Then the white lattice on the stoep buckled and collapsed. That sweet smell of grass fire, which I always loved, now makes my stomach clench and brings before my eyes the furious fall of our house.

They found me eventually, hauling me out of my hiding place and dragging me over to the officer in charge. He cast disinterested eyes at me until his gaze rested on this book. Pulling it from me, he opened it and threw it on the floor. He gestured towards a wagon which was being loaded with sacks from our barn. I just managed to scoop it up before I was pushed into the wagon. I knew those sacks were full of our potatoes and cabbages. As the wagon began to trundle out of the yard, I asked the driver where we were going. He was a black man, dressed like a burgher, and he spoke Afrikaans to me. He told me they were taking me to the camp close by, the one called Goshen. I asked if the others were going there too. He looked at me strangely and shook his head. 'No, child. You are now alone. They've gone to Winburg.'

Hannah sat back in her chair, her thoughts skittering around what she had found. She knew there had been concentration camps in the South African War. They were run by the British as refugee camps for Boer women and children displaced by the British farm-burning policies. She remembered her fierce ouma saying that, though the Nazis took concentration camps to another level, the British had used them before Hitler had been out of short pants. Hannah had never taken it any further, never read or researched that part of South Africa's history at all. More than that, it had been local; it probably happened within a hundred kilometres of where she was sitting. Bethlehem, where the box of books had come from, was the closest town to Leliehoek, after all.

Closing the ledger and carrying it to the shop desk, she typed into the Google search page, *concentration camp, South African War, Goshen*. A thrill of anticipation bubbled as the page loaded. A list of options appeared, references to the war, to the camps, but all had the search word *Goshen* missing. Underneath these came references to Goshen, but they were unconnected to the war. She changed the search words to *Goshen, Orange Free State*. A link appeared at the top of the list and she clicked on it. A scenic shot of fields with red-gold sandstone cliffs in the background. The page was titled 'Goshen Farm, farming for the future by restoring the past'. Below this banner were posts about game auctions and stock sales. She clicked on 'Contact Us'. Farm telephone numbers below the name Alistair Barlow. The address, a post office box in Leliehoek.

Hannah jumped as Barbara peered into the room from the doorway. 'Sorry, didn't mean to startle you.'

'No, I'm just silly. I was so engrossed, I forgot you were here.'

'Nice to hear I'm forgettable,' Barbara said with a grin. 'I'm off. Going home to make myself some lunch and have a little siesta before the rugby. Don't stay locked up inside all day.'

'What rugby?' said Hannah, her eyes glued to the screen.

Barbara rolled her eyes. 'When I said it's good to be eccentric, Hannah, I didn't mean there are no limits. If you are going to make any kind of conversation with any men in the district, you had better keep up with the rugby. Eccentric to them means supporting the Sharks instead of the Cheetahs.'

'I'd better do some research, then. I mean, my primary motive in coming here was to meet men after all.' Hannah looked up, a smile tugging at her mouth.

With a grin and a wave, Barbara let herself out the door.

Hannah returned to the screen, clicking on maps and finding directions from Leliehoek to Goshen. A flag appeared, not far out of town. She took note of the road to get to the farm and then shut down the computer.

As she retreated to her apartment, Hannah's stomach reminded her that it was past lunchtime. She took her chicken and rocket sandwich out onto the deck where Patchy hadn't moved an inch since early that morning. Pulling a wrought-iron chair into the shade of the umbrella and drawing her feet up, Hannah reimmersed herself in Rachel Badenhorst's story.

As the wagon rolled away from the house, I stared at the crate of jars from our pantry, some with shaky labels written by Ouma Anna before she died last year. Pickled green beans and chutney and stewed peaches we would never taste. My mouth waters now at the thought of those jars, the sweetness and bite I've almost forgotten after weeks of camp food. Her berry jam on hot, thick slices of my bread. Remember Ma saying I had the touch when it came to baking bread? Somehow my kneading hands could draw the dough to rise light and soft as air. Oupa Jakob called it Rachel's Best Bread. My mouth has forgotten it now, even though my mind has not. I came with no money, so I can't buy extra rations, and the work I do in the latrines just pays for mealie meal once a day.

My old dress hangs on me. It may be just rags, but I'm better off than most. I work in the camp fields some days. The soldiers bring us seed, and we grow decent vegetables, but most of the produce goes off in wagons to the army. Only people with money get to buy from the soldiers. I sneak a carrot or a cabbage leaf. I see the children who only eat mealie meal. Their gums swell and their teeth fall out; the babies' joints ache so that they cry when they move. They don't last long. I'm strong and clever, and now I'm a thief. Would Ma and Pa be proud of me? Pa's Bible reading haunts me. We knew passages by heart, and sometimes I say them over and over. It takes me back to the voorkamer, to the candlelight and our family's voices saying the Psalms.

How long wilt thou forget me, O LORD? For ever? How long wilt thou hide thy face from me? How long shall I take counsel in my soul, having sorrow in my heart daily? How long shall mine enemy be exalted over me? Consider and hear me, O LORD my God: lighten mine eyes, lest I sleep the sleep of death; Lest mine enemy say, I have prevailed against him; and those that trouble me rejoice when I am moved.

But I can't finish it, Wolf. I can't say I trust in His mercy. My heart cannot rejoice. I will not sing to the Lord. He has not dealt bountifully with me. Ma would slap me for that. It is ungrateful and blasphemous, but I am angry and I don't know how I will ever be peaceful again. I am alone. I am useful but alone.

Hannah surfaced to the slight chill on her skin. Great charcoal clouds now obscured the sun. The light had shifted to a surreal green. The garden had a glow to it she had never seen in the Cape. And she thought of Rachel, who would have lived through afternoons just like this, but seen them through a pall of hungry misery. The aloneness of Rachel's voice pulled at Hannah. It drew a deep recognition, a feeling Hannah knew well but refused to let surface. Even in the midst of a family, a full and busy life, Hannah sometimes felt it too. Not being invisible exactly, but living unacknowledged.

Fat drops of rain began to fall around Hannah, spotting the deck slowly at first, and then faster and harder. Hannah gathered her things and ducked into the kitchen, leaving the French doors open. The earthy scent of the rain infused the room. Sheets of white rain now drummed on the corrugated-iron roof, punctuated by flashes of lightning. Thunder rolled in the distance.

Half an hour later the storm had moved on, leaving lighter flurries of rain which then dwindled to nothing. The sun ventured out and cast flashes of reflection off every dripping branch. Who wouldn't prefer this to the days and days of grey winter wet that the Cape weathered? She glanced at the journal lying open on the table. Rachel had prodded something in her, something tender, like a bruise you couldn't help pressing. What on earth would come of it?

April 1901, Goshen Camp, Orange River Colony

Dear Wolf,

Goshen. This is not what I pictured when Pa read to us from the Bible. Goshen was the best land in Egypt, given to Joseph to settle his family, wasn't it? A blessed place, a refuge from famine. Here I am, in Goshen, with no family. I have to spend every effort to find food. What horrible joke is this?

The camp is so close to home – we travelled just a short distance on the cart to get here – but it is a wild, hidden place, a plateau with a hill between us and the road. No one will find me, even if you and Pa went back to the farm, why would you look here for me? The wind whistles ice across the hillside; there is no escape from it. I have a coat now. It does not fit me well, but it is thick and warm enough. Gone are the niceties of burying people in their best. Survival trumps respect, doesn't it? Wolf, will you still like me when we meet again?

We found a bag of tree seeds yesterday, in amongst the other seed. Another delivery error. I joined the camp children and we planted those seeds in a line across the edge of the camp, a windbreak none of us will see grown. I tend those trees, though they have no benefit for me. Just a tin of water and they have taken. Tiny, spindly baby trees that grasp on life. They are like me, thirsty and desperate to cling on, but tough, showing a tenacity absent in the people around me. Something draws me to keeping those little trees alive, though it seems impossible even to think of a time beyond this camp. I know that so many of us won't survive to see it.

People dig graves every day. Mothers burying children and children burying mothers. There are now rows of graves outside the camp. The British like to order everything, even death. The strength of those left behind determines how the graves look. Some are marked with flat stones from the veld, names carved in deep grooves into the stone. Some are heaped with small stones. And then, for those who have no one to mourn them, the earth mounds are just left to flatten over time. I don't have anyone to bury, and when I'm dead it won't matter who buries me. I'll be piled into one of those holes with the other unclaimed dead. No one will visit my grave with a stone for every visit, a mark of memory. Perhaps this journal is my mark. Perhaps someone will read this and think of me, Rachel Badenhorst, of Silwerfontein, aged thirteen years.

I wish it to be you, Wolf.

CHAPTER SIX

Hannah opened her eyes and reached over to the bedside table, checking the time. Eight o'clock. And Sunday. No reason at all to get out of bed. She rolled over and closed her eyes again, smiling at the prospect of another hour in bed.

Patchy jumped up softly, padding up to Hannah's head. With one paw, she gently batted at Hannah's face. Hannah groaned and pulled the quilt up over her face. Patchy eyed her through a gap in the sheets, and then a paw prodded Hannah's cheek again.

'Okay, okay, I'm getting up!'

Stumbling down the passage, she tripped over the Victorian iron doorstop as she headed into the kitchen. Both Patchy and Tim received a curse as she nursed her toe, the nail torn and bruised.

Sipping her strong cup of tea, she opened the French doors and stepped onto the deck. The sun was already deliciously hot on her skin, the garden humming with life after the rain.

Her thoughts wandered to the journal. Why not spend today exploring the site of the camp? She gobbled her breakfast and pulled on her running shoes, envisaging a walk up a hillside to the memorial site. Twisting her hair into a ponytail and, with her scribbled notes folded into her jeans pocket, she locked the cottage.

Just outside of Leliehoek, she took a tar road to the right, and drove for ten minutes before seeing a sign post for Goshen Farm. A dirt road ran between pastures on either side. Around a corner, the fields dropped away to a wooded ribbon which, she guessed, followed a stream. The road curved and, crossing a cattle grid, she found herself in a park-like garden where lawns stretched between the shades of old trees. She passed a quaint stone cottage, where standard iceberg roses stood in a row along the drive, and flowerbeds rambled up against the walls of the little house.

Further along the drive, she caught sight of a much larger house, also of tawny sandstone. A wide veranda sprawled along three sides of the house. It too was set amid a striking garden, but it was far more utilitarian, with agapanthus plants and succulents massed in huge groups, giving it a more formal feel than the warm softness of the cottage. The drive ended in a circle that had a sundial and aloe garden at its centre.

She took a minute to admire the setting. The house looked over the garden towards the steep red-gold cliff faces of a mountain. Trees grew thickly at its base along what she thought must be the river she had seen earlier. She slammed her car door shut, and then froze as a storm of barking came around the house. First to appear was an enormous ridgeback who galloped straight for Hannah, as though intent on swallowing her whole. She braced herself, squeezing her eyes shut in terror. When, a second later, she opened them again, the huge dog was standing in front of her, sniffing her jeans and wagging his tail. By this time, two Labradors had joined them and proceeded to gambol around her, their tails thumping her legs. She gingerly offered the dogs her hand to sniff, and was rewarded with licks and broad grins from all three.

As she looked up from stroking the ridgeback's head, she saw a tall, lean man standing in the farmhouse doorway. His brows were drawn down into a frown, darkening his face.

'Um, hi,' said Hannah, smiling uncertainly and trying to direct the ridgeback's nose out of her crotch.

The man came down the three steps and, as he drew closer, she could see that a white scar ran from his nose, slicing his right cheek and pulling the corner of his mouth down. It destroyed what must once have been a beautiful face.

'Visitors are by appointment only,' he said curtly.

'Sorry,' Hannah stumbled over her tongue. 'I was looking for Alistair Barlow? I've just arrived from Cape Town—'

'I thought I made it clear in my email a few weeks ago that I wasn't interested in your eco-tourism venture.'

'Um, actually, no—'

He cut her off again: 'What do you mean, no? This isn't a debate.' His eyes hardened to a flinty glare.

'Um, no, I mean I'm not here about a tourism venture … I'm looking for the camp site.'

'There is no camping here.' His voice dropped to a scary softness. 'Get the fuck off my farm.'

Realising she was not going to rescue this, Hannah got into the driver's seat, started the engine, and drove off. She looked in her mirror and saw the man staring after her. His hands were shoved deep in his pockets, the dogs sitting at his feet, looking up at him, their tails thumping the ground.

Hannah was furious. She drove back over the cattle grid, the rumbling of the tyres over those bars jarring, just like her thoughts. What the hell was that? That horrible man. Maybe she should just turn the car around and go back. Shred that cold façade with the hot words that were boiling out of her now. She thought of a million things she could have shouted at him, but she had been completely tongue-tied. He had walked all over her, told her to get the fuck off his farm. Nobody had ever spoken to her like that. *Well, you bastard. I will not. I'll find the camp site myself.* She swung the Mazda onto a track that trailed between two sloped fields. Her little car bounced and scraped along the track, and she slowed to a crawl. The storm had softened the track, and what were clearly tractor tracks had now become two parallel ditches of mud. Anger fuelled her determination to keep going along the track which was deteriorating fast. Eventually, the Mazda ground to a halt, tyres spinning in her increasingly futile attempts to rev the car out of there. She gave up at last and, opening her door, managed to leap from the cab to the grass edge of the track. From this angle, she could see that her car was well and truly stuck. This made her even angrier. She had left her cellphone in her bedside drawer, loving the freedom of not being contactable. That had come back to bite her. Dammit!

She slammed the Mazda's door as hard as she could, reaping tiny satisfaction from the car's shudder. Then, turning back, she made her way down the track towards the farm road, keeping to the grass verge. By the time she came to the road, her running shoes were sopping wet, the hems of her jeans mud-soaked. She stopped at the end of the track, debating with herself whether to make her way back to the farmhouse for help or head for the main road. Thinking that she would rather take her chances with potential axe-murdering motorists than approach the farm owner again, Hannah turned for the road.

Five minutes later, walking resolutely down the farm road, she heard the approach of a vehicle. It came into view before she could scramble and hide, so she kept walking, her head high. The Isuzu pickup drew alongside her and a good-looking older man hung his elbow over the window frame.

'Can I help you with something?'

Hannah stopped and looked into warm eyes, crinkled at the corners. He was wearing a two-toned khaki-and-blue shirt. A Jack Russell lay across the seat behind the man's shoulders, its stubby tail wagging against the man's sunburnt neck.

'My bakkie got stuck up the track. I need a tow, I think.'

'That, I can help you with,' he said, smiling. 'Hop in. I'm Neil Barlow and this is Jim Beam.' He put a hand behind his neck to the little dog.

'Hannah Harrison,' she said and grinned at him in relief.

He looked quizzically at her as he drove off down the road. 'I'm at a complete loss as to who you are and how you got stuck on the farm. We don't see many young people here any more.'

'I'm new in town,' she said, wanting to steer the conversation away from exactly how she had ended up stuck on the track. 'I'm managing the bookshop in Leliehoek.'

'Tim's shop? For how long?'

'Well, Tim and Chris are going to try life in Australia. If they settle there, then ...' Hannah shrugged.

Neil looked back from the road to her. 'Isn't that interesting. It's about time we had another beautiful girl in town.'

'That's the best welcome I've had since I arrived,' said Hannah, laughing. 'So, who is the other beautiful girl?'

'That would be Sarah Breedt – she stopped my heart when I first saw her.'

'So you're a ladies man, Mr Barlow.' Hannah looked out her window and couldn't help feeling a little disappointed in this charming man.

He smiled across at her. 'My name is Neil, please. And I'm one lady's man. Sarah married me forty years ago, and I'm still flummoxed that she chose me in the first place.'

'Oh,' said Hannah, 'your wife.'

'I saw a sign in a shop – you know those knick-knacky shops?' Hannah nodded, smiling as he continued. 'The sign said, "Every love story is beautiful but ours is my favourite." That's true for me.'

Hannah felt drawn to indulge him, and was beginning to get an inkling as to why Sarah might have chosen him. 'Are you going to tell me?'

'Well,' he said, settling in to his tale, 'we met on a train from Pietermaritzburg. Sarah had been at university there and was on her way home to Leliehoek, and I was finishing my studies at Cedara College of Agriculture and going home to Johannesburg.'

'So you had a farm in the Transvaal?' said Hannah.

'No.' Neil glanced at her, his eyes twinkling. 'There was no farm in the family at all. My parents wanted me to be a businessman and I just wanted to be a farmer. The thought of their intelligent, good-looking son' – Neil winked at Hannah – 'being a farm manager was definitely not in their plans for me. Anyway, by the time Sarah and I reached Ladysmith, instead of changing trains for Joburg, I changed my ticket to spend more time with her. We arrived at Bethlehem station together, and Sarah's parents just assumed I was a long-standing boyfriend from university, not some stranger she had picked up a few hours previously.'

'And what happened?'

'At the end of the Christmas holiday, Sarah returned to finish her last year of studies and left me working for her father on Goshen. She graduated that year and married me. We moved into a cottage that Sarah's granny had lived in, and you know what?' Hannah shook her head. 'It felt like I was home for the first time in my life. Thirty years later, we moved back into that cottage to allow my son to have the farmhouse.'

Hannah coveted the sweet simplicity of his story. Her story was messy. Too many bruised relationships she was limping away from.

She indicated the turn-off to the track up ahead and stared at him in surprise as he drove straight past it. 'My car is up there,' she said, pointing up the track again. 'Aren't we going to tow it?'

'Yes, we are, but this bakkie doesn't have a winch on the front. I'm going to pick up my son's Hilux. Is that okay?'

Hannah hoped her non-committal murmur passed for a response while she slid a few inches down in her seat. She could feel her cheeks flush as they headed up the driveway and took a road Hannah hadn't noticed earlier, one that led behind the main house.

They pulled into a farmyard where tractors and equipment were parked in a large shed. A kitchen garden, planted with herbs and vegetables sprawled from the back of the house, and a paved path divided the garden, leading to what looked like a kitchen door. Neil crossed to another farm vehicle, a white Toyota Hilux with railings around the bed at the back. He checked for keys. 'I'll be right back – my son is much more responsible with keys than I am. Give me a minute.'

He hadn't taken a step when the kitchen door opened, and there stood the tall man from earlier. He frowned at Hannah and looked at his father, before saying, 'What's going on, Dad?'

'This is Hannah Harrison. I found her marching down the farm road.' Neil gestured across to her, smiling at the younger man. 'She's taken over Tim's shop in town. Her bakkie got stuck up in the donkey pasture, and she needs a tow.'

Neil's son stared at Hannah. 'What the hell were you doing up that track? I told you there was nothing here for you.'

Those million things Hannah had thought to say to him fled and her mouth gaped in shock while she wondered how she could possibly be surprised at the rudeness of this man.

'I see you have already met my son, Alistair,' Neil said dryly. 'I'm afraid he's lost the manners I raised him with, and seems not to have inherited any of my charm.' He touched Hannah's arm briefly and smiled. 'I'll be your knight in shining armour today, be it an old, creaky one.' He turned to his son, who was standing, arms folded, defensiveness rolling off him in waves. 'Come on, boy,' Neil said cheerfully, 'get those keys – we have a quest.'

When Alistair disappeared inside, his three dogs responded to Neil's whistle, leaping and scrambling onto the back of the vehicle. Jim Beam jumped neatly into the cab and settled in his usual place on the seat back while Neil leant across the seat to open the passenger door for Hannah. She climbed in while he attempted to clear miscellaneous items from the dusty footwell. Boxes of sparkplugs were shoved into the cubby hole, a pair of binoculars dumped on the seat between them.

'Sorry about the mess, Hannah,' said Neil. 'My son needs a woman to improve his habits.' He waggled his eyebrows at her, and she shook her head, but couldn't help a grin for him.

Alistair returned, throwing the keys to his dad, who caught them one-handed out the window. He then walked around to Hannah's side, opened the door, and waited for her to move up on the seat to make space for him. His mouth was pulled into a sneer, daring her to refuse. She glanced across at Neil, who grinned at her. She shifted up on the bench seat so that she was sitting in the middle and wondered, awkwardly, if she should put her right leg over the transmission into the driver's side, but then decided that, as much as she did not want to be squeezed against Alistair, having someone she'd just met change gears between her legs was a little more intimate than she was comfortable with. Alistair wound the window right down, hooked his left arm out the window frame, and shifted as much of his body as was possible away from Hannah.

'I would still like to know what you were doing up in the donkey pasture after I told you to get off the farm,' said Alistair.

Hannah snapped. 'What's your problem? I came to ask permission from you to visit the memorial site and you jumped down my throat before I could even get my name out.'

Alistair was glaring at her. 'What the hell are you talking about? First you ask if there's camping on the farm and now you're talking about a memorial. There's nothing on this farm that would interest you. But more than that,' his voice rose, 'I told you to get off the farm and you deliberately drove off the road into the donkey pasture.'

'For heaven's sake,' Hannah spat back at him, 'I didn't know it was a donkey pasture. There was not a donkey in sight—' She broke off to mutter, '"That's one thing about our Harry. Harry hates everybody."'

Neil laughed out loud, 'You can quote *Dirty Harry*? You're not old enough to know those movies.'

Hannah tried to shift away from Alistair. 'My father's a fan,' she said as she gripped the edge of the seat as hard as she could, bracing her body against the motion of the truck as it rolled and bounced.

Her miserable Mazda came into view and, as soon as they drew to a stop, Alistair jumped out, getting away from her as quickly as possible.

Hannah watched as he walked around the small blue Mazda, seemingly assessing whether to tow it forwards or back. He returned to Hannah's side of the car and swept his arm in a wide, sarcastic bow which, combined with his hard angry look, had Hannah scrambling out. He yanked the seat forwards and scrabbled around behind it, pulling out two strips of old carpet. He threw one to Neil and the two men hunkered down at the Mazda's back wheels to slip the ends of the carpet strips under the tyres.

The dogs had jumped off the pickup and were ranging around in the field, noses to the ground and tails wagging high in the air. Hannah stood on the grass verge above the track with her hands in her back pockets, helpless and embarrassed.

While Alistair unwound the winch cable and set about attaching it to the towing eye of the Mazda, Neil came across to stand with Hannah.

'So where are the donkeys?' said Hannah, wanting to distract him from her flushed face.

He smiled at her. 'There haven't been donkeys here for fifty years, but the name stuck for some reason.' Neil was quiet for a moment and then he glanced at her. 'What's this about a memorial?'

Hannah kicked the toe of her running shoe into the grass tufts on the verge. 'I heard there was a concentration camp from the South African War on this farm.'

'Where did you hear that?' Neil's brows had lifted in surprise.

'I didn't hear it exactly,' she admitted. 'I found a reference to it in the shop. I was clearing out some old stuff.' She felt the need to explain, but couldn't bring herself to mention Rachel's journal with Dirty Harry in earshot. 'I thought there might be a memorial to the camp,' she said. 'I suppose it piqued my interest enough to want to explore.'

'You wasted your time,' said Alistair, as he came back to the truck. 'And a lot of ours. There's nothing like that on the farm.' Then, just as abruptly: 'Dad, you get in the Mazda and reverse slowly when you feel the car starting to move.'

'I can do that,' said Hannah.

'You stay where you are,' said Alistair, leaning into the truck to manage the winch. 'You've caused enough trouble.'

Neil shook his head at his son's rudeness and, with a squeeze of Hannah's arm, climbed into her car.

Hannah folded her arms across her chest and narrowed her eyes. '"You're a legend in your own mind, Harry,"' she said under her breath.

The winch pulled and Neil slowly began to reverse. The tyres found traction on the strips of carpet, and the car slid out of the mud as easily as she had driven into it. This made her feel even more stupid. Alistair didn't look her way as he approached her car again to unhook the winch cable.

Neil, still in Hannah's driver's seat, reversed the car up onto the opposite grass verge and swung it around, skirting Alistair's truck. He leant out of the window. 'I'll drive this back to the house. See you there.' Alistair and Hannah could only watch him make his way down the slope.

They drove in silence to the house. The tension was palpable between them and, as soon as he had parked the pickup at the back door of the farmhouse, Alistair disappeared inside without a word. Hannah, muttering curses, made her way across the yard to Neil, who was leaning against the bonnet of her mud-covered car. He smiled as he handed the keys back to her. 'Don't worry about him. He's more comfortable with his dogs than with people.'

Hannah grimaced. 'They've got him used to giving orders and being blindly obeyed.'

Neil laughed. 'Not a whole lot of obedience in you, though.'

She coloured again. 'Sorry I caused so much trouble for you today. I really appreciate the help.'

'It was a pleasure, Hannah Harrison, made completely worthwhile by seeing my son knocked off his even keel. He's been despondent lately, and that worries me more than seeing him angry.' Neil looked to the kitchen door, his face suddenly older.

'Okay then.' Hannah awkwardly jingled her keys. 'I'll be off home. Thank you again, Neil.'

'You don't want to stay for lunch, as late as it is? I'll introduce you to the other beautiful girl in Leliehoek.'

'No, I've put you out enough for one day. Thanks for the offer though. Another time?'

'I'll hold you to it,' he said, closing her car door firmly.

Neil found Alistair in the kitchen, peering into the fridge.

'Your mother has lunch waiting for us. Come on over to the cottage. But leave the mood behind, please. I've seen enough of it for a day.'

Alistair closed the fridge door and gave Neil a filthy look.

'What?' Neil said. 'Was I supposed to leave her walking down the road looking for help?'

'Dad, you encouraged her, downright charmed her.'

'She's a pretty girl who needed help – why wouldn't I?'

They left the farmhouse through the front door. Neil glanced at his son. 'The real question is, why you wouldn't help her? What are you holding against a girl you've hardly met?'

'She irritated me.'

'More like she got to you,' Neil said, smiling.

'Drop it, Dad.'

They reached the cottage where the kitchen was filled with the smell of bread fresh out the oven. Sarah was ladling thick brown soup into bowls.

'It's bacon and bean,' she said. 'I know it's better in winter, but I just felt like making it today. Neil, please pick up the salad and take it out to the veranda. I thought we could eat there.'

Neil leant over to kiss Sarah's cheek. 'It looks wonderful, my girl.'

She smiled but didn't look up from dishing up the soup. 'Alistair, can you carry the bread? And you'll need a bread knife.'

The table was set with cotton mats and flowered side plates. Alistair and Neil sat across from each other and were spreading butter on thick slices of hot bread.

'Neil, you don't need the butter,' Sarah said, frowning at him.

'Don't put it out if you don't want me to eat it.'

She ignored him and moved the salt out of his reach.

The soup was thick and fragrant, and there was silence at the table while the two men concentrated on their meal. 'What have you been up to this morning?' Sarah said, delicately spooning her soup from the opposite side of her bowl.

'We met the girl who's taken on Tim's shop,' Neil said. 'We towed her bakkie out of the mud.'

'Here?' Sarah looked in surprise between Neil and Alistair.

'She was trespassing,' said Alistair curtly.

Neil rolled his eyes at his wife. 'Alistair took exception to her being on the farm. She had heard somewhere that there was a Boer concentration camp site in the area. I liked her, actually. Seems sweet. Pretty too.'

Sarah's brows crinkled. 'How strange that those old stories should surface off the farm. I've only ever heard them here.'

Alistair put his spoon firmly down. 'What stories, Mum? I've never heard anything like that?'

'I haven't heard them for years and years, not since I was a girl really.' Sarah buttered her bread and neatly cut it in half with a knife. Alistair looked across at her in disbelief.

'And?' He had found this day disturbing on a number of levels. Riding in the truck next to Hannah had stirred emotions in him that he hadn't felt in years. Despite her trying her hardest not to touch him, an accidental brush of her arm against his had scalded him. He put down his spoon and pushed his right arm under the table. The faraway look in his mother's eyes did nothing to soothe his disquiet.

'You know that, as a child, I used to play with Kobie and Lena? I was in and out of their house in the workers' compound a lot. There were stories that their mother had told them, to scare them into behaving, I thought.' Sarah put her spoon down. 'She would say that the ghost woman from the camp was looking for her children, and that Kobie and Lena had better be good or the woman would come for them. Kobie and Lena swore that they saw the ghost woman on the plateau, but I never did. And then I forgot all about it, till now. How strange,' she said again, before picking up her spoon quietly.

'Come on, Mum, that's superstitious nonsense. We would know, after all these years on the farm, if there had been a camp here. The camps are all documented and accounted for anyway. The closest one was at Winburg.'

Neil wiped the remains of soup from his bowl with a crust of bread. 'Stories all start somewhere, though. Just because we lose the beginning of the thread doesn't mean it never happened. That wind pump up on the plateau is pretty old.'

Sarah smiled across the table at him. 'I remember my grandfather telling me about that metal one arriving in a kit all the way from America. It was a big event on the farm.'

Alistair frowned at his parents. 'How is it that I don't know any of this?'

'Anyway,' Neil said, not so deftly shifting the conversation, 'I hope we see more of that girl. Maybe we should invite her round, Sarah?'

Alistair pushed his chair away from the table. 'Just warn me, please. I'll make sure I'm out of the way.' He came around to Sarah's seat and dropped a kiss on the top of her head. 'Lovely lunch, Mum, thanks.'

May 1901, Goshen Camp, Orange River Colony

Dear Wolf,

At night, I dream of the farm. I dream of you, my brother and my best friend. I see you in my sleep. You come in from the veld with your face brown from the sun, and the smell of wind and grass on your clothes.

I think of our playing together as children, hiding from the little ones and feeling so grown up that we could build forts and swim in the river on our own. Then we were older. I had more work to do in the house and you were out helping Pa. Sometimes I brought lunch to you in the fields, where we lay on the grass and talked about being grown up. You wanted to breed horses. You said Pa would listen when you were older because your plan was good. I lay with the grass tickling my neck and looked at the sky. It was clear and bright, and I couldn't imagine anything beyond the moment. Being happy with you.

Now I dream of food, of being warm. I even long for the cauldron of washing, that boiling soap that made my eyes sting. Hot water and being properly clean is a thought too luxurious to allow myself in the daylight. I would never get out of my blanket if I let the dreams take me in the day. I wake every morning thinking I'm home. I open my eyes and the awful truth hits me that it is the nightmare which is real.

Do you long for the past as I do? Do you dream of me, Wolf?

CHAPTER SEVEN

Patchy woke Hannah early again the following morning. The creeping sun on the deck drew her outside to curl into a chair with her cup of tea. Her thoughts returned to the previous day, as they had many times since she'd left the farm. That man. That bitter, arrogant man. How had he got like that? She pushed the thought aside. Who cares. If she could avoid him, all the better.

The morning brought a steady stream of curious visitors to the shop. Barbara managed the till and shamelessly exploited the unusual surfeit of customers, persuading them to buy a paperback or a knitting pattern before they left the shop, while Hannah tried to be as friendly as possible while deflecting their personal questions. In all her years with Todd, she had perfected the art, and spent much time talking in depth about the other person. By the end of the conversation, the person left feeling like they had really engaged her but, in actual fact, had learnt nothing about Hannah at all.

When the shop quietened down by lunchtime, Hannah's kitchen had already accumulated numerous foil-covered dishes and various bottles of pickles and jams. As overwhelming as the people and their questions had been, Hannah had never experienced such a welcome from strangers before. She wondered if her Cape Town friends would've been as happy to see her as the residents in this new town were.

'Barbara, do you mind if I sneak out and get a take-away coffee? I feel like I deserve one after that.'

Barbara looked up from the computer, her bright orange reading glasses perched on the end of her nose. A beaded string looped from each earpiece and matched her Ndebele-style necklace. Her eyes crinkled and she said dryly, 'You survived the vultures – you do deserve one. Go ahead, get me one too? Black, three sugars?'

Hannah crossed the street and walked along the edge of the square where enormous plane trees projected deep green shade across the lawn. The bistro next door was open for lunch. Tables and umbrellas were set up on the deck, edged with boxes of tumbling geraniums and bright petunias. The school year was wrapping up in the next month. Holidaymakers from Gauteng would arrive at their country getaways and the town would burst open with activity.

Cutting across the corner of the square, she passed a blanket shop. Rows of multicoloured Basotho blankets hung on display. Hannah's mother had inherited four Basotho blankets from Hannah's ouma, blue with black lions marching across the width. They were used every winter and Hannah could hear her mother in her head: *Sixty years old and still as warm as when they were bought!*

She wondered if her parents had tried to contact her. She hadn't checked her phone since arriving in Leliehoek. Its battery had no doubt died by now. She brushed the thought of her parents aside, pausing in front of a pink-and-white-painted shop. A sign hung above the door, 'Coffee and Cake'. White-painted tables and chairs filled the interior. The décor was eclectic, glass jars jostling with old-fashioned tea tins and pink-and-white daisies. The effect was girlishly charming.

A large glass cabinet filled with beautiful pastries, cakes, and iced biscuits ran the width of the shop. The decadent smell of fresh brewing coffee filled the room. A waitress came out from the kitchen, carrying a tray with floral cups and two tea pots covered in crocheted pink tea cosies. She smiled at Hannah. 'I'll be with you in a minute.' Two older ladies were seated in the window. They only paused in their stream of chatter to smile at the waitress, before digging into enormous slices of carrot cake.

'May I help you, sweetheart?' the waitress asked, returning to the counter.

'I'll have two coffees to go, please.'

The waitress began pulling levers and twisting knobs on a coffee machine. 'My kids say this beast is straight out of Willy Wonka's factory.

They could be right too.' She looked up at Hannah. 'You visiting Leliehoek?'

'Um no, I'm working at the bookshop. I arrived on Friday.'

The woman's face lit up. 'Oh my goodness, you're Hannah! Of course, I should have known … I mean, you wouldn't have your surfboard in the middle of the Free State, would you?'

'Pardon?' Hannah tried to hide her confusion.

'Oh,' said the woman, 'it's just that the picture of you in my head was in a wet suit with a surfboard under your arm.'

Hannah nodded slowly. 'I suppose, coming from Cape Town, people might assume I'm a surfer.' Though nobody ever had before.

'I'm also from Cape Town, but not Kenilworth,' said the woman, putting two take-away cups and lids in front of Hannah, and gesturing to a large ceramic milk jug and bowl of sugar.

Hannah was too mystified by the interaction to reply. How did this woman know she surfed, and where she'd lived? She clipped the lids onto the cups and pulled out her wallet to pay.

'I'm Kathryn, by the way. My parents still live on the Flats, but I haven't been back to the Cape for years.' She shook her head at the money in Hannah's hand. 'Your first visit to the shop is on me. Tell Barbara I made red velvet cupcakes just for her.' Kathryn turned and began packing the cupcakes into a white box.

Hannah glanced at the cabinet full of beautiful cakes. 'You make all of these?'

'Aren't they gorgeous?' Kathryn grinned. 'Who would've thought that a girlie from the Flats would end up with a boutique bakery in the Free State? Not me, anyway!'

It dawned on Hannah for the first time that she was speaking to the owner of this lovely place. 'It's an amazing shop. I can see it's going to be a disaster for me.'

Kathryn giggled in delight. 'Wrecking people's diets is my goal in life. Why would you live a life of denial when there is lemon meringue in the world?'

Hannah picked up her coffees and the cardboard box, laughing. 'You are so right. Thanks for these, Kathryn.'

'See you soon, Hannah,' she said, waving cheerfully. 'So glad you're here. There's something in the air, and it's all to do with you. Exciting times, I think.'

Hannah turned and left the shop, her brows drawn. What was it about that woman? So strange, but not bad strange. Just a light unsettling that stirred something in Hannah, like a warm breath on her skin. She shook off the feeling as she crossed the square back to the shop.

Barbara had opened a foil-covered quiche and warmed it in the microwave while she tossed some salad onto plates.

'I met Kathryn,' said Hannah, sitting down at the table and picking the cherry tomatoes off her plate. She popped them into her mouth one by one as Barbara lifted two large slices of quiche onto their plates. 'She sent your red velvet cupcakes.'

'She's a honey,' said Barbara. 'Bakes like a dream. I think she keeps the Women's Guild afloat single-handedly. People come just for the tea afterwards.'

'At the church?' said Hannah.

'St Luke's, the Anglican church. She's very involved there. It amazes me how someone who has had as much trouble in her life as she has had, can be so warm and open. She's a special girl.'

'She's had a hard life?' Hannah put a forkful of buttery pastry and asparagus into her mouth.

'It's a rough story, but I'll leave her to tell you. All I'll say is that she's triumphed.' There was silence between them for a while as they ate their meal, sipping their coffees.

'I'm going to spend the afternoon on the computer,' said Hannah. 'I'll be in the shop for the rest of the day. If you want to go home, it's fine with me.'

'I think I might just do that, thanks. I need to get to the bank in Bethlehem. And tomorrow is book club here.'

Hannah looked up. 'Book club?'

Barbara smiled at what Hannah knew was a slightly panicked look on her face. 'On a Tuesday afternoon. We have about fifteen women who come regularly. They buy a book and, when they're done, they re-view it for the group. It's great for sales.'

Hannah sat back in her chair. 'Do we have to get anything ready?'

'Not really,' said Barbara, looking over her orange reading glasses. 'They take turns bringing eats and we provide tea and coffee. There are some women who have never done a review, and I doubt they read a book at all, but they're here every week. It's fun – you'll enjoy it.'

'Hmm,' was all Hannah could manage.

After Barbara had left, Hannah searched the history section of the shop, pulling out books on the South African War. There were a number with chapters on the camps. Sitting at the table in the reading room, she began to jot down relevant information in a notebook next to her.

When the British army had occupied the Boer capital, Pretoria, in June 1900, they had thought the war was largely over. In fact, it was only the beginning of a new, brutal phase. The style of battle shifted to guerrilla warfare. Mobile groups of Boers, commandos, were difficult to pin down, and the war looked set to drag out indefinitely. In response, Lord Kitchener embarked on his scorched earth policy with the intention of cutting all supply lines and support for the Boer commandos. Farms were burnt, crops destroyed, and stock killed. Floods of refugees began to pour into the camps, which had been set up initially to manage the crisis. But poor administration, inadequate rations, and the subsequent waves of disease set in motion a misery which saw the deaths of more than twenty-six thousand people. Most of these were women and children.

The photographs brought the history painfully to life. Hannah pored over the pages. A homestead with a pall of smoke hanging above it, and bundles of linen and furniture piled outside, three British soldiers posing formally in the foreground. A line of soldiers on a stone wall with guns raised shooting cattle. A field of horse carcasses, a man standing with his foot propped up on one, like a hunter. Women in deep-brimmed white kappies sitting exposed in a row of open cattle trucks about to leave for the camps. And then the children. Naked, skeletal bodies arranged before the camera. A little corpse held tightly by her blank-faced mother. Hannah felt nauseated. How could she not have known the scale of what happened?

She began searching for a reference to the camp called Goshen. She found lists and tables and graphs all detailing official records of the camps. She found maps with black dots marking the camps across South Africa's landscape. There was no camp called Goshen.

When the shop doorbell tinkled and a customer came in to browse, she packed up the pile of books and moved across to the computer. On Google, she found herself sidetracked by other journals from the war. There was one account of a mother who had hidden her children in caves to escape the British camps. They had managed to evade capture until the end of the war, though the memory was punctuated with the pain of desperate times. By late afternoon, Hannah had found nothing about Goshen Camp, but her head was whirling with pictures and stories from the war. It occurred to her that perhaps the journal had been written as a piece of fiction. It lacked the blunt voice of other women's real testimonies and was altogether more personal. It was as if the other accounts were protest pieces, full of bitterness against the British for wreaking such destruction on their people. Perhaps Rachel's story was no more than a writer expressing her own pain through the horror genre of the camps. Perhaps it would be better just to leave the story alone.

Hannah cashed up and retreated to her apartment. The house was quiet and still warm from the afternoon. Patchy stretched and yawned on the kitchen table. Hannah picked up the journal. The covers of the book were worn, but there was no indication of when or where the ledger had been printed. It certainly looked authentic, but then you would never know whether the account inside was written during the war, or ten or twenty years later. With no facts to back up the writing, it could be a work of fiction. Or perhaps this person had been in a camp and changed all names to avoid trouble. But that didn't fit with what she had seen this afternoon. There was nothing careful about the virulent writings of other Boer women from that time.

Hannah opened the ledger to where she had left off reading. The cramped writing crept on and on across the pages. The words jumped at her, and she couldn't help picking up the story again.

I make myself useful. I make friends by being helpful and hope that an extra ounce of rations will come my way. I carry buckets of water. I collect fuel for the neighbours so I can sit by their fire. I watch the children when their mothers are too tired to get up. I show them games that we played on the farm, and tell them stories. I show them how to write their names.

The medical officer visited last week and found I could write. It is useful to him that he can leave me here and visit less, not worry about keeping records himself. Now I make lists. Endless counts of sick people and dead people. Why do names on paper mean more to the British than the people who belong to those names? The lists can't save them, but somehow they have saved me. I get paid for my lists, and now I can buy a tin of meat every now and then. I will help anyone with any chore, but the food I keep secret and eat quickly, hidden under my blanket. I know these secret tins are my only chance to survive this camp.

It shames me to see children getting thinner and thinner until their knees and feet are enormous lumps on their stick legs, but I won't share. I won't sacrifice myself for nothing. One tin between so many would go nowhere, and then we'd all be dead. Surviving is no reason to boast – it's not heroic or brave, just selfish. Would Oupa Jakob be proud of me?

You and Pa and even Paul are on commando, fighting for our farm and family. You are heroes and Paul is only ten. Did you know that when you left to defend Naauwpoort Nek, Paul packed his bag and moved into the barn? He said he couldn't stay in the house like a baby or a girl. When Pa came back that last time, I remember Ma standing on the stoep watching Pa cross the yard to the barn. He called Paul down. I can see them now in the encroaching twilight, one tall and tired, and one little and fierce. He promised Ma that Paul would stay with him. That he would keep Paul safe. He's probably safer out there with you in the veld than in camps like us. I wish Pa would come for me.

There are so many ways to die here. Children are going the fastest. Once you are weak from hunger, you have almost no chance. Lists of names with measles, measles, measles. People start with a cough and a runny nose; then a rash comes. Then a fever hits them, and they start coughing up green phlegm; then they shiver uncontrollably and then they die. That's the way most go.

At least our water is clean. I hear the newcomers speak of bad water in other camps, water that makes your stomach so sick you vomit yourself to death. We have a good well, at least. They need water for the vegetables and we carry buckets to water them. Guards let families have a bucket a day. We drink and cook and wash with that one bucket. I carry the buckets for anyone who asks, so the guards at the pond know me and lose count of the times I come. This is the way I sneak extra, and the women are grateful – they think kindly of me. But I am not kind. I am a schemer, and everything I do is about what I can get, how much longer I can last.

Hannah looked up from where she had settled at the kitchen table. Her mind elsewhere, she stared out the window at the garden, now dim in the last light of the evening. She couldn't help feeling that Rachel's voice was too compelling to be fiction. It touched Hannah across the years, real and honest and oddly familiar.

CHAPTER EIGHT

H annah waited for the book club ladies to arrive. Even though she
stood nonchalantly at the till, her stomach curled at the thought
of being on display for the curious. She was good at putting on a casual
front, having learnt to do so with Todd and his endless social gather-
ings. But small talk in a crowd of new people did not come naturally to
her.

She had laid the reading-room table with one of Tim's embroidered
cloths and set out his mismatched antique cups and saucers. Glass jars
filled with herbs and flowers from the garden brought a light waft of
scented geranium and rosemary. Maybe she could pull off the afternoon, despite her inadequacies.

'Oh, Hannah, this looks gorgeous. You've put so much effort in – far
more than I ever do,' said Barbara when she arrived.

'Is it too much? I wasn't sure.'

'No, honey, it's lovely.' Barbara put her arm around Hannah's shoulders and squeezed her. 'You'll be fine here, you know. People are kind
and mostly gentle.'

Hannah felt her eyes prickle with tears. It surprised her. She hadn't
expected a maternal gesture from Barbara; she couldn't remember the
last time her mother had done anything like it. Wiggling away, she
clapped her hands together and said, 'Right, I'll just go and put the kettle on. We still need to fill up that urn.'

By three o'clock, the reading room was buzzing with laughter and
chatter. Dainty cake plates were piled with tartlets, scones, and savoury
pastries, the women tucking in with gusto. Hannah thought of the girls
her age in Cape Town who picked at half a health muffin, leaving the

nuts while sipping their compost-smelling matcha. They might be in skinny jeans showing flat stomachs but they certainly didn't have as much fun as these older women. Past the point of worrying about their thighs, the book club members were relishing being together, away from their housework and their husbands.

One woman, dressed in three-quarter beige trousers and a classic white-cotton shirt, approached Hannah. Her hair was silver white and styled in a sleek bob to her shoulders.

'Welcome to Leliehoek, Hannah. I'm Sarah Barlow. I think you met my husband, Neil, the other day.'

Hannah looked at this lovely woman and wondered how two such warm, secure people could produce a son as grating as Dirty Harry.

'Yes,' said Hannah, 'Neil was so helpful. Well, more than helpful really. He got me out of a jam.'

Sarah looked at Hannah with interest. 'Would you like to come to tea on the farm? Perhaps see it in less stressful circumstances?'

Hannah's eyes lit up at the thought of getting back onto Goshen. 'I'd love that, Mrs Barlow. Thank you.'

'Please, call me Sarah rather.' Her eyes creased gently. 'Mrs Barlow was Neil's mother and a tricky woman to like.'

'When would it be convenient for me to come?' Hannah hoped she didn't sound overeager.

'Are you busy in the shop tomorrow morning?'

Barbara had clearly been eavesdropping, her voice carrying from across the table as she said, 'I'll be here, Hannah. You go on ahead.'

'There you are, then,' said Sarah. 'Come at ten o'clock.'

Hannah smiled at the older woman. 'I look forward to it.'

The next morning Hannah was up early. Having put a good few hours into entering the new stock from the cardboard box she'd unpacked a few days earlier, she had registered the shop with an online book auctioneer and already had responses to the books she'd put up for auction. Some of the bids were surprisingly good. Perhaps she should also go through the second-hand stock on the shelves – there were bound to be books of value which would do well on auction. A trip to Bethlehem would be necessary soon to buy packaging so that she could ship the sold items to their buyers. The Leliehoek post office might become busier than they realised. She smiled at the thought of the historic post office with its equally ancient postmaster managing a flood of new work.

At half-past nine, she stood in her bedroom deliberating over her white T-shirt and old jeans. She looked down at her flip-flops and wondered again if she should buy some proper shoes, pretty sandals maybe, that would look less scruffy. Eventually opting for a cotton knee-length skirt, she twisted her hair into a plait that brushed her neck. The flip-flops would just have to do.

By twenty to ten, she was on the road, her palms sticky on the steering wheel. She wondered if she should have bought flowers. Something as a gift for Sarah. But then she remembered the exquisite garden growing around Sarah's cottage – arriving with a sad bunch from the supermarket would be embarrassing. Hannah turned off the road at the Goshen sign and drove up the farm road, glancing up at the donkey pasture as she passed it and shrinking a little at the thought of her antics a few days before. She hoped Alistair was out this morning.

Sarah came down from the stoep to greet her and they stood for a few minutes while Hannah tripped over words of admiration for the view and the garden.

Sarah brushed off the praise gently. 'The sad thing is, when you have lived somewhere your whole life, it just is what it is, no matter how beautiful. Does that sound horribly ungrateful?'

'No,' said Hannah, liking this woman. 'I felt the same about Cape Town. I looked at Table Mountain every day, numerous times a day, and I stopped seeing it – let alone hiking up it.'

'Exactly. Come on in. Would you like to see the cottage before we have tea?'

'I'd love that.'

The stoep floor was patterned in Victorian tiles that created tumbling cubes. 'My mother hated this floor,' said Sarah. 'She said it made her nauseated eating out here.'

'It's quite Escher-like, isn't it?' said Hannah, liking the optical illusion playing out on the floor.

'It's exactly like his drawings,' said Sarah, looking at Hannah in surprise. 'My father loved it and wouldn't let Mum touch it. Like many Free State farms, this cottage was the original dwelling. My grandfather bought the land and then built this cottage in 1910. He and my grandmother lived here until the family could afford a more substantial house. He told me that when he built this cottage, he scavenged all the flooring and roof beams from dump sites.'

Hannah ran the dates in her mind. 'So this wasn't a farm during the war?'

'I don't think so,' said Sarah. 'I know he bought the land cheaply from the government who wanted to get rid of it. I always assumed this was the first dwelling to be built here, but the worker housing is also very old.'

Hannah studied the antique tiling. 'I suppose so many houses were destroyed in the war, there must have been building materials around that could be reclaimed.'

Sarah followed her gaze and said, 'That never occurred to me ... I'm sure you're right. Like I said before, when you grow up in a place, things disappear in your consciousness though you see them every day.'

She led Hannah into the house. The passage had wide wooden floorboards. They had been sanded and sealed, and glowed golden brown.

'We've done quite a bit of remodelling. Made the bedrooms en suite and opened up the kitchen. The original house was rather dark.' The cottage was immaculate. Antique furniture complemented homemade quilts on the beds, but it was unfussy and simple, which made it altogether charming.

The kitchen was clearly Sarah's favourite room. An original anthracite stove dominated the room. 'We had the stove reconditioned when we moved back in here – it's such a joy to cook with now.'

'I wouldn't know where to begin,' said Hannah, laughing.

'It looks intimidating, but cooks like a dream when you get the hang of judging temperatures,' said Sarah, busying herself with filling a silver tea pot. 'Would you prefer muesli or buttermilk?' She pointed to two large jars of rusks on the counter.

'Muesli definitely,' said Hannah.

'Neil calls them horse rusks because of all the bran and fruit in them.' She shook her head but her smile softened the disdain.

They sat at the veranda table, Hannah facing the garden. She sipped her tea and thought how easy it was to be with this quiet, gentle woman. It put her relationship with her own mother into stark contrast. Maud Harrison constantly seemed to be measuring Hannah, assessing whether she was performing. Conversation was never just easy talking but invariably became intense, a debate that was won or lost. Being with her mother was exhausting.

'Do your parents still live in Cape Town, Hannah?' said Sarah, as if reading Hannah's thoughts.

'Yes, they both lecture at UCT, though they're on sabbatical at the moment in England. Seeing a bit of my brother, who lives in Cambridge.'

'Is he studying there?'

Hannah concentrated on setting her cup back in the saucer without spilling. 'No, he has a fellowship at the university. He's a rising star in the archaeology department. A golden boy.' She said this without sarcasm, but didn't look at Sarah.

'Neil said you were interested in South African War history in this area.'

Hannah looked up, relieved Sarah had turned the conversation away from her family. 'Yes. Though I don't know very much – I'm only just beginning to read about it.'

'Did something specific spark your interest?'

'I found something in the shop which references a camp called Goshen. I can't find any other record of it, though, so I seem to be at a dead end.' Hannah dipped her rusk in her tea, leaning over her plate as she bit into the biscuit to avoid messing on Sarah's pristine cloth.

'You know,' Sarah said after a few moments, 'the old farm workers had stories. I always dismissed them as ghost stories to frighten children … but perhaps there might be something to them. There is an elderly man on the farm called Kobie. He and his mother before him were both born on the farm. If anyone knows anything, it will be him.'

Hannah helped herself to more tea from the pot, projecting a casualness she didn't feel. 'Could I talk with him sometime?'

'Of course,' said Sarah. 'I saw Kobie in the yard this morning. I can take you up there to find him.'

They walked around the side of the house and up the drive past the bigger farm house. 'If you go up to the sheds, you'll find Kobie there. And then maybe you should find Alistair at the house and ask him to take you around the farm.'

Hannah didn't want to tell Sarah how disastrous her previous encounter with Alistair had been. 'Um, okay. But if he's busy, I can come back another time. Maybe Neil could show me ...'

'Alistair's not doing anything that can't wait an hour. Besides, it'll be good for him to get away from his desk. He's been tied to it the past few days.'

'I don't want to be a bother.'

'Nonsense. You go chat to Kobie.'

Sarah watched Hannah cross the yard and disappear into the shed, before she turned towards the main house. Manipulation was not normally something she practised, and now she hoped the consequences of throwing Hannah into Alistair's path would not be disastrous for them both. Perhaps Neil was right and she should stay out of it. But she liked this girl, and hoped Hannah might be able to shake Alistair out of his blundering pain.

'Alistair?' She knocked on the back door. 'Are you home?'

'No, I'm out,' came the reply.

Sarah muttered under her breath and made her way down the passage to his study. She stood in the doorway, watching him work. He didn't look up from his computer screen.

'Alistair.'

He lifted a finger to signal to her to wait, then carried on typing numbers into columns. Sarah sighed and crossed her arms across her chest.

Eventually, he sat back in his chair and ran his hand through his hair, making it stand up in the crest which signified a desk-bound morning. 'What is it, Mum?'

'I want you to hear me out before you fly off the handle.'

'That sounds ominous.' He picked up a pencil and began to tap it on the mouse pad in front of him.

'I want you to take Hannah up to the plateau.' He carried on tapping the pencil, staring at her. After a moment or two, she blurted, 'Aren't you going to say anything?'

'I'm waiting to hear you out before I fly off the handle.'

Sarah huffed in irritation. 'Alistair Barlow, sometimes I do not know where you came from. And yes,' she added, seeing his smirk, 'I already know everything and more about the birds and the bees.'

'Wow, everything and more?' Alistair's smirk stretched into a grin.

'Oh, you!' was all Sarah could manage as a blush crept up her neck.

'Why do you want me to take her up to the plateau?' The fun in his eyes drained away again, and Sarah wished she could hang on to it, even at her own expense. 'Are you encouraging her in this crazy idea that there was a camp here? Really?'

'What's the harm, Alistair?' Sarah said.

'The harm? The harm is that I don't want this farm to become a laughing stock in the community because of some ludicrous stories. I don't want strangers walking all over the farm looking for so-called ghosts.'

'Could it be that you don't want to meet someone new, Alistair? That you keep your fear of another relationship like barbed wire around you?' She backtracked when she saw pain widen his eyes. 'I'm sorry, that was unfair.'

'You really know how to twist the knife, don't you, Mum.'

'Please just take her, Alistair. When she sees that there's nothing there, she'll lose interest.' She hoped she sounded more convincing than she felt.

'If I do, will it get you off my back too?' Alistair sighed.

CHAPTER NINE

Hannah peered into one of the sheds and, when her eyes had adjusted to the gloom, she saw a small man sitting on a paint tin with his back to her. He was painting something onto an orange plastic ball and, when she approached, the smell of fibreglass resin singed her nostrils. Not wanting to startle him, she called out, 'Excuse me, I'm looking for Kobie?'

The man looked over his shoulder at her. His face was lined with deep grooves from the sun. 'Ja, Miesies, ek is hy,' he said and, when he smiled at her, she could see that his front teeth were missing. She switched to Afrikaans.

'Do you have a minute to talk with me?'

He gestured to another paint tin. As she lowered herself onto it, she found the seat was surprisingly comfortable.

'Mrs Barlow said I could talk to you about the farm. She said you've been here the longest.'

He nodded and returned his attention to the fibreglass patch he was applying to the ball float. 'I lived here my whole life – 1939 till now. My mother was also born here, 1921.'

Hannah watched his weathered hands brush the resin up and down. The stringent smell brought tears to her eyes but seemed not to bother him at all. She thought carefully about how she should approach the conversation.

'Kobie, do you know anything about the war here, the South African War?' He nodded, and she continued, 'I've heard there was a camp on the farm from those days.'

Kobie lifted his head and, for the first time, looked directly at her.

His eyes were older than his years, somehow, thought Hannah, struggling to grasp what she saw.

'I know these stories,' he said simply.

'Can you tell me?'

He sighed deeply and looked away from her, over his shoulder. She followed his gaze to the rocky cliffs which climbed the view over the valley. 'My ouma, my mother's mother, lived with us. She was a young girl when the British came over the land. After the war, she had no parents, no family at all. She never told us what happened to them. Never spoke about those days. But in her last years, her mind drifted away from us. We had to watch her all the time, or she would wander out the house and get lost on the farm. She started speaking about soldiers and tents. She spoke of people walking like skeletons. She said weeping had soaked into the ground. That grief had scored the rocks. It frightened my sister and me. And then, when we started seeing things, we remembered her words.' He looked back at Hannah and smiled, perhaps at how wide her eyes had grown, and Hannah realised she had been holding her breath.

Kobie dropped his brush into a glass jar of thinners and closed the tin of resin, hammering the lid with the heel of his hand. He leant down to inspect the patch on the float.

Hannah tried to rein in the excitement which seemed to flick through her like a live charge. 'What did you see?'

Kobie sat back up and looked at his gnarled hands, picking off bits of resin. 'When the oubaas ran big herds of sheep on the farm, I would walk or ride out to check them. I was often on the plateau at sunset. Especially when the dark comes early and the cold drops like a stone onto the veld. I've seen strange things. Not every time I was out, but some.' The silence stretched unbearably before he softly continued. 'Once, I smelt strong smoke, like I was in the smoke, but there was no fire. Once, up on the plateau, the wind carried a thick smell of sewage, so bad I had to cover my nose. There are no people up there, Miesies, no drains, nothing.'

Hannah's thoughts scrambled. 'Could it have been manure on the fields that you smelt?'

'Manure is sweet – even pig manure – but human shit is different. It made me want to vomit. Do you understand?'

Hannah nodded, sorry she had interrupted.

'A few times, I have heard far-off keening. You know what keening is? It's not weeping. It's a sound that comes out of someone's stomach – a sound they can't control, might not even know they are making. It tears out of them when they are too stunned by grief to talk. It is a deep, old sound that makes your hair stand up.'

Hannah felt the flesh on her arms and scalp rise. Kobie looked at Hannah, his own eyes wide now. 'A few times across my life, I have seen women on the plateau. One was small and her dress came to here.' He gestured to mid-calf. 'She wore a kappie, you know this kappie? Like in the old days. The bonnet with the deep rim? I couldn't see her face. She was carrying buckets, two heavy buckets. She walked and then disappeared, even though I was frozen in the same place.'

Hannah ventured carefully, 'And you saw her more than once?'

'Yes, a few times. Always in the same place, she walks a short way with her buckets and disappears. Like a movie reel at the bioscope, over and over. And there was the other woman who frightened me when I was young. She just walked. Tall and thin. She wore a long dress to her ankles and a kappie. My mother used to tell us she was looking for her children. I don't know why my ma said that.'

The stories intrigued and thrilled Hannah. Yet her rational brain struggled to make sense of them. There was no doubt in her mind that Kobie was telling the truth, that he believed what he had seen. But did she? She had never considered ghost stories to have any root in reality, but then she had never heard one first-hand and witnessed the conviction on the teller's face.

'Kobie, have other people seen these things?'

'My mother and my sister, Lena. We have lived our lives on the farm and we know every corner. I tell Miss Sarah when we were children. But white people, they don't like things they can't explain. And if they can't explain something, sometimes they don't even see it.'

Hannah saw the truth in his statement and thought of her parents, who debated and argued things into or out of existence, proud of their open-mindedness. How ironic that they were completely closed to the idea of the supernatural. Staunch in their academic atheism. She wondered where she stood now. She felt Leliehoek changing her. As if a different, brighter person were emerging from a dull, old husk.

'Miesies, I don't know what happened, but I do know that place on the plateau is restless – that something hangs in the air.'

Walking down from the sheds towards the farmhouse, Hannah took a deep breath, pulling her shoulders back and lifting her chin – as if drawing herself up to her full height would give her the necessary courage to face Alistair Barlow. She felt a clench of nerves as she knocked on the front door.

The sound of dogs on wooden floorboards rushed at the door, and she braced herself for the onslaught as the door opened. But the three big dogs just pushed themselves around her legs, sniffing her feet, their tails wagging furiously. She tried to stop a tail from lifting her skirt as she looked up into Alistair's face. The white scar pulling his cheek crooked unnerved her. The picture of him in her mind had been dominated by his anger and now, seeing his face composed and deliberately neutral, the twisted mouth looked wrong. She felt the unfairness of his disfigurement, and pity welled up in her. Alistair stepped out onto the paving stones rather than inviting her in. Shoving his hands in his pockets, he waited while she looked at him. It was as though his pride had him stubbornly meeting her eyes and daring her to look away first. But she didn't look away, instead saying, 'I'd like you to take me up to the plateau. Kobie's been telling me about the farm, and I want to see the plateau. Will you take me?' She gritted her teeth and forced out, 'Please.'

'Okay,' said Alistair.

'Oh,' she said, caught on the back foot now as she scrambled for words. 'I thought you would say no. I thought you hated the sight of me.'

Hannah glimpsed the hint of a grin at the corner of his mouth. *The bastard's enjoying this*, she thought, clenching her fists at her sides.

Alistair turned and reached for his keys just inside the door. 'I changed my mind.' He brushed past her as he headed for his pickup and she had to trot behind him to keep up, wondering as she went whether he had changed his mind about saying no or about hating her.

Instead of going back down the drive towards the farm road, Alistair drove past the sheds. He continued on to a track that wound up around the hill behind the house. They drove in silence. Hannah opened her window. In the wing mirror, she could see the dogs' heads pushed through the railings of the pickup, their tongues lolling and nostrils flaring as they tracked the farm smells. 'What are your dogs' names?' she said, keeping her eyes on the mirror.

She felt him glance her way before he said, 'The ridgeback is Grant, and the Labs are Lee and Jackson.'

'I wouldn't have taken you for a Confederate supporter.'

'No, not at all,' he said, his mouth twisting into a small smile. 'Just a military history fan. They were outstanding generals.'

As they climbed higher, the grassland opened up into swathes of red-brown grass. A small herd of blesbok grazed down the slope. They turned their broad, white faces to the vehicle, the largest snorting and moving back a few paces. As he saw the Toyota moving away from them, the big male relaxed and dipped his head once more to the grass.

They reached the fence and slowed to a stop. Hannah was already scrambling out to open the gate and enjoyed the surprise on Alistair's face. *Yes, Harry, you think you know what kind of girl I am. You don't.* But she had to use all her strength and stand on tiptoes to pull the wire loop over the top of the pole. She could feel her skirt riding up the back of her thighs and hoped he was looking the other way. Once she'd pulled the wire gate across and dropped it in the grass, she stood with her hands on her hips, her hair escaping from the plait into wisps around her face as she waited for him to drive through.

He leant across and spoke through the passenger window, 'Leave it, we can close it on the way back.'

She caught him glancing at her exposed leg as she swung into the cab and she pulled her skirt as far down her knees as she could. The truck jerked as he fumbled the gears and he swore, his hand smacking the gear stick into place. Had he always been this angry, she wondered, or was his bitterness connected to his scarred face? It was not something she could ask without risking her life.

'Do you feel lucky, Punk?'

'Excuse me?' said Alistair, glancing across at her.

Hannah blinked, realising she had spoken aloud. 'Nothing.' She slid down a bit in the seat, fixing her gaze on the view from the window.

They crested the top of the hill. A plateau stretched before them. A wind pump stood next to a concrete reservoir, its blades turning gently in the mild breeze which stirred the grass into a whisper. The sun was high and the sky, a rich cobalt blue. The dogs had leapt off the back of the Toyota and now ranged around the vehicle, not venturing far.

'There's really not much to see.' Alistair was leaning on the bonnet of the Toyota, watching Hannah. She walked the few paces over to the reservoir and peered over the top into the pool of water. Trailing her hand in the water, she disturbed the surface into ripples that fanned across the pool. The water was cool – deep and inviting. She tilted her head upwards to a line of old gum trees that stretched away across the plateau. The ground beneath them was bare and knobbled with roots, their trunks striped in pale ribbons of grey and pink and orange.

Alistair's voice reached her from the pickup. 'I always wonder who planted such a straight line. It's a windbreak, but why here and not at the house?'

Hannah turned to face him. 'It was the kids.'

He straightened, the shock on his face stark. 'What?'

'The camp children planted these trees. I read about it.'

His eyes darkened. 'Where are you reading this stuff? Where are you getting these crazy ideas?'

Hannah turned her head to look at him, her face serious. 'I found a journal in the shop, written by a Boer woman. A girl actually. She writes that she was interned at a camp called Goshen. The writing is so vivid, Alistair. The problem is I can't find any official record of the camp. No mention of it in any book or online document I have managed to lay my hands on. It's so frustrating! And then Kobie tells me these creepy stories about seeing women up here and smelling raw sewage and hearing keening on the wind. I just want to unravel the threads and find some truth at the bottom of it all.'

Alistair's mind rushed and tumbled. How could this be true when he had lived here all his life and never heard any mention of it? He had long been interested in the war history of the area and was well read. He knew the set piece battles by heart, had visited the sites many times. He had picked up shell casings and bits of saddlery in the veld, keeping his small collection in a drawer in his study. What if this mad story were true? What if his own farm were part of the history he loved so much? The spark of excitement was snuffed by the thought of the people who would come to the farm, the attention that would turn again to him. And they would come – there was no doubt. Hannah was already here, and that was bad enough. He glanced across at her, her gaze fixed on the stand of trees. It would mean spending more time with her, having her walking in his fields, riding in his pickup, and coming into his house. His heart contracted and fear won over.

He didn't like the words as they came out his mouth: 'It's a waste of time.'

Hannah's face fell and she turned searching green eyes on him, the disappointment clear. 'You don't believe me.'

Alistair kicked the heel of one boot rhythmically against the tyre behind him. Looking down at his feet, he remained quiet.

'What about Kobie's stories then?' Hannah persisted, turning her body to face him. 'Do you think he's lying too?'

'I don't think either of you are lying. I just think you've got hold of stories. Fiction. Folktales. You said yourself there are no facts to back them up.' He looked up at her and he felt like the liar. Once, he would have been open to any adventure, been up to exploring any possibility. Now it was too threatening. She was too threatening.

Hannah said nothing on the return journey, and Alistair felt guilt curdle in his stomach, preferring the sparky, angry girl to this composed, quiet one. When they rolled to a stop in the farmyard, she opened the door and, with a tight smile that didn't light her eyes, she said, 'Thank you for taking me up there, Alistair. I'm sorry I wasted your time.' Before he could respond, she had disappeared around the side of the house to where her car was parked.

Alistair slammed his door hard. Bloody woman. He hardly knew her; why should he be feeling guilty? The image returned to him of Hannah standing at the gate, hands on her hips, escaped hair soft around her face and slim legs bare, with ridiculous flip-flops. Who wears flip-flops in the Free State? What disturbed him most, though, was that, far from looking out of place, Hannah had looked alarmingly at home. What he actually wanted was to see her here again. For the first time in eight long, dark years, Alistair recognised this feeling. He was attracted to her. He pushed the thought away, telling himself he wasn't ready – maybe would never be ready for another relationship again. He opened the tailgate for the dogs to jump down and Grant, instead of leaping off, put his big head on Alistair's shoulder. Just rested it there. Alistair stroked both hands down Grant's head and ears, taking comfort from the dog's huge heart.

Later that afternoon, Hannah strolled over to Coffee and Cake, hoping she would catch Kathryn before she too closed up her shop. She told herself she needed something sweet to cover the emotion of the day. Something pretty and girlie and delicious to restore her balance. Poking her head through the door, she saw Kathryn putting the chairs up onto the tables and getting ready to sweep. 'Oh, sorry, I was hoping you'd still be open.'

Kathryn looked up, a big smile lighting up her face when she saw Hannah. 'I'm officially closed, but I'm dying for a cup of tea myself. Want one?'

'Desperately,' Hannah said and smiled at Kathryn's laugh.

'Sounds like my day too,' Kathryn said.

Hannah perched on a tall barstool at the counter while Kathryn made quick work of the sweeping.

'Choose something out of the cabinet, anything you like,' said

Kathryn, ducking her head to retrieve a napkin from under a table. 'There are plates on the shelf.'

Behind the counter, Hannah found two mugs and two side plates. Not sure how the hot water tap on the coffee monster worked, she went as far as popping teabags into the mugs. The selection in the display cabinet was overwhelming. Rows of intricately iced cupcakes, slabs of chocolate brownies, and glazed pastries vied for her attention. She eventually settled on a lemon meringue pie, artfully constructed in a small glass jar so that the meringue puffed out the top and the yellow lemon curd made a sunny stripe across the middle of the jar. She dipped a teaspoon into the jar and closed her eyes in delight.

'My goodness, that is just delicious,' she said, watching Kathryn finish up, and licking the back of her spoon.

Kathryn smiled at her as she pulled a lever on the coffee machine and filled their mugs. 'Those little jars are sweet, hey. I'm always on the lookout for new ideas – Pinterest and I are like this,' she said, crossing her fingers. She handed Hannah a mug of strong tea and sipped her own.

'You're not having anything to eat?' said Hannah, indicating the second plate.

'It's the only downside to my business,' said Kathryn with a rueful smile. 'I spend so much time making these things, and then all day smelling them, I just can't bring myself to eat any of them. Offer me a samosa or some hot chips, though, and I might bite your whole hand off.'

Hannah chuckled, scraping the last of the buttery crumb crust from the bottom of the jar. Heaven. Kathryn watched Hannah over the rim of her cup, as if waiting for her to reveal why she was really there.

'Sarah Barlow invited me out to the farm for tea, and then I had an altercation with her son.' Hannah felt her mood sink again at the thought of Alistair's brittle words which had quashed her hopes of pursuing Rachel's story.

'The elusive Alistair …' Kathryn said. 'I'm astonished you managed to even have a conversation with him, let alone an argument.' At Hannah's raised brows, she continued, 'Let's just say he keeps to himself. He's always polite, but he keeps walking with a quick hello, never stops to go beyond that. What were you arguing about?'

Hannah deliberated for a second, and then decided to tell Kathryn about Rachel's journal and the references to Goshen. Kathryn listened with her head cocked to the side, dark eyes intent, like a little bird. Hannah found herself relaxing as she spilled her encounters with the Barlows and Kobie into the space between them.

Kathryn waited until she finished and then asked gently, 'What is it you want from all this, Hannah?'

Hannah looked down at her mug to avoid the searching gaze. 'I'm not entirely sure. I came to Leliehoek on a whim. And I love it. Being here, I mean. And the shop. Then I find this journal, and for the first time in a very long time I'm excited about something. This girl has grabbed hold of me in a way I don't fully understand. She's living through the worst possible experiences, and yet she's resilient. And there's something about her – a pathos, a loneliness I find myself relating to. It sounds feeble when I say it out loud.'

'No, not feeble. The word *vulnerable* comes to mind, and I would guess you haven't been that in a long time.' Hannah looked up in surprise and met Kathryn's intelligent brown eyes. 'It happens when you put yourself out on the line, and it sounds to me like you are venturing into unfamiliar territory – on many fronts.'

'What do you mean?' said Hannah, sitting back in her chair and folding her arms across her body.

'You are completely alone here. You've left all the expectations of your past behind, and now you're pushing into places that are wholly your own pursuit. It seems to me like you are opening yourself up. Maybe Alistair is one of those new fronts?' Kathryn smiled at Hannah's bewildered face. 'It's a good thing, Hannah.'

Hannah stared at Kathryn, wondering how she could possibly have so much insight into her life. They had really only just met, and yet Kathryn spoke with an understanding which Hannah's parents – or Todd, for that matter – had never had. She wasn't sure how comfortable she was with it.

As if reading her mind, Kathryn reached out and touched her arm lightly. 'Sorry. I sometimes speak without filtering what I hear.'

'Let me just clear something up, though,' Hannah said bluntly, trying to cover her confusion. 'I am not interested in starting another relationship. Especially with a self-absorbed bully of a man.'

Kathryn raised an eyebrow. 'I agree. You've had one of those already, but Alistair Barlow is not like him, I promise you.' She picked up their mugs and disappeared into the back, leaving Hannah wondering how Kathryn could know anything about Todd.

She called from the back, 'Our church is having a fête on Saturday. Can you help at all?'

Hannah was happy to change the subject. 'What do I have to do?'

Kathryn reappeared, grinning. 'It would be great if you could manage the bookstall. We have had piles of books donated and the proceeds go to church funds, mainly supporting a farm preschool nearby.'

Hannah rather liked the idea of a small town church fête. She followed Kathryn out the front door and watched her lock up the shop. 'Thanks for the tea, Kathryn. And for listening too – you're good at it.'

Kathryn looked up from locking the door and grinned at Hannah. 'Let's pop over the road to the church now and I'll show you the books. We'll probably need to sort them or price them or something before the weekend. You can meet Douglas – he might tickle your fancy.'

'I don't need anyone near my fancy, thanks very much,' said Hannah darkly, though Kathryn's shout of laughter had her mouth curving into a smile. They crossed the road and Kathryn opened the wooden lych-gate. A slate-paved path led to a stone church, but instead of going to the front door, Kathryn led the way around the side to a more modern building set towards the back of the property. A sign pointed to the church office, and another to the church hall. Kathryn stuck her head into the office door and called, 'Douglas?'

A man's voice answered from the hall next door, 'I'm in here.'

The hall was piled with an assortment of loaded plastic bags, boxes of strange kitchen gadgets, and four trestle tables of old books. An athletic man in his early forties looked helplessly at the heaps of stuff. He was dressed in shorts and a Red Hot Chili Peppers t-shirt. He smiled widely at the two women as they came in. 'I hope you've come to rescue me, Kathryn. I'm completely at sea with all this crap.'

'Hannah, this is Douglas. He's our new minister.' Hannah looked at the man in surprise. He was unlike any minister she had ever seen and, as he came over to shake her hand, she saw his face compose itself with over-the-top charm.

'I am so happy to make your acquaintance,' he said, a dimple appearing at the corner of his mouth. 'Please tell me you have come to help turn everybody's junk into a decent fête. People in Joburg would never dream of buying second-hand rubbish, so I've never done this before. I'm beyond desperate.'

'Don't look at me,' said Hannah, laughing at his pathetic, pleading expression. 'I've hardly been in a church, let alone run a church fête.'

'Perfect!' Douglas crowed. 'We can use your mercenary, worldly principles to make heaps of cash out of this dreck.'

Kathryn was poking through the piles, opening bags and hauling out old clothes and curtains which she was holding up to the light and discarding into two piles. 'Oh shut up, Douglas,' she said with a toss of her head. 'How about getting to work rather than flirting with Hannah.' Douglas winked gamely at Hannah, who laughed and shook her head at the inconsistency of this man and his role.

Then she got stuck into the piles of dusty books, and by the time she had sorted them into categorised wooden crates, it was dark outside and she was filthy. Kathryn had managed to unearth two clothes rails on wheels and she had filled them with dresses and coats, arranging them in a colour order which looked so attractive, Hannah wanted to browse through the dresses herself.

Douglas tried to sort the bric-a-brac but, with no appreciation for what he was doing, Kathryn eventually sent him off to buy them supper. He returned, bumbling in through the door with a carry bag in each hand, a bottle of wine under his arm. 'I didn't know what you liked, so I got a selection,' he said cheerfully. He unpacked the food onto a free trestle table and, by the time the women had washed their hands, a feast was awaiting them. They tucked into pizza, salad, and an enormous box of hot chips, which was accompanied, rather incongruously, by a very good red wine and slabs of chocolate.

'I thought ministers weren't allowed to drink,' Hannah said to Douglas, who was now stretched out on his side on the hall floor, reclining on his elbow and looking more like a feasting Roman than a priest.

'That's the Methodists,' he said with a grin. 'I chose the Anglican church precisely for the reason that we drink wine every Sunday. Red wine is biblical, after all.'

'You give rocks what people think of you, even if you weren't allowed,' said Kathryn, sitting cross-legged on the floor, guarding the box of chips on her lap.

Douglas smiled across at her. 'True. My wife couldn't handle the scrutiny, though.'

Hannah's brows shot up in surprise. 'Your wife?'

Douglas kept his gaze on Kathryn. 'My wife, Kristy, hated the fishbowl life which comes with church work. She felt constantly watched and judged. She left me three years ago for an accountant who works office hours.'

Hannah glanced between Kathryn and Douglas, wondering at Kathryn's silence and a certain spark in the air. Douglas sighed dramatically, breaking the tension, and launched into an impression of Donkey from *Shrek*, singing at the top of his voice that he was all alone.

Kathryn shook her head and Hannah burst out laughing.

June 1901, Goshen Camp, Orange River Colony

Dearest Wolf,

A different kind of man came into the camp yesterday. Reverend Charlie from a new church in Bethlehem. It is called the Methodist Episcopal Church. I don't know what that is – all we ever knew was the Dutch church where Pa would go to nagmaal. Unlike any black-robed dominie I've seen, this man wears a brown suit with a stiff, clean shirt underneath. He holds himself upright, proud and comfortable in his skin. I had forgotten what that looks like. He spoke to us of freedom and not living under the hand of any other man. He spoke with a kindness we don't hear in the camp. He looked at me directly, met my eyes when he spoke – and I knew that he saw me. Really saw me. A year of looking past one another and finally, someone who sees me, Rachel Badenhorst. He said he'd come back. Said he had connections in America who would send money for us. I want so badly to believe him.

CHAPTER TEN

Hannah walked across to the church early, and found Douglas co-ordinating a group of men as they pitched canvas gazebos and set up trestle tables under the spreading plane trees in the church garden. She lugged the crates of books from the hall to her stand. Luminous price stickers and a homemade sign were the final touches. Douglas sauntered over, relaxed in his black-and-red Killers т-shirt, a lightning bolt emblazoned on the back. Hannah wondered what his parishioners would make of it.

'You're amazing,' he said, his arm casually pulling her into his side. 'New in town and already jumping in, boots and all.' Hannah allowed him the familiarity, certain his interest lay with someone else, and en-joying his charm, for what it was worth.

She smiled up at him and gestured to the church grounds now buzz-ing with people setting up stalls. 'Looks like you pulled it off.'

He threw his head back and howled in an outrageous accent from the American South, 'It's a miracle from the Lord, hallelujah!'

Hannah, laughing, punched him on the arm. 'You are the most ir-reverent person I know, and also happen to be the only priest I know. How's that possible?'

Douglas quickly moved out of range, rubbing his arm and grinning at her. 'I need to go set up my music equipment – my fans await.'

'I hope he matches his music to the audience,' said Kathryn, coming up behind Hannah. Her wildly curly dark hair had been caught up in a bun at the base of her neck, leaving black tendrils loose about her face. She was holding the hands of two small children, both as striking as their mother, with dark, curly hair and big brown eyes, but framed by faces much fairer than Kathryn's smooth brown complexion. 'This is Matthew and Emma-Jane,' she said, pulling them in front of her and stroking the tops of their heads. 'Say hello to Hannah, guys.' The children greeted Hannah shyly and slid round their mother's legs till they were hiding behind her. Kathryn turned and crouched down in front of them. 'Granny and Gramps are at the jumble stall inside the hall, and I'll be making pancakes right over there. Go and explore, but don't take a single step out the gate, you hear?' The twins nodded, but were off like two hares springing away from their mother's catching hands.

'They are beautiful, Kathryn,' said Hannah, watching them dart between the tables and guy ropes.

'Yes, they are,' smiled Kathryn, 'and they keep me on my toes.'

'Is their father around?' Hannah kept her gaze on the two children in an effort to keep her tone light.

'We're still married, but he's been gone five years now. Disappeared just before the twins were born. We only found him last year.' Her face held shadows of pain as Hannah met her eyes.

'Why did he leave?'

'He's schizophrenic … living on the streets in Durban. A friend saw him begging at an intersection, but he won't come home. We've all tried. He nearly broke his parents.' Kathryn shook her head and swatted her hands around, brushing away the past like a stinging insect. 'I'd better get cracking with my pannekoek – I'll send some over. Cinnamon sugar?'

Hannah nodded, with a smile for her new friend. 'And a bit of lemon, please.'

By mid-morning, the church grounds were full. Douglas's surprisingly talented busking drifted over the busy stalls. Help for Hannah had arrived in the form of a small, neat man who introduced himself as Moses Motala. Quietly spoken and highly efficient, he was soon managing the stall pretty much single-handedly. Listening to his interactions with customers and friends, Hannah eventually figured out he was the mayor of Leliehoek, and liked him all the more for his humility and friendly nature.

She caught glimpses of Alistair helping his father cook eggs and bacon. He didn't look her way, even when Neil raised his spatula in a big wave across the lawn.

Hannah waved in return, a smile on her face for Neil, though her thoughts had clouded over. Bloody Alistair.

Her irritation was arrested by Douglas's voice over the sound system, 'And now, a song for the new girl in town. For Hannah Harrison.'

Hannah's head jerked up, and a flush spread rapidly up her neck as his clear, mellow voice began a reggae song in her honour.

A deep belly laugh erupted from Moses, and he clapped his hand onto Hannah's shoulder. 'What do you think of our priest? He's a blast of fresh air for this town.'

'He's a blast, all right,' muttered Hannah, holding her hands to her hot cheeks.

The end of the song brought scattered applause and whistling for Douglas, who bowed dramatically, and then blew a cheeky kiss towards Hannah and another to Kathryn, who stood watching him with her arms folded and good-humoured exasperation on her face.

Hannah turned back to her books, but not before she caught a glimpse of Alistair Barlow. He was watching her, a frown darkening his face before he quickly composed himself to face his mother holding a roll for him to fill with egg and bacon.

By early afternoon, the fête had wrapped up. Hannah and Moses packed up their stall, pleased with themselves. Huge reductions and special deals towards the end of the day had cleared the books. Amused patrons had walked away with their arms full for a few rands. When a group of men arrived to take down the gazebo and move the tables back into the hall, Hannah wandered out through the gate to stand on the pavement.

The Dutch Reformed church stood over the road, an imposing building compared to the little Anglican church. Hannah slipped through the gate into the grounds. Here, a large cemetery filled most of the property and Hannah strolled among the gravestones, glancing at the inscriptions with interest. A thought occurred to her and she moved to the older part of the cemetery, where the headstones leant over and the engravings became less clear. She walked along the lines of graves until she stopped in front of three graves lying alongside one another. The first was the newest, and the headstone was carved in the shape of an open Bible. One side read, *Daniel Stephanus Badenhorst, 1910–1961, beloved husband*, the other side, *Maria Jacoba Badenhorst, 1915–1965, beloved wife*. The second and oldest headstone was a simple weathered stone marker, and Hannah had to bend low and trace the letters to be sure of the name, *Danie Petrus Badenhorst, 1855–1920*. The last headstone was an ageing marble cross set on a plinth with *Corlie Johanna Marietjie Badenhorst 1882–1939* engraved on the horizontal bar of the cross. Below, on the plinth, was another name, *Wolf Daniel Badenhorst, 1885–1943*.

Hannah's heart tripped at the sight of that name. *Wolf.* She quickly searched the rest of the cemetery but could find no other Badenhorsts and then, thinking that Rachel might have married and changed her name, she checked again for any graves marked *Rachel*, but there were none. Her mind filled with questions: Was it just coincidence that there was a Wolf Badenhorst buried here? Coincidence that his dates set him perfectly in the frame of the South African War? This Wolf would have been fifteen years old at the outbreak of war, and Hannah knew that boys much younger rode with the commandos, though perhaps unofficially. But if this was Rachel's Wolf, where were the others whom she wrote about? Where were little Lizzie and Oupa Jakob and wild Kristina? And where was Rachel?

Hannah wandered back towards the gate and, as she came around the corner of the church, she nearly bumped into a large, older man unlocking the church door.

'Ekskuus,' he said, smiling, a grasp on her arm to keep her from overbalancing before he let go quickly. 'Kan ek help?'

Hannah replied in Afrikaans. 'I was looking in the cemetery, and I was wondering if the church keeps records of births and deaths?'

The man looked quizzically at Hannah. 'We have the registers in the vestry – are you looking for something in particular?'

'I can come back when it suits you, though. I don't want to trouble you.'

He smiled, his eyes behind spectacles crinkling in the corners. 'I'm waiting for the flower lady to bring the arrangements for tomorrow's services. Now is good, actually. My name is Morné,' he said, holding out his enormous hand for Hannah to shake. His grip was firm and dry.

He led Hannah through the dim, quiet church. Tall stained-glass windows reached for the roof, casting soft patterns of glass onto the carpet. At the front of the church was a door to the left, and Hannah stepped into a room crammed with odd things. Flower vases competed for space with a wooden crib, straw spilling through the slats onto the carpet. A tall cupboard filled one wall and, when Morné opened it, Hannah caught a glimpse of silver jugs and chalices. Hannah, who had only been in church a few times to attend the weddings of friends, now found herself intrigued at the paraphernalia stuffed into this little room. From one shelf, Morné drew out three thick, bound registers, and set them on a table. 'Take your time. I'll be in the church. Call me if you need anything.'

Hannah settled down at a table and opened all three registers until she found the oldest one, whose dates were closest to the time period she was looking for. The first entry began in 1903, and she scanned through the entries until she came to the marriage of Wolf Badenhorst and Corlie du Plessis in 1909. In the entries of the following year, she found the birth of their son, Daniel, and then three more children over the next few years. In the next register, Hannah found the entry of Daniel's marriage to Maria Brandt in 1934; they had their first daughter, Gisela, that same year. Like in the graveyard, Hannah could find no earlier references to other Badenhorsts, no earlier marriages of other daughters, and no deaths, apart from those she had seen in the cemetery.

Before she could open the third register, Morné had stuck his head into the room and smiled apologetically. 'Sorry to interrupt, the flowers have arrived.'

'I think I'm done too,' Hannah said, stretching her arms above her head. She glanced at her watch and was startled to see she had been hunched over the registers for an hour.

'Find what you were looking for?'

'Not really.' Hannah closed the books and handed them to Morné, who slid them back into the cupboard. She watched him thoughtfully. 'What happened to the farming families around here during the South African War? Were the locals affected much?'

'Oh yes,' he said, his back to her as he locked the cupboard, 'very much so. Most were on commando or sent to the camps. My impression is that the farms were abandoned. It took years for them to be resettled. And some families never returned.' He stood back for Hannah to precede him through the door into the church before he pulled it closed behind him. 'My great-grandfather was sent to Ceylon as a prisoner of war. He never went back to the family farm near Bethulie. Settled in Bloemfontein after the war, where there was work.'

As they walked back through the quiet church, Hannah breathed in the strong scent of lilies from an enormous arrangement on a pedestal. 'Did anyone from this area resettle here?'

Morné opened the church door for her and came out behind her. 'I've been here for twenty years and have never found out much about those days. The old folks are long gone, and the younger generation's not so interested, especially since 1994. Who wants to dig up that old Afrikaner stuff?' He locked the church door and stood with Hannah on the pavement. 'The one family I know of who has stuck it out since those days are the De Jagers on Silwerfontein.' Hannah tried to keep her face neutral, her heart tripping at the name of Rachel's farm. It hadn't occurred to her to pursue Silwerfontein. She had been so caught up with Goshen. Morné went on, oblivious to her struggle to keep her composure. 'Karl de Jager's father married the Badenhorst girl and took over her family farm.'

'Who was that?' managed Hannah, not believing what she was hearing.

'Gisela Badenhorst. She died last year. A fierce old lady, stalwart of this church. Strong as an ox until her granddaughter Marilie was killed. Marilie was married to the Barlow boy, Alistair. Have you come across the family?'

CHAPTER ELEVEN

Hannah was crossing the road to the square, heading for home but so deep in thought she didn't look up when Kathryn called across to her from where she was packing the last of her cooking equipment into her car. When Kathryn raised her voice and yelled like only a girl from the Flats could, Hannah stopped and changed direction towards her.

'Why didn't you tell me about Alistair's wife, Kathryn?' said Hannah, coming to a halt right in front of her, her eyes flashing, mouth tight.

'I didn't think it was important. You said you weren't interested in him.'

Hannah slumped against the car next to Kathryn, resting her head on the window frame. 'I'm not interested in him. I'm interested in his farm, and now it turns out he married into Rachel's family. Every which way I turn, I bump into him. And he's so mean to me.' Aware that she sounded petulant, she looked at Kathryn, who was visibly struggling not to smile.

'The twins are with their grandparents and I'm starving. How about you cook me some supper?'

Kathryn parked her car outside Hannah's gate and they walked up the back steps to the kitchen door. Bending down to stroke Patchy, Kathryn promptly sneezed. 'I love cats so much and I can't be near them – isn't that the most unfair thing you've ever heard?'

'Right up there with world hunger and wealth disparity,' said Hannah dryly, though her mouth tipped in the beginnings of a smile as Kathryn laughed out loud and said, cheekily mimicking Hannah's earlier tone, *You're so mean to me.*

Kathryn settled herself at the kitchen table with a glass of white wine and watched Hannah move around the kitchen, putting together omelettes and salad.

'So I've got a journal written by a girl called Rachel Badenhorst from Silwerfontein. She's separated from her family and goes to a camp called Goshen. The mother, grandfather, and children go to another camp, Winburg, I think. The father and two brothers are on commando. One of those brothers is Wolf, and I found his grave today in the Dutch Reformed church cemetery, along with his wife and son. Another grave there could be their father's, but Rachel just calls him Pa.' Hannah talked as she grated cheese and pulled sundried tomatoes from the fridge. 'I'm not sure if Danie Badenhorst is Pa. And I don't know how to find that out.' She piled the filling and fresh rocket into the pan and folded the omelette in half. Pulling two plates from the cupboard, she slid the omelette onto one plate and set it in front of Kathryn. 'The dominie, Morné, told me that Silwerfontein was the Badenhorst farm until Gisela Badenhorst married a De Jager.'

Kathryn nodded, looking up from her plate. 'I knew Gisela. She died last year only. She was an amazing lady, strong but fun. She farmed on her own after her husband died, until Karl was old enough to take over.'

Hannah kept her eyes on the pan, finishing the second omelette. 'And Karl was Alistair's father-in-law?'

'Yes, Karl and Esme are still on Silwerfontein ... well, kind of. They have a house in Wilderness in the Cape, and Esme prefers to be there than in Leliehoek, especially since Marilie was killed.'

Hannah sat down at the table with her plate and took a sip of wine. 'And Marilie was married to Alistair when she was killed. Is that why he's so awful?'

Kathryn sighed. 'Hannah, he's not awful. He's a mess. A lot happened around her death, and he's had a very rough time. Don't be too hard on him.'

'I'm not hard on him – he's hard on me!' She pushed her half-finished plate away. 'He won't give me access to Goshen, and now I find that he's inextricably linked to Silwerfontein too. I can't win.'

Kathryn put her knife and fork neatly together on the plate. 'Look, Karl is a nice man. See if you can meet him and ask him about his family. Maybe there are letters or photo albums or something that will help. Alistair doesn't have to be involved.'

Hannah tilted her head to the side, deep in thought.

Kathryn put her hand on Hannah's arm to draw her gaze. 'Hannah, just be careful of his wife, Esme. She's bitter and can be nasty.' Hannah saw Kathryn's expression intensify and her eyes become deeply serious. 'Be ready for an attack.'

A chill raised the hair on Hannah's arms and she shivered. Glancing behind her at the closed door, she shook off the feeling, then leant across the table and poured them both another glass of wine. Wanting to lighten the mood, she raised an eyebrow at Kathryn. 'I have a slab of Lindt dark chocolate in the cupboard. Could you bear it? Or do I need to eat the whole thing by myself?'

The opportunity to meet the De Jagers came sooner than Hannah expected. She was finishing up in the shop when she heard the *beep* of a car remote. A large white BMW had parked outside the shop. A personalised number plate read, ESME, in green letters. The doorbell tinkled and a petite woman came in. She was dressed in skin-tight jeans and a small vest, and looked to be in her late fifties. Her peroxided hair was cut short in the back and blow-dried into a bouffant style in the front. The smell of hairspray and musky perfume filled the shop as she clattered into the reading room on high wedge sandals. A few minutes later, she appeared at the till with a stack of romance novels. She tapped with long acrylic nails on the counter and didn't make eye contact when Hannah introduced herself. Hannah dawdled over ringing up the books, wrestling with how to start a conversation.

She blundered in: 'I'm interested in the South African War history of the area and I've heard your family goes back generations here.'

'My husband's family,' said Esme, her tone dismissive as she stretched one hand to examine her nails.

'Would it be possible for me to come to the farm and chat with your husband?' Hannah ventured, gingerly.

'We're far too busy. We're off to Wilderness soon, so ...' A bored expression settled on her face.

Hannah, feeling a strong dislike creep over her, pushed, 'Are there perhaps Badenhorst records or memorabilia in the house? Family's important, after all.'

Esme's eyes froze over. She leant over the counter towards Hannah and spat, 'You know nothing about family! Fokken stay away from me.' She stormed out of the shop, beeped her car open, and threw the novels onto the passenger seat. Hannah stood in the doorway, watching the car disappear in a spit of gravel. She focused on a figure standing outside the supermarket. His face turned to her, pale.

Alistair strode across the street, taking the stairs two at a time. Stopping on the stoep, one hand gripping the balustrade, eyes dark, he said, 'What the hell just happened?'

Hannah, still shocked by Esme's outburst, and now feeling a slow slide of guilt, crossed her arms across her waist. 'I just asked her about the old Badenhorsts and if there were any family records from the war.'

Alistair thumped his fist against the pillar of the stoep. 'You said you'd drop it!'

'No, I did not!' Hannah pushed herself away from the doorframe, her hands clenched at her sides. 'What's your problem, Alistair?'

His eyes narrowed. 'You've been here what – a week? And you think you have the right to poke into other people's lives. You know nothing about us!'

Alistair took two steps towards her, his body threatening, but she was too angry to notice. She glared up at him, meeting stormy eyes. 'I'm not poking,' she spat. 'I'm just trying to find out about Rachel Badenhorst, and every which way I turn, I come up against your bloody ego. You just can't stand anyone getting in your face. If you would help me instead of fricking exploding every time you see me, I might get out of your hair a whole lot faster!'

His scarred mouth curled into a sneer, but his tone evened out. 'If only that were possible. You see, I can't help with delusions. The camp story is a fantasy and I've never heard the name Rachel Badenhorst. You've got your knickers in a twist over a few ghosts and a piece of fiction.'

'My knickers have nothing to do with it, no matter how much you might wish otherwise.' Alistair's eyebrows shot up but she continued, 'You do not get to tell me what I can and can't do. Who I can and can't speak to.'

'Fine! Then stay away from Goshen.'

'So you control whom your parents get to see, too? I don't think so. I bet I can call up your dad any day of the week and get a guided tour of the farm.'

'Hannah, I swear to God, if you use my parents for your own ends ...' He reached for her, but his hands curled and clenched in the space between them and he took a step back. 'Just you try manipulate them – you'll see the worst of me. I promise you.'

She tilted her head to the side, her eyes wide, though her words slid with sarcasm. 'There's a worse side of you? And I thought the twisted half was bad enough.' As the words left her lips, she wished she could pull them back. She watched his face receive the blow. He seemed to stagger, all anger leaving his body like a breath exhaled.

As if injured, he stumbled away from her back to his Toyota and drove off, hunched over the steering wheel. She walked back into the shop, locking up as she went. In her kitchen, she automatically switched on the kettle and stood staring out at the garden. Her heart still thumped and her stomach churned, nausea and guilt so thick in her, she didn't notice the kettle subside on the counter next to her.

Thirty minutes later, Hannah knocked on Alistair's front door, shame and nerves tangling. The dogs thundered down the passage and scrabbled on the other side of the door, but no footsteps followed. Hannah retreated down the steps to her car but paused at the driver's door. She had been awful. Yes, he'd provoked her. He'd been unfair in his accusations, but neither justified her nastiness. She glanced back at the house and sucked her lower lip between her teeth. Dammit. She headed around the house and stepped through the herb garden at the back door, rosemary scenting the air as she brushed past. The stable door to the kitchen was half-open and the dogs had beaten her to it. Grant stood on his hind legs, a crocodile grin on his face. She reached to stroke his head and saw Alistair sitting in the dim kitchen, elbows propped on the table.

'Not now, Mum,' he said, his hands pressing into his eyes.

'It's me,' said Hannah.

For a few seconds they stared at each other, and then Hannah said quietly, 'May I come in?'

He shrugged, getting to his feet as she stepped inside the kitchen.

'Alistair, I came to apologise ...' Hannah shook her head, hating the weary pain in his eyes. 'You made me so angry. I should never have said those things. I don't know why I did.'

He drew in a breath and ran his hand into his hair, tugging on a chunk at the front. 'It's the truth, after all – isn't it? I am twisted. And angry. And a bully.'

Hannah had prepared herself for rage, had wondered if she would even make it through the door. This beaten man disabled her. She leant against the counter.

'It was Esme, or rather my talking to Esme, wasn't it?' Her voice softened. 'It's about your wife?'

'What have you heard?'

'Nothing. I mean, I heard that she died.'

'She was killed,' he said, his tone flat.

'Yes.'

He looked past her, to the yard, and she felt him retreat somewhere else.

'What happened to ... to haunt you like this?'

Alistair slid to sit on the floor. His face paled, naked with a pain that brought tears to Hannah's eyes. Something seemed to loosen in him as he said, 'Marilie ...' He swallowed. 'My wife. We married young. Too young, really. We were so careful not to fall pregnant in those first years.

We were loving our lives. Had such big plans. She was showjumping competitively, doing really well. And then, when we thought the time was right, we couldn't fall pregnant anyway. We spent a fortune on specialists and treatments but for nothing. Marilie became obsessed, then bereft, then depressed. I started suggesting we look at adoption, but the chances of getting a white child are pretty much nil in this country.' He must have caught Hannah's frown because he smiled a small, sad smile. 'Marilie wouldn't consider a black baby. We started fighting.' His fingers rubbed across his eyes and pinched the bridge of his nose. He looked straight at Hannah. 'We were fighting that afternoon – I told her to get over herself. I actually said, *Would you rather be a racist than a mother?*' He shook his head. 'If I'd held back those words … She wrenched away, told me to get away from her.'

Hannah's heart ached for him, the way he sat crumpled in his own kitchen. She wanted to cross the room and touch him, but fear won. There was too much emotion in the room. Too intense for her to go near.

Alistair picked at the fabric of his jeans. 'Her groom was loading her horse for an event. She stormed away from me and took over the loading, but she was so angry, she tried to rush the horse. He must have picked up on her emotion because he wouldn't go in. And then, suddenly, he backed off the ramp and knocked her over. Her foot got caught in the lead rein and, with her screaming at the groom, the horse spooked and bolted. He dragged her a few paces and then started kicking and stamping on her to get away.' Alistair's voice cracked. 'The groom was trying to get to the horse and I was trying to get to Marilie when the bungee cord holding the horse snapped and whipped. It sliced my face.' He lifted his hand to cover the white scar. 'I didn't notice. By the time we got to her, she was dead. Her skull smashed on the driveway.' He drew a shuddering breath. 'It was my fault.'

Hannah slid down to the floor across from him. They were both silent for a few moments, before Alistair said, 'My dad sat with me on the driveway until the ambulance came, holding a towel to keep my face together. I had her head in my lap, trying to keep her brain in her skull.' He gestured to his face. 'This is to remind me what I did.'

Hannah brushed her eyes with her sleeve. 'And Esme?'

'She made Karl shoot the horse. Rooi Baron. I can't imagine how Karl managed to do it, but he did – for Esme. How Marilie loved that horse. Sometimes I wondered if she loved him more than she loved me. Esme never forgave me for Marilie's death. I can understand that. I don't hold it against her. But she's unstable – maybe she always has been – and what happened pushed her over the edge.' He tipped his head back against the cupboard. 'Better to stay away from her, Hannah.'

Hannah uncrossed her legs and stretched them out on the kitchen floor. She met his gaze. 'I'm sorry I caused trouble, Alistair. Kathryn warned me and I just barged ahead anyway. I was so convinced the De Jagers hold the key to unlock Rachel's story.'

He stayed where he was, looking too wrung out to react as he had earlier. 'Why are you so determined to keep going? Did you come to Leliehoek for this?'

Hannah sighed. 'I really didn't. I ran away from my life. Came here on a complete whim and the minute I drove out of Cape Town, I felt a weight lifting off me. All the expectations of my parents and my supervisor and …' She was about to mention Todd but changed her mind, not wanting to bring him into the room. 'It all lifted. I was on my own with my destiny in my own hands for the first time.' She smiled. 'That sounds so clichéd.' She looked down at her hands. 'When I found Rachel's journal, an excitement lit in me. I haven't felt that in years.' Pausing, she tilted her head before saying, 'Actually, I can't remember ever feeling it.'

'How is that possible?' he asked.

'How is what possible?'

'That you, of all people, haven't been passionate about anything?'

Hannah shrugged. 'People in my life have always made decisions for me and I went with the flow. I followed the academic path my parents had chosen for themselves. I got involved with someone before I had even figured out who I was for myself. Instead, I became what he wanted.' She smiled at him. 'So all this … passion … is new.'

'As much as it irritates me, it suits you.'

Hannah pushed herself up off the floor and crossed to him, offering him a hand up. 'I'll remind you next time you get angry with me.'

Taking her hand, his eyes serious, he said, 'Can we be friends, Hannah?'

She smiled up at him, liking that her hand felt small in his, liking it perhaps too much. 'We can try. But you must know first that Rachel has her hooks in me and I won't give her up.'

He dropped her hand, shoving his fingers into the back pockets of his jeans. 'What will you do if you discover that this camp really did exist?'

Hannah leant back against the counter. 'I don't know. I haven't actually thought that far. I suppose we'd have to get some experts in.'

His face darkened immediately. 'No people on the farm. I don't want cars and strangers. No.'

Hannah took a step towards him and put a hand on his arm. 'What if we keep it really quiet? No fanfare. Just an historian?'

'We don't,' he amended it quickly, 'you don't even know if the journal is true. You prove that Rachel was a real person and then I'll think about it.'

Hannah felt the immediate conflict. She had gained ground with him; he was going to consider the possibility. But what if she couldn't prove that Rachel was real? She had found nothing so far. More than a little dismayed, she nodded.

CHAPTER TWELVE

By the time Hannah arrived home, it was dark outside. She drew the curtains and then stopped in the passage, hovering over the phone. Should she call the De Jagers or not? Putting Alistair's and Kathryn's warnings aside, she pulled a sticky note from her pocket and dialled the farm number, holding her breath while the phone rang. *Please let it be Karl. Please let it be Karl.*

'Yes?' Esme's tight voice cracked across the line and Hannah's heart sank.

'Hello, Mrs De Jager. I'm phoning to apologise for upsetting you this afternoon. I was out of line, I'm sorry.' The silence on the other end unnerved her and she blurted out, 'It's Hannah Harrison, from the bookshop?'

Esme's voice, though muffled to a whisper, spat bitterly, 'I saw you go to Goshen today. You're hunting my daughter's husband, aren't you? You move quickly, bitch—'

Hannah slammed down the phone. Her chest tight with shock, she pressed trembling hands into her solar plexus, trying to breathe.

Her evening was restless after that. She couldn't settle to anything. When she realised she had been staring at the computer screen for half an hour without registering a thing, she eventually gave up on the movie she had started. Changing into her pyjamas, she crawled into bed, picking up Rachel's journal and opening it to where she had left off a week previously.

> I write to take my mind off this place, as if I can write a
> different world into being. I wish I could. I would write

away this camp, this war. All the hatred and misery and death. I want things which I do not know if I will ever have again. My family. I do not want to just be with them; I want to be on the farm. I want all the things of the past. The talking, the laughing, the playing, the singing. Ma always said, 'I want does not get.' I don't care any more about manners – I want it all. I always thought war bred heroes, but it doesn't. It breeds selfishness. I am the best example.

At its harshest, it strips life of normality. I watch the soldiers stationed at this camp. I'm sure at home they are normal people with mothers and sisters and grandmothers. They must do normal things like kiss their children goodnight. Like go to church and sing hymns with their wives. Here, they are strapped into uniforms and helmets. They look at us like we are a species foreign to them.

Even the medical officer, when he comes, does not like to touch us. He snaps at the mothers, telling them if they keep their children clean and feed them properly, they won't get sick. Like it is our choice to be dirty. Like it is our choice to starve. He tells them to stop using the old medicines their mothers taught them, and their mothers before them. But there is never enough British medicine, just stories about supplies and rations. What do they expect us to do? He says blame the commandos for blowing up the railways. But did the Boers start this war? Did the commandos burn our homes and herd us off the land into these places?

Hannah awoke in the middle of the night, unsettled, as thoughts and emotions gathered and shifted around her. She knew her brain was trying to process the day, but that clean, rational explanation didn't lighten her mind's stumbling from one thing to another. Her bedside light glowed next to her, throwing shadows onto the walls. She had always hated this time. This weird, lost time, when everyone else was asleep and she lay alone. Todd had teased her – made fun of having to close the cupboard doors on the black caverns they became in the night. As a little girl, she had been stranded in her bed. The terror wouldn't allow her body to leave the safety of the sheets. So she had to lie there, paralysed by gut-twisting fear. Reading had been the only way through it. Now she reached for the journal again.

> It is so cold. Our rough shelters do little to ward off the wind. I think of you all the time, Wolf. Where are you? I hear stories about the prisoners of war. That the British are sending burghers to far-flung places, to Bermuda and Ceylon. To India? Is this true? Are you still here? I would rather think of you hunched against the wind in the lee of a rock than setting sail for a place from which you might never return.
>
> How I long for the house with its thick stone walls. We lay in our beds listening to the wind raging around the house, loving the sound because inside we were warm and safe. Our home has been lost, Wolf. There is no thatch house, no stable, no horses, no fields. Even if we all could meet back there again, so much has gone.
>
> I am changed too. Not lost yet, but almost.

Hannah must have fallen asleep for a few hours because she awoke as the light began to creep under the heavy curtains of her room. Her head thumped, her tongue thick with a metallic taste. She kicked the wretched iron doorstop on her way to the kitchen for a glass of water. *That thing has to go*, she promised herself.

Hobbling, she retrieved her leggings from the floor and a clean T-shirt, and sat on her bed, about to pull on her running shoes, when she changed her mind, sliding her injured toe into flip-flops instead. She hadn't gone for a run since she had arrived in Leliehoek. But not today, with the restless night still pounding behind her eyes and her toe bruised and throbbing. It wasn't five o'clock yet, but she felt compelled to get out of the house.

As she started her car, she thought how wonderfully still the small town was at this time. Glancing across the square, she could see Kathryn's lights on. No doubt she was hard at work already, her ovens filling the shop with scents of cakes and pastries. But Hannah turned left at the corner and headed out of town, finding herself driving towards Goshen. Soon, she was climbing the hill behind the house, and she wound down her window to breathe in the fresh morning air. The sun was climbing too, and with it came the grass birds, clinging to the grass stems, bending the heavy seed heads with the weight of their little bodies. The morning light brushed the hillside in bright gold, and Hannah felt herself relax, congratulating herself. As her headache disappeared, so did the vague nausea. She wished she had brought something to eat. A rusk with a cup of coffee would've been perfect.

Instead of opening the wire gate for her car, she parked there and ducked through the triangular gap at the bottom of the fence, deciding to walk on to the plateau rather. The sun was at her back and wonderfully warm. As she crunched through the wet grass, each step raised the scents of dew and dust that tangle together in summer. She indulged a memory and stopped to pull a long stem from its stalk, biting the soft green end and relishing the sweetness.

The wind pump and reservoir came into view as she crested the plateau. The light sat gently on them, quiet seeping from the still air. What was it about this place that was so compelling? What was this almost visceral connection?

Walking around the reservoir until she came to a concrete water trough, she stepped up onto it to look over the edge of the reservoir where the pipe trickled water into the pool. The wind pump stood tall overhead, its metal frame weathered and rusted in parts. The blades were still, reflecting bright silver in the sun. Hannah folded her arms on the wall and rested her head on them. From this angle, with the stand of gum trees behind her, the view stretched over the plateau to the hills beyond. No sign of human habitation anywhere. Isolated. The silence grew heavier and seemed to hang in the air.

With a deafening clank, the wind pump blades swung into motion. Hannah started and fell off the trough. The wind pump was now shrieking, faster and faster. A freezing wind blew over the plateau and into the gum trees behind her, raising a skeletal rattle through their grey leaves. She picked herself up and rubbed her arms, now white with goosebumps. Her ears rang with the metallic scream of the wind pump. Glancing back towards the trees, she noticed in confusion that they stood completely still. Her brain wouldn't compute what she saw, and the temperature plummeted further. The rush of wind through the trees whistled around her, but the trees stood unmoved. She looked from side to side, expecting to see the grass folded over in the face of the wind. It was undisturbed. Backing away, she broke into a run. Her flip-flops slipped in the wet grass, and she tripped over tussocks, but kept on till she got to the fence. She ducked through and saw Alistair's pickup pulling up next to her own, the dogs milling around her legs.

Alistair slammed his door and came striding towards her, concern in every movement. He must have felt the chill in her arms as he grasped her, and he began to rub them vigorously. 'Are you okay? What happened?'

Hannah drew a breath and felt her heart slow its frantic pace, relief replacing the crazy fear. 'I'm fine. Just spooked.' She looked up at him. 'But I didn't imagine it. One minute, it was beautiful and sunny. Then the next, the temperature dropped to freezing and the wind pump started up.' She looked back towards the plateau. 'It's still going – can you hear it? But there's no wind. And it's warm here.'

Alistair's eyes were puzzled. 'It can be unsettling up there. I don't come up unless I have to.'

Hannah felt his gentle diplomacy and it irritated her enough to snap, 'What are you doing here then?'

He stepped away from her. 'I take the dogs for a run every morning and I saw your car from the bottom field. I came to see you – I mean, to see if you were okay.'

She pulled herself up, 'You still don't believe what I'm saying, do you? Nothing could possibly be up there. Kobie and I have just imagined it all. Right? Why would I need help?' She looked past him.

Turning from her, he walked to his Toyota, wrenching open the door and pulling a fleece from the seat. He came back to where she was still standing, stony and remote.

'Put this on, you're cold.'

'I'm fine.'

His face dark, teeth gritted, he growled, 'Put it on.' She angrily pushed her arms into the huge sleeves and he zipped up the front roughly. He shoved his hands deep into his pockets and glowered at her. Furious, and not sure exactly why, Hannah turned towards her Mazda. Alistair followed her and firmly closed her door. He stood back as she drove off without a further word between them.

CHAPTER THIRTEEN

Hannah was setting up for book club the next afternoon. She and Barbara had spent the morning together, serving the odd customer and registering the new stock Hannah had ordered. Older townspeople, who didn't own computers, still thought Amazon was a jungle in South America, and Loot something to do with pirates, and depended on Hannah ordering specially for them. The courier service had delivered the stock that day, and Hannah had begun to phone customers to let them know their books had arrived. She set out catalogues and a few reviews of the latest published books, hoping the book club might find something interesting.

The doorbell tinkled and Sarah Barlow looked into the reading room. 'I know I'm early – I wondered if you might need some help?' She began to unpack a wicker basket, placing on the table plates of scones, and cheerful jars of cherry and gooseberry jam.

'Those look wonderful. Are they your jams?'

'I make them every year, even now that I won't let Neil touch them. I produce far more than I should. Please keep these, Hannah.'

Hannah smiled at her, appreciating the sunny atmosphere which seemed to follow Sarah. 'That would be great, thank you.'

'May I get the tea things for you?' said Sarah.

'Thanks, they're laid on trays in my kitchen.' Sarah bustled out and Hannah stood back from the table, checking the cloth and flowers, still a little anxious that she might not hit the mark with the ladies of Leliehoek.

Sarah returned with the tray of cups and saucers, and began to set them out, placing a teaspoon on each saucer and turning the teaspoons so that they lined up in identical rows. She glanced at Hannah. 'That's a very old ledger you have on the kitchen table. Did you come across it in the shop?'

Hannah sighed. She should have put it away. She was still smarting from her encounter with Alistair yesterday, and had run out of ideas which might lead her closer to Rachel. Taking a breath, she folded her arms across her waist as she leant back against a bookshelf. 'Remember I told you I had found something in the shop which referred to a camp called Goshen?' Sarah nodded. 'That ledger is a journal, written by a Boer girl called Rachel Badenhorst of Silwerfontein.' Hannah saw Sarah's eyes widen. 'It means something to you?'

Sarah was quiet for a moment. 'I know Silwerfontein – I grew up there almost as much as I did on Goshen. Karl is a bit younger than me, but our families have been neighbours for generations. His mother, Gisela, and mine were very close.' Sadness passed over her face as she said, 'After so many generations of running together as kids, Marilie and Alistair were the first ones to marry. It was like losing my own child when she died. Two, actually. Alistair became a different person after that.'

Hannah laid her hand lightly on Sarah's arm. The older woman smiled back at her, then gave a small shake of her head. 'It split the families too. We pulled Alistair back into ours, defending him fiercely from …' She paused, then: 'As well as I know the family, though, the name Rachel doesn't ring a bell. Gisela was the last Badenhorst before she married Bryant de Jager.'

Hannah nodded. 'Alistair said I have to give him some kind of proof that Rachel was a real person, that this journal is not a fictional account. If I can do that, he'll consider allowing me to look into the camp on Goshen. I've been wondering if there aren't photos or letters or something at Silwerfontein which might tell us about her.'

'But Esme is the obstacle?'

Hannah's mouth lifted in a small smile of acknowledgement, but she didn't say anything more. She didn't want anyone to know about the phone call. It had been too personal an attack, and Hannah still felt a niggle of guilt about provoking it. 'I've found nothing so far. I really want to get into that house.'

Sarah lifted a hand. 'It's impossible with Esme there. Maybe Karl ... Let me think about it, Hannah.'

The doorbell tinkled and the book club ladies began to arrive, filling the shop with chatter and the clink of tea cups. Hannah didn't get the chance to say anything further to Sarah, but she felt a faint glint of excitement that someone, at last, seemed to be interested in Rachel too. Perhaps having Sarah in her corner would turn the tide.

On the surface, she calmly managed the afternoon, refilling tea pots and replenishing plates of tartlets and cheese muffins. And beneath it, she enjoyed the feeling of anticipation – a sense that something was about to break open for her.

Later that evening, her house phone rang. Hannah paused in her supper preparations, wondering who had her home number. She padded barefoot into the passage to answer. Sarah's voice came down the line, bright and excited: 'I've arranged it! Esme's in Wilderness and it's just Karl at home. I asked if I could look for some of his mum's recipes.'

'That's so sneaky, Sarah! And completely genius.'

'I know!' Hannah could hear the grin in Sarah's voice. 'Can you manage a visit to Silwerfontein tomorrow?'

'Barbara is in the shop tomorrow afternoon – I can come out then.'

'Meet me here first and we can go together.'

Hannah replaced the receiver in its cradle and returned to her plate of reheated lamb casserole, one of the many contributions to have come out of the freezer from her welcome a few weeks before. Savouring the stew, Hannah's mind turned to the following day. She had no idea what to expect – what they would find – but her sense of anticipation grew, and she wondered if perhaps this was indeed her break.

The next morning crawled by. The shop was quiet, and Hannah was not able to settle. She was making herself a sandwich in the kitchen when Barbara came down the passage.

'Hello, Hannah-Belle,' she said breezily as she helped herself to a wedge of cheese. 'That has a nice ring to it.'

Hannah looked sideways at Barbara. 'Hannibal Lector comes to mind, not quite the image I try to project.'

Barbara grinned back at Hannah and munched her cheese. Hannah bit into one half of her sandwich, balancing the other half with her keys as she slung her bag over her shoulder. She waved and left Barbara cutting a thick slice of bread, slathering it with Sarah's cherry jam.

At Goshen, Sarah was waiting for her and they climbed into her Ford to drive to Silwerfontein. Though the farms shared a boundary, it took twenty minutes to drive back to the main road, take the next farm entrance along, and reach an avenue of old oaks which lined the road to the farmstead. Hannah wondered when they had been planted. Could they have been young trees when Rachel and Wolf played there?

The avenue ended at old stone gate posts, which stood as sentinels on either side of the drive. Passing through, Hannah could see the house. Built from similar sandstone as the Goshen house, this dwelling was laid out in a horseshoe shape with two wings jutting forwards, topped by gables. A veranda ran around the inside of the U, shaded by pergolas with old wisteria creepers twisting across the beams.

As they pulled to a stop in front of the house, a cloud of small dogs erupted from the front door. Hannah climbed out the car, wincing at the high-pitched cacophony of three dachshunds and two Yorkshire terriers. An enormous man followed the dogs down to the car, opening Sarah's door for her. His grey hair curled around a warm, sun-beaten face. When he hugged Sarah hello, she disappeared into his huge arms. He was heavily built, but so tall he could carry off at least twenty kilograms more than most men. He was dressed in what Hannah imagined was his uniform, a short-sleeved checked shirt with khaki shorts and dusty farm boots. Even in the middle of winter, he probably just threw on a fleece and went about his business. He came around the car and held out his hand for Hannah to shake.

'Hannah, this is Karl. One of my oldest friends,' said Sarah, smiling fondly at him.

Karl met Hannah's eyes and, despite the warmth of his smile, she could see deep sadness in the depths, of a sort that would never go away.

'Aangename kennis,' he greeted her with the traditional Afrikaans welcome.

Slinging an arm around Sarah, he led them around the side of the house. Hannah, walking behind them, was sure he would not have been so unreservedly friendly if his wife had been home. They followed a path and came to a small house set towards the back of the garden. It too was built of sandstone blocks. A simple rectangular house with a steep-pitched roof of grey corrugated iron. White wooden trellises formed a balustrade to the stoep and prolific old-fashioned pink roses scrambled along their lengths.

Karl turned back to Hannah. 'We call this the "Ou Huis". It was my mother's after I got married.' He took a ring of keys from his pocket and unlocked the front door, stepping back onto the stoep. 'I'm afraid it's been mostly shut up since she died. Esme can't stand, what she calls, the old lady smell, and I just don't know where to begin or what to do with all the old stuff.' He shrugged his shoulders helplessly.

Sarah patted him on the arm. 'Don't worry, I probably know this little house better than you do. We'll be fine.'

Karl smiled at her. 'Ma certainly loved you. I think when you brought Neil home that holiday, all sorts of plans went up in smoke. For both our mothers.'

Sarah smacked her palm on his arm. 'A good thing I did, then! We would've bickered each other to death.'

Karl laughed and raised one brow suggestively. 'I don't know about that – we used to agree you had the finest legs in Leliehoek.'

Sarah shook her head. 'Don't listen to a word he says, Hannah. He's always teased me relentlessly.' She turned her back on him and went into the house, leaving Karl grinning on the stoep.

'I'll send over some tea for you,' he said and walked away, the buoyancy in his step disappearing as he approached the main house. How hard his life must be now, alone, with a wife like Esme, thought Hannah.

The Ou Huis was neat inside but completely still. An abandoned atmosphere had settled there. Hannah felt the emptiness, as if this house longed to have someone living in it, loving it. It was furnished with old, heavy furniture, upholstered in brown velveteen. Each chair had a white-lace doily set neatly over the back. Ornaments crowded a glass-fronted cabinet and a book case was filled with red bound Reader's Digest books and Christian devotionals. Sarah called from the next room. The bedroom was furnished simply with a high single bed and a large wardrobe reflected in the wings of a glass-topped dressing table. Photographs crowded there, narrow white-and-gilt-scrolled frames leant on cardboard stands. Hannah picked up a wedding picture. The couple stood on the steps of the Dutch Reformed church in town. The bride's smiling face was crowned with a fifties-style veil falling below her lace-covered shoulders.

'Who is this, Sarah?'

Sarah, crouching in front of a smaller book case, squinted up at the photograph. 'Oh, that's Gisela and Bryant, Karl's parents.'

'She was gorgeous. Like, film-star gorgeous,' said Hannah, peering at the beaming couple.

Sarah smiled. 'And still beautiful in her eighties. Marilie resembled her.'

Hannah replaced the frame and noticed, at the back of the collection, another photograph. She picked it up and studied another couple. Alistair and Marilie. For the first time, Hannah saw how lovely Marilie had been. Petite with blonde hair pulled smoothly back into a short ponytail. She was dressed in riding gear, a smart black jacket, and cream jodhpurs, and she held the bridle of her horse. She kissed the side of its head where a large rosette had been attached to its bridle. A bright ribbon medal hung around her neck. Alistair stood behind her, large in comparison, and he was looking at Marilie. His unspoilt mouth smiled at his wife, but there was something else in his expression – a sadness or longing Hannah couldn't quite interpret.

Sarah had pulled out three heavy, leather-bound photo albums. She staggered to her feet and glanced at the frame in Hannah's hands.

'There she is. Beautiful. Talented. And completely in love with that horse. I loved her like my own daughter, but she held herself away. From everybody, except that horse. You know she made the Olympic showjumping team? She died a few months before the Games.' Sarah shook her head and carried the albums to a round table in the living room. 'Come on, let's see what we can find in these.'

Hannah returned the photograph to its place, with one last glance at the man, who, even then, seemed to be injured.

Each album had a metal clasp on the side. Thick board pages held two photographs back to back on each side of the page. Sprays of flowers curled on each corner, sketched and painted delicately in watercolours. Someone had written captions below some photographs – small, faint pencil names and dates. Hannah began paging through the first, peering at the names. 'These are mostly De Jagers,' she said to Sarah who was looking at another album.

'That would be Bryant's family, Karl's father. And this album seems to be the Van Rensbergs. Karl's paternal granny was a Van Rensberg.'

Hannah kept on going, checking each picture, and then pushed the book away, sighing. The last of the three albums was plainer than the others, but the first page made her heart jump. A man sat in a spindled chair, dressed in a black suit. A white flower was pinned on his lapel. His serious face looked out at the camera. Standing slightly behind him, a young woman had her hand placed on his shoulder. Her light dress had long fitted sleeves to her wrists and a high neck. The waist seemed so cinched, she held her breath tight and high. A pale, pretty face looked away from the camera. The pencil named the couple Danie Petrus and Aletta Badenhorst. Married 1880.

'This is it, Sarah!'

Sarah scooted her chair closer to Hannah. On the next page, an older couple sat, their chairs angled towards each other. Jakob and Anna Badenhorst. The man's bushy white beard, full and neatly clipped, reached his chest. He didn't smile but his eyes looked soft somehow, as if he were about to smile. His wife was more severe, with dark hair parted unforgivingly down the centre of her scalp and pulled back tightly off her face. She sat upright in her chair, her black high-necked dress stiff and formal. 'The diary speaks of Oupa Jakob and Ouma Anna – this must be them.'

Hannah felt she should open her eyes as widely as possible to believe what she was seeing. Quickly turning the page, she found a family portrait. The two couples, slightly older than on the previous pages, were seated on chairs in the foreground. On one side stood a boy, tall and strong, his young face tanned and smooth. He stared into the distance past the camera. A baby sat alongside him, on Aletta's lap. A frilly white smock covered tiny feet as the child peered at the camera, fine blonde hair curling in wisps. This portrait was set outdoors and, peering closely, Hannah recognised the white trellises, similar to the ones outside this very room. Hannah read aloud, '*The Badenhorsts, 1891*. This is the family, Sarah,' whispered Hannah, poring over the picture, trying to absorb every detail. 'These are the people she writes about.'

'So who is who?' said Sarah, leaning forwards. 'This is taken nine years before war breaks out.'

'I would say these are Rachel's parents, Danie and Aletta,' Hannah said, pointing to the younger couple. 'This older couple would be Oupa Jakob and Ouma Anna. The boy would be Wolf, which would make the baby Rachel? I think she fitted between Wolf and the rest.'

They turned the page and found two more photographs of the family. On the left, a formal shot of the men and two boys, one an older Wolf. The men were seated, with the boys on either side. All were wearing slouch hats and held rifles at their sides. The facing page held a picture of two small girls. One stood, her dark hair wild and curly, escaping the confines of an enormous bow that sat crooked at the back of her head. Her fine-featured face was exquisitely fair, with large dark eyes set beneath fine brows. She had bunched up her dress on one side to reveal buttoned boots. The other girl was a toddler, seated on the floor with a white smock spread around her and a painted wooden dolly clutched in her arms. The next page was empty and, through the frame, they could read on the back of the previous picture, *Kristina en Elizabeth, 1898*. 'These are the two youngest, Rachel's sisters,' said

Hannah. 'I wonder if the missing picture was of Rachel. There's one of the boys and one of the girls, and then this gap. Why is nothing simple, Sarah?'

The last photograph was a wedding portrait of Wolf and Corlie, taken ten years later. Wolf's face was hardened, his eyes shadowed. He stood stiffly with his hand resting on a high-backed chair. His new wife perched on the chair. White-lace sleeves reached smooth, pale forearms, and her hands held a posy of white flowers. Her fair hair was piled on her head which she held firmly set. It was her face that struck Hannah: she was pretty, but something around the mouth spoke of determination, a slight petulance which made Hannah feel a touch of sympathy for Wolf.

'Gosh, but this is solemn for a wedding picture,' said Sarah, echoing Hannah's thoughts. 'I know they weren't supposed to smile, but they hardly look the blushing new couple.'

'They were tough times, I suppose,' said Hannah, leaning back in her chair. 'Seven years after the war, trying to make a new start, rebuilding your home and farm. They would have been scraping an existence together.'

'And probably both traumatised,' added Sarah. She turned the page, but there were no more photos, the board pages empty, just frames with vacant holes that sank to the back of the album. 'I wonder what happened to this family.'

Hannah was opening the drawers below the display cabinet when they were both startled by a knock at the door. She stood guiltily. A woman dressed in a neatly pressed blue-and-white uniform, brought in a tray which she set on the table.

Sarah jumped up and grasped the woman's hands. 'Lena, it's been such a long time since I was here. I've missed you.'

'Oh, Miss Sarah, things are bad here.'

Sarah's eyes softened in sympathy. 'I'm so sorry, Lena.'

'There are no visitors any more, and I worry for Mr Karl. The madam is angry all the time. Shouting for me, shouting for Mr Karl …' Lena shook her head.

Sarah jogged their hands up and down to draw Lena's eyes to hers. 'Why don't you come home? There will always be a place for you there.'

'I can't leave Mr Karl. No new girl will stay a single day with her. At least I know how things go in the house. I know what he likes to eat. I look after Mr Karl.'

Sarah pulled her into a hug. 'Karl is lucky to have you.'

When Lena had left, Sarah poured tea and helped herself to a square of moist coconut cake. 'Poor Lena. I don't know what to do. Esme is so brittle, so thorny; nobody can get near her. She refuses to see any thera-pist, won't consider medication. And she seems to be getting worse as time goes on, not better.' She sipped her tea and stared out the window over the garden. 'And, let's face it, I'm the last person she'll accept help from. I think she always felt threatened by me because I grew up with Karl. Because I got on better with his mother than she ever did. And then Marilie's death just wrote me off, along with Alistair.'

Hannah had gone back to the cabinet and, kneeling, opened the linenfold drawers again. One was filled with all the random bits and pieces which accumulate in drawers. Rolls of ribbon, a pair of binoculars from the forties, an old biscuit tin with an assortment of fountain pens and elastic bands. The second drawer was deeper. Stacked on one side were some cardboard files, labelled with stickers that read, *Tax*, *Banking*, and *Correspondence*. From the other side of the drawer, Hannah drew out a large Bible. Its leather covers were worn soft, perishing at the creases where it had been opened and closed for a hundred and fifty years. Gently, she turned the first pages. The pages were tissue-paper thin, the writing in beautifully printed old Afrikaans. A few pages in, she came to the ragged edges of a page that had been torn away. She could see it had been some kind of register, faint, printed lines reaching the tattered ribbon in the centre. The next page was intact. A marriage register that began in 1850. Hannah ran her finger down the list and found the marriages of Rachel's grandparents, her parents, then Wolf. Further down, she saw Gisela, then Karl and Esme, and lastly Marilie and Alistair.

'These old Bibles usually used to have birth and death registers in them, didn't they?'

Sarah turned to her. 'I think so – have you found something?'

'I think the birth and death page has been torn out. Such a pity. It would have answered most of our questions about the Badenhorsts.'

'Now what?' said Sarah, taking another square of coconut cake.

'We're still just guessing about Rachel. We have one picture, but with no name identifying her.' Hannah sank into a velveteen rocking chair with her mug of tea. 'That's not much for Alistair, is it?'

'It might have to be enough. Finish your tea, Hannah. We should go. We've been here a while, and I don't want to trouble Karl.'

'Should I find a recipe book to make our ruse slightly believable?' Hannah grinned at Sarah, who nodded, colouring slightly.

Sarah picked up the tea tray and left to return it to Lena in the main house, while Hannah went through to the kitchen at the back of the little house. A rounded corner shelf sat near the old-fashioned stove and was stacked with recipe books. She pulled one off the top of the pile and left the house, pulling the door closed behind her.

Alistair wiped his wet hands on the back of his jeans as he approached his mother's house. The pungent smell of roasting rosemary drifted from the kitchen, making him smile. Inside, Sarah bustled around the room, pushing a pan of sausages into the oven to bake alongside a tray of butternut wedges. At the table sat Hannah, paging through a book. Alistair stopped in the doorway, suddenly unsure whether to escape back to his house or enter the room. Neil, peeling potatoes, looked up as Alistair hesitated.

'There you are,' said Neil. 'I was about to come call you.'

'I followed my nose,' said Alistair, watching Hannah look up and smile at him. He stepped into the kitchen and took the knife his father held out, beginning to cut the potatoes into a pot.

Glancing over at Hannah's book, he noticed the pages were old and fragile, browned at the edges, and spotted here and there with marks and crusty bits.

'What is that?' he said.

Sarah opened the oven door to poke a skewer into the butternut.

'We were at Karl's today,' she said. 'We borrowed one of Gisela's recipe books.'

Alistair caught Hannah's quick smile for Sarah, before she turned another page. Then she jerked forward to peer at a page.

'Sarah, it's her! Rachel wrote this. It's her bread recipe she speaks about in the journal.'

'Let me look.' Sarah took the recipe book, held it at arm's length and squinted at the page. She then rifled through the rest of the book, stopping towards the end. 'You see,' she said, pointing to another page, 'this is Gisela's writing at the end. It could have been her mother's book.'

'Or even her grandmother's, Wolf's wife. That would put it in the same timeframe as Rachel.' A smile spread across Hannah's face and Sarah beamed back at her.

'What's going on?' said Alistair, laying down the knife and moving to the table. Hannah turned to him, smiling smugly and handing him the open recipe book. At the top of a page, in neat spidery writing, was written and underlined in a sweep of ink, *Rachel's Best Bread.*

'A recipe? We're going to open a can of worms over a bread recipe?'

'It would seem we are,' said his father, still patiently peeling potatoes.

Sarah swatted at him with her oven gloves. 'We found an album with photographs of the old Badenhorst family, one with Rachel as a baby. And then this recipe book with the very recipe she talks about in Hannah's journal.' She waggled her mitted hand. 'She was real, Alistair, which means the camp is likely to be real too.'

'Okay, okay.' Alistair raised his hands in surrender. Hannah's face lit up with a smile, delight dancing in her eyes. She was clearly loving every minute of his defeat. He bowed a low, mocking scrape, offering the book back to Hannah like a medieval courtier. 'What now, Captain, my Captain?'

She knocked him gently on his bowed head with the recipe book. 'Now I shall call my brother to recommend an historian.'

'Remember the deal though?' Alistair straightened and folded his arms across his chest, his light mood threatening to unravel.

'Yes, of course. No media, no strangers, no circus.' Hannah's grin was infectious and Alistair couldn't help but smile back. Underneath, though, a niggle of dread began to uncurl. He had held his life so tightly for the past eight years, held it in a fist. Nothing had been outside of his control and he had felt safe. Until now. On so many levels. Giving strangers licence to his farm was enough to tip him over the edge but then there was Hannah. He shut down that line of thought. He wasn't ready.

He kept the tone light that evening, hiding the churn inside and maintaining a friendly banter with Hannah and his parents. He liked seeing her there. Relaxed and laughing. He liked seeing his mum and dad respond to her, drawing her out further with talk of growing up in Cape Town, childhood holidays in Betty's Bay. Maybe he and Hannah could manage a friendship. Maybe, if he kept his distance, they could keep it like this. Easy and light like warm water at the top of a sunny pool. She had kicked her shoes off under the table and, when she rose to help Neil carry the dishes through to the kitchen, Alistair watched her retreat bare foot down the passage, her legs long and slim in the old jeans hugging her hips. She lifted the dishes to dodge Grant bounding past her and, as she raised her arms, her T-shirt slid up a few inches revealing the small of her back and a hint of underwear, a line of lace sliding above her jeans. This was the problem, he thought. Friendly did not describe what she evoked in him.

CHAPTER FOURTEEN

Days slid by, and Hannah had not heard a word from her brother, Joseph. She had rushed back from Goshen and emailed him that same evening. Every day since, she had called him at every number she could find. Voicemail picked up every time she tried his UK number. She had left messages with his secretary at the archaeology department and, as a last resort, she had called her mother at the rented apartment in Cambridge. The conversation had not gone well.

'I have no idea where Joseph is, Hannah. I've been trying to contact him for five days now, with no response. If you children only knew how frustrating it is that you never answer your phones! Why have them, I want to know. And then I hear from Todd that you've left Cape Town!'

'You spoke to Todd?'

'He's the only one in this family who seems to care about keeping me in the loop.'

'Todd is not part of this family, Mum.'

'For the moment, at any rate. I'm sure you'll come to your senses eventually.'

'Me? Todd had an affair, Mum! What should I have done?'

'All men dally, Hannah. It's in their genetic code. We can't let that stop our living successful lives.'

'I can't accept that. I want more than that. Don't tell me Dad—'

'Of course not! Your father is hardly aware that the world is still turning. He's only vaguely present in the relationships he already has. It would never occur to him to take up with another woman. But I digress. Hannah, what were you thinking, abandoning your life in Cape Town for some grubby little town in God knows where?'

Hannah's fingers tightened on the receiver as her mother continued: 'I can't believe you would give up on all the work you have put into your thesis. Research is for the long haul – it's exhausting, but you have to stick to it. Persevere, Hannah.'

'What for, Mum?'

'What do you mean, what for? You can't get anywhere in the academic world without a PhD, you know that.'

'What if I don't want to be in that world?'

'Hannah, stop this indulgence at once. You are thirty years old and without even a foothold in the university. Once you get through this PhD, you'll take on a lectureship and start publishing, and everything will fall into place. How soon can you get back to Cape Town?'

'I'm not going back anytime soon, Mum. I'm happy.'

'Happy? What has that to do with anything?'

Hannah had put the phone down quietly, knowing her mother would be sputtering with rage and also knowing she didn't have Hannah's number in Leliehoek.

Now Hannah was in the shop when the doorbell tinkled and Kathryn popped in with two take-away coffees.

'I needed a break from the shop – I haven't looked up since half-past four this morning. I hope Maisie can cope. She only started last week.'

Hannah smiled and looked over her shoulder from where she was selecting the more valuable books to photograph and auction online. 'Things getting busier now that it's holidays?'

'Hell, yes. Town is filling up and holidaymakers are gorging.' Kathryn slouched in one of the chairs at the fireplace, closing her eyes. 'I can't keep up. At least tomorrow is a public holiday. But Christmas is coming far too soon.'

Christmas. Hannah hadn't thought about it much. The idea of Christmas didn't thrill her. In fact, the last few years had been dismal. Coming back from London and leaving Todd had meant an end to the glamorous parties. All that fake Christmas cheer which just covered up everybody's selfish agendas. Hobnobbing in that crowd was all about being seen with the right people, wearing the right clothes, and getting some kind of thrill from flirting with other people's spouses. Then Hannah was left with Christmas at her parents' house, which wasn't much better. How do two atheists celebrate Christmas? The tree, the fairy lights, and the stockings had all disappeared when Hannah and Joseph had got older. That nefarious character, Father Christmas, had never been subscribed to, even when the children were little. All in all, Christmas in the Harrison household had been a non-event. For Hannah, it had always been a morning associated with disappointment.

'What are your plans for Christmas, Hannah?' said Kathryn.

'The shop will close, I suppose – I hadn't really thought further than that.'

'Can I book you to come for lunch at our house?'

'You hardly need to book me. I would love to come.'

'Don't get your expectations up, though – we have a lot of fun, but it's not in any way civilised.'

Hannah smiled at her friend. 'It sounds perfect.'

'And tomorrow, too, if you want to. You will close the shop for the day, won't you? Why don't you come over, hang out at my house for the day.'

'I'd love to. But let me bring lunch.'

'Nah. We'll forage in the fridge. Throw something together.'

Just then, the shop doorbell jingled again and both girls turned to see a tall, rangy man walk in. He was wearing dusty boots and creased cargo pants, his T-shirt printed with the silhouette of a dinosaur riding a bicycle, ET like, across an enormous moon. As he turned his unshaven face, Kathryn took a breath. 'Oh my goodness,' she said, goggling.

Hannah dropped her books and flew across the room into a hug which swept her off her feet and swung her around.

'What are you doing here?' she said, when he had released her onto her feet, breathless from his squeeze, her face alight with pleasure.

'I could ask you the same thing,' he said dryly. He looked over her shoulder to Kathryn, raising one eyebrow. 'But first, how about an introduction?'

Hannah rolled her eyes. 'Kathryn, meet my brother, Joseph, who remains the same, regardless of how many years go by.'

Kathryn, for the first time that Hannah had witnessed, remained speechless. A wide grin lifted her brother's mouth and crinkled his eyes, taking him from gorgeous to devastating; Hannah knew Kathryn would be thinking the same.

'You didn't answer my calls,' said Hannah.

'I thought I'd answer in person,' said Joseph casually. He pushed the door to the stoep open to pick up an enormous duffel bag which he heaved back into the shop. 'May I put this down somewhere?'

Hannah pointed down the passage towards her apartment and, once he had jostled his bag past her, she turned to pull a face at Kathryn. Kathryn had yet to string two words together and now she merely flapped her hands at Hannah, gesturing for her to follow her brother.

Joseph had dumped his duffel in the passage and was looking into each room. Hannah, as a reflex, turned on the kettle.

'How long can you stay, Joseph?' she said.

He sank into a chair at the table. 'I'm taking a few weeks in South Africa, letting some things settle in Cambridge.'

Hannah dropped a rooibos teabag in a mug for him. 'Still plagued by women?'

He shrugged. 'She got a bit possessive, a bit neurotic. Better if I'm not around. Hopefully she'll realise her husband is a nice guy, really. She should turn her attentions to him.'

Hannah shook her head in disbelief. 'Josey, your rock-like heart. Does the trail of destruction you leave in your wake not bother you at all?'

He grinned at her over the rim of his cup. 'It's because I have a rock-like heart that I can walk away unscathed. I can recommend it, actually.'

Hannah ignored him. 'Where will you stay?'

'Here.'

She looked up sharply. 'I only have one bedroom and I'm not giving it up, not even for you.'

'Good for you. This place suits you, Hannah. You seem different somehow.' He frowned at her, his head tilted to the side. Then he shrugged the thought off. 'I'm happy on the floor or the couch. Do you mind if I crash right now? I haven't slept since I left Cambridge two days ago.'

Hannah glanced across at him and realised his eyes were shadowed with fatigue beneath the mischief. She softened. 'Take my bed for the afternoon. I'll wake you up for supper.'

As he unzipped the duffel and began rooting for a change of clothes, Hannah stood in the passage doorway, watching.

'How come Mum didn't know where you were? I thought she would be seeing as much of you as she could.'

'I told you already, she got a bit possessive, a bit neurotic.'

'The woman you were fleeing was Mum? Joseph Harrison, you are too much!' Hannah couldn't help the laugh which gurgled to the surface. She left him stripping off his shirt in the bathroom and turning on the shower. Throwing a clean towel into the bathroom doorway, she pulled the passage door closed behind her.

'Phwoar!' said Kathryn as Hannah returned to the reading room.

'Stay away, Kathryn. He is a piece of work where women are concerned. He has had a perpetual string of women since he was sixteen, and probably broken every single one.' Catching sight of Kathryn's smile, she added, 'And don't think you'll be the one to change him, either!'

Hannah resumed her sorting as Kathryn lay back in her arm chair. 'Don't worry. He reminds me of Chris when I first met him – astonishingly good-looking with all the confidence-slash-arrogance that goes along with it. Consider me severely burnt in that regard.'

CHAPTER FIFTEEN

The next morning, Alistair opened Hannah's garden gate, the squeak of the hinges rousing a sleepy tortoiseshell cat from its nap on a deck chair. It stretched its front paws out and yawned, giving Alistair a sceptical look, before beginning to clean itself. He climbed the steps and rapped on the kitchen door. Everything looked quiet through the glass doors. His scarred reflection stared back at him, and he wondered if he still had time to escape back to his car. He'd barely made it back to the deck steps when the door opened behind him. With a nervous smile, he swung around, then stopped, paralysed at the sight of a good-looking man, sleep tousled, wearing only tracksuit bottoms.

'Hi,' said the man casually, reaching his arms above his head, his torso rippling in a stretch very like the cat's.

'Hi ...' said Alistair, his brain stumbling for words, 'I was looking for Hannah, but I'll try her later at the shop, I think.'

'Who are you?' said the man, his tone friendly.

'I was wondering the same ...'

'I'm Joseph.'

'Okay ...' Alistair waited for Joseph to add anything which might explain who he was, but Joseph just stood looking at him, completely at ease.

'What should I tell Han when she gets back?'

Wanting to get away from this awful encounter, Alistair could only mumble, 'Don't worry,' before turning to the gate just as Hannah came through it. Her face was flushed, her running gear damp with sweat. Her hair had escaped the ponytail to curl in moist wisps in her neck and around her face.

'Hi, honey, how was your run?' Alistair heard Joseph call from the deck.

Hannah shot her brother a confused look. Alistair turned back to the deck where Joseph was grinning down at them. 'You know, I was missing Han so much, I just had to come and see her. She's so damn gorgeous, isn't she?' He yanked her ponytail as she came past him and pulled her into his side.

'Shut up, Josey,' said Hannah, wresting herself away from him. 'What can I do for you, Alistair?'

'It's obviously not a good time,' said Alistair in a rush to leave, 'Thanks. I mean … bye.' He stumbled down the path. Damn. He knew he shouldn't have come. Agreeing to be friends didn't mean he could expect her to be single. Of course she'd choose a man like Joseph. Laid back, good-looking, affectionate. No way to compete with that.

Hannah punched Joseph on the arm. 'You are such a bastard!'

Joseph, laughing, turned back into the house, rubbing his arm.

'Wait, Alistair!' Hannah jogged out the gate and reached him as he unlocked his Toyota, catching his arm. She felt him jolt and he pulled away, putting some distance between them. Her heart stammered for a moment and she blinked. What on earth was that? Awkwardness hovered.

'Sorry. My brother is a complete idiot. He loves messing with people, especially me.'

'I thought—'

'I'm so sorry. I've spent much of my life apologising for my brother. I love him, but no one can infuriate me like he can.' As she smiled up at Alistair, she could see the tension dissipate from his face. He let out a breath and leant against the side of his car.

'I came to ask if you would like to go and see Surrender Hill?' He looked up at the sky. 'It's a beautiful day. Maybe this afternoon?'

'What's Surrender Hill?'

He smiled. 'A battle site, relatively close by. It's where a large portion of the Boer army surrendered to the British. I'm taking Douglas to show him. And today is Day of Reconciliation – seems appropriate somehow.'

In more ways than one, she thought, wondering if they would ever figure out a relationship which wasn't fraught with emotion. She nodded. 'I'd love to come.' Then her face fell. 'But I made plans with Kathryn.'

'Bring Kathryn.'

When she came back into the house, Joseph was sitting at the table eating an enormous bowl of cereal. Patchy sat next to him on the table, watching him adoringly and purring.

Hannah shook her head in disgust as she passed him on her way to the shower. 'Even cats? Really?'

'I can't help it.' He shrugged.

'What are you doing today?' she yelled from the bathroom.

'I've got some calls to make, emails to send. I probably need to let some people know where I am. You?'

'I'll be out this afternoon.'

Later that afternoon, they set off from the bookshop. Hannah and Kathryn rode in Kathryn's car, her twins strapped into their seats. Douglas and Alistair drove ahead in Alistair's Hilux.

Alistair dropped his speed so that Kathryn could follow. She was either a very cautious driver, or she was distracted. Alistair would put his money on the latter. He glanced in his rear-view mirror again, and could see Kathryn gesticulating wildly as she told a story. Hannah threw her head back, laughing with an abandon which made him envious. There was always tension between him and Hannah. Even though they were no longer openly fighting, Hannah was still a long way from being as relaxed with him as he would like.

Douglas turned his body to face Alistair and leant against the passenger door.

'What's going on with you and the beautiful Hannah?'

Alistair felt his brows shoot up. 'Nothing. Why would you ask that?'

'It's certainly not nothing. There's enough spark between you to warrant carrying a fire extinguisher. Whether it be lust or anger, it's not nothing. Have you seen anyone since Marilie's death?'

Alistair shook his head, really not wanting to go down this road. 'You're not shy of getting straight to the point.'

'No one? Not one? And it's been what, five years?'

'Eight,' said Alistair, feeling his hands begin to clench on the steering wheel.

'Eight years is a long time to be alone. I've been married and divorced in half that time, and even I'm thinking it's time to move on.'

Alistair grasped this shift in conversation away from himself. 'To someone local?'

'Maybe,' said Douglas, a smile curving his mouth.

'Someone local to the car following us?' said Alistair, raising an eyebrow.

'Maybe.' Douglas's smile now widened into a grin.

'You do know that Kathryn's not a simple case? There's a husband somewhere. The twins. If you're going to get back into the dating game, she's not the one to play around with.'

Douglas's good humour didn't falter. 'Do I look like a player?' Alistair glanced across at him, choking on a laugh when he saw Douglas's exaggerated leer. Douglas composed his face and continued: 'Anyway, we're talking about you.'

Alistair looked away. 'It's complicated. Hannah's not a simple case either. She's not an open book.'

'Your book,' said Douglas, 'is glued shut, my friend.'

To Alistair's relief, the brown sign to Surrender Hill appeared on the side of the road, and they slowed to turn into the grassy field which was signposted as parking. Kathryn followed. As soon as her car had pulled to a stop, the twins piled out and galloped up the slope. They made straight for a stone plinth with a brass plaque cemented onto the top. The children ran their fingers over the raised letters and traced the circular medallion marking a national monument. Climbing onto the plinth, they both balanced on the top, turning in a circle and looking around at the grassy hillside. The sky met spectacular sandstone formations and hilly grassland in all directions.

Alistair pulled a wide-brimmed cricket hat from behind the seat of his Hilux. He unlocked a farm gate with a key from his pocket and led the others up the hill. The sun was hot on their backs but a slight breeze lifted the heaviness. The children followed, picking grass and chasing each other to and fro. Halfway up the slope, Alistair turned, his voice carrying on the breeze.

'Let me give you a bit of background.' He cleared his throat. 'By July 1900, the war had been going on for nine months. The Boers had won significant battles in the early stages but British troops were pouring into the country and most of the towns in the Free State were occupied. The British General Hunter began advancing south towards Bethlehem. The great Boer General De Wet decided to abandon Bethlehem, and took to the hills of the Brandwater Basin.' Alistair stopped to pick up a stick and sketch a diagram in a patch of sand. 'Brandwater Basin is a kind of horseshoe shape – we are standing on the right prong, looking inwards.' He stood up again, and pointed with his stick at the mountains surrounding them in every direction. 'The Witteberg to the west, the Drakensberg behind us, and the Rooiberg, which we are looking at. This basin is a natural fortress where the president of the Free State thought his commandos could rest. General Hunter soon made it a giant trap. There are only six ways in and out of this basin, some of them only narrow paths. General Hunter planned to take each pass, trapping the Boer army inside.'

The others, who were now sitting in the grass, looked around with new insight at the view.

'De Wet, astute as he was, realised the danger. He divided the commandos and planned to get everyone out over a couple of days, in different directions. He took President Steyn and two and a half thousand men, and escaped on the first night. He managed to get four hundred and sixty wagons and carts within a mile of a British camp, moving in silence.'

Kathryn shook her head. 'That's incredible.'

Alistair continued: 'The problem, though, was that without his decisive strong leadership, the Boer generals left behind began to fight among themselves. The Boer leadership model was far flatter and less structured than the British military. Old General Prinsloo assumed command, but other Boers supported Paul Roux instead. They wasted time, the idiots, and soon it was too late. The British captured the first, second, and third passes. Unsurprisingly, Boer morale dropped horribly.

'General Hunter was just brilliant. De Wet would have been the only match for him, but he was long gone. Hunter feinted, by taking a column and heading for Naauwpoort Nek – you know, the pass near Leliehoek?' Alistair pointed his stick towards a mountain range in the distance. 'The Boers quickly split their force to send reinforcements there. At the last moment, Hunter veered right and moved on Retief's Nek, catching the Boers by surprise and bombarding their position. Major Generals Macdonald and Hamilton captured Naauwpoort Nek and Golden Gate. By 24 July, the basin was closed and the Boers were trapped. They had been completely outmanoeuvred. They took up a position on this farm, then called Slaapkranz, and the British met them here on 28 July. They blitzed the hillsides with artillery.'

Hannah looked around her, the breeze lifting a quiet rustle down the slope. The picture of that battle was strangely vivid, the assaulting roar of shells pounding the earth and rifle fire scattering the hillside. The contrast of that day and this heightened her senses, and it was not difficult to imagine a sharp smell of cordite burning her nostrils.

'The next day, Prinsloo offered the surrender of all commandos in the basin. This angered the commandos loyal to De Wet and Roux, and one and a half thousand men managed to escape with their horses. De Wet was furious when he heard of the surrender. If the generals had followed his instructions, things might have been very different.'

Hannah thought of Rachel's account of the loss of Naauwpoort Nek; of the resulting influx of British and the farm burning. Could that have been avoided?

Alistair began to speak again. 'On 31 July, the Scots Guards, the

Royal Fusiliers, and the Royal Irish stood in formation on this hillside as a guard of honour to receive the Boers. They unfurled the Union Jack and waited for the Boers to appear. The Boer generals Prinsloo, De Villiers, and Crowther appeared first, tall and upright on their horses. Then came the commandos. Proud men, dressed in dusty civilian clothes with slouch hats, they approached, throwing down rifles and ammunition in front of the British. And the men kept coming, lines of men on horses, winding down the steep slopes. Over four thousand men, including elderly men and young boys surrendered across the basin.' Alistair turned to face the others, emotion clear on his face.

'A British soldier wrote that the Boers halted in the road – and we're talking about that road,' he said, pointing to his left. 'Imagine that road without the cutting. Dry, rutted gravel heading over the crest of this hill. An older man, tall and composed with a sandy beard, rides along the line of Boers, shaking hands here and there. When he reaches the head of the column, the men raise their hands in a kind of salute and say, as a goodbye, just the word, "Generaal". It was General Prinsloo saying goodbye.

'Two million rounds of ammunition and thousands of Boer rifles were burnt, and it is said that the bare patches of earth, which you can see near the plinth over there' – he pointed to the memorial plaque near the cars – 'are where those piles of metal melted into the ground, making the soil barren for over a hundred years.

'The prisoners were marched to the closest towns and put on trains to Cape Town. From there, they were shipped to POW camps overseas to return only when the war was done. Many would die there, and the rest would not know if their wives and children were still alive or not. Because, of course, now began the awful process of civilian internment into the camps.'

Hannah looked up at Alistair from where she sat in the grass. She had been gripped by his narrative, transported back to the battle which had raged in that very spot. Her skin raised to goosebumps, though the sun was warm on her skin. 'So the war carried on after the surrender?' she asked.

'Yes, this surrender had two big implications. One was that, over the next few days, the British moved to take Harrismith to the east, which crucially opened up the supply line from Durban. The other implication was that it cemented the idea of guerrilla warfare in the Boer mind. They were always going to be disadvantaged by set-piece battles which favoured the structured British. Now began the stage of war where the Boers' mobility, horsemanship, excellent marksmanship, and knowledge of the terrain would be their greatest allies. They kept the British on their toes for almost another two years.'

Douglas raised himself on one elbow. 'I've heard it said that almost every Boer soldier was as good a shot as the best British snipers. Imagine facing that stuck in a column, exposed in the veld.'

Kathryn spoke for the first time. 'I guess those Boers would have grown up on horses with rifles in their hands.'

'And,' added Alistair, 'many British soldiers in the lower ranks would have come straight from mines or factories. Just being in the sun was a major challenge, let alone firing at invisible enemies scattered over the hillsides.'

Hannah's mind was racing with scenarios, thinking of Rachel's father and brothers. 'Do you think all the men from this area would have been shipped off to the POW camps?'

'That would have depended on which commando they belonged to, and which general they were following. I know that some Boers from the Leliehoek area went to Ceylon – families still have mementoes from their great-grandfathers' internment. But then, some might very well have managed to stay uncaptured until the end of the war.'

Douglas lay back in the grass and was staring at the sky. He took a long grass stem from his mouth. 'It's strange to think we are all products of that time – it certainly shaped the future of South Africa, much of it for the bad, but not all. I'm a mix of Afrikaner and English blood, and yet my great-great-grandparents would have sat on different sides of the war.'

'Mine too,' said Hannah. 'Even my ouma wasn't too thrilled when my mother married an Englishman.'

Alistair smiled at her. 'My great-great-grandfather Barlow came out with the Lancashire Fusilier's 2nd Battalion as an eighteen-year-old.

When he returned home to England and his struggling family, he decided his fortunes might be better back in South Africa. I think it was the same for many young British soldiers. They had seen space and opportunity out here which they would never see at home.'

Clouds were forming in the distance. Hannah wondered how the sky could seem so much bigger. She remembered London's sky, a tiny sliver of grey wedged between buildings. This ridiculous blue expanse was simply breathtaking. She understood why British soldiers would leave that for this.

Out the corner of her eye, Hannah saw as Douglas leant over on one arm and tickled Kathryn's ear with his grass stem. 'What about you, Kathryn?' he asked.

She batted the grass away and looked over her shoulder at him. 'I don't know much about my ancestors – my parents and grandparents never wanted to talk about the past. Too much apartheid pain, I suppose. But I think there are slave roots way back and Dutch blood, all mixed up. That's the way of the Cape, hey?'

Alistair reached out a hand to pull Hannah up. 'How about we open up that picnic basket, Kathryn?'

'Good idea,' said Kathryn, scrambling up and nudging Douglas with her foot. 'Come on, the kids have probably found the picnic already, they've gone awfully quiet.'

They ambled down the slope and found the twins stretched out on the bonnet of Kathryn's car, warming their backs now that the breeze had freshened and the sun had slipped behind a cloud. Alistair and Douglas pulled camp chairs and a folding table from the back of the pickup and set them up in the lee of the vehicle.

Kathryn pulled out a large flask and plastic cups. Two old-fashioned cake tins revealed large choc-chip cookies in one and a magnificent carrot cake in the other. Hannah sat in a camp chair and pulled her knees up to her chest. After seeing the contents of the picnic basket, she decided Kathryn should be invited on all outings. She finished a generous slice of cake and licked the cream cheese icing off her fingers. As she stared up the slope, Hannah wondered when she had last had such a good time with friends. She was accepted just as she was. There was no feeling of being less. Less glamorous, less successful, less clever. Had she lived so many years under that word? She leant her head back into the chair, closing her eyes, content.

What felt like the very next moment, she jumped in fright, nearly falling out of her chair, as a soccer ball hit the side of the Toyota next to her head.

'Sorry!' shouted Douglas, laughing at her wide eyes and gaping mouth. Hannah realised she must have dozed off and missed the beginnings of a game. They had marked out two sets of goals, and Alistair and Emma-Jane were taking on Douglas and Matthew. She relaxed back into her chair and watched the four of them race around. The two men eventually picked up their respective team mate, using the twins as croquet mallets to kick the ball at the opposite goal. Shouts of laughter echoed across the impromptu pitch, and Hannah couldn't help smiling at the natural way these two men responded to Kathryn's children. The game ended with Alistair tackling Douglas to the ground and the twins piling on top of them, shrieking in delight.

Kathryn was packing up the picnic when the twins, each hanging on one of Douglas's arms and standing on a foot, begged him to ride back with them in Kathryn's car. Hannah caught Kathryn's eye and raised one eyebrow, smiling at the colour that crept into Kathryn's face.

'Stop pestering the man,' said Kathryn, becoming more brisk in her packing.

Douglas picked up the twins, one under each arm like two rugby balls. He posted them on the back seat to much shrieking and giggling, then pressed his nose against the glass and pulled ridiculous faces.

'You enjoyed yourself today, Hannah,' said Alistair, hauling the folding table over the tailgate.

'Every minute,' she said, rewarding him with a happy smile which reached her eyes. He had watched her this afternoon, and had found himself wanting to touch her. Wanting to step behind her. Put his arms around her. Pull her against his chest as they stood on the hillside, looking out at that huge sky and grassy slope rolling away beneath them. He had wanted to pull her into his lap as they sat with their tea. Wanted that simple physical affection couples have in the company of friends – that relaxed intimacy which comes with being secure and easy together. Wanting her like that had brought his years of isolation sharply into focus. He had shut down completely after Marilie. He had shunned the few opportunities that had come his way over the years, not being able to think about any kind of encounter, even for the sake of sex without strings. He had managed without the sex, but now he missed the affection with a pang that was painful.

He looked across as Kathryn started her car. Douglas was about to get into her passenger seat and he gave Alistair a salute with a cheeky wink.

'I guess that means I'm coming with you,' said Hannah. 'Is that okay?'

'Of course, it would be silly to squeeze five people into Kathryn's car,' he said, kicking himself for not saying what he should have – that he wanted her with him.

Hannah climbed into the cab and shivered. The sky had darkened, threatening a storm, and the afternoon had cooled further. She pulled from her bag the blue fleece she had borrowed on the plateau. 'Sorry it's taken so long to return it.'

He turned the key in the ignition, leaning over the steering wheel. 'Put it on again – it's getting cold.'

She smiled wryly at him and slid her arms into the sleeves, zipping it up to her neck and lifting her hips to pull it under her buttocks. The hem came to mid-thigh, hiding the denim shorts she had on underneath. He found the sight of her in his top with bare legs below unsettling. Erotic. He amended his earlier thoughts. In moments like these, he did miss sex. A picture of pulling her across to him and pressing her down into the seat blossomed in his mind, and he smothered it before he lost control, his fingers clenched over the steering wheel. They were quiet for a while, Alistair pushing thoughts away and trying to focus on the road in front of him.

'You tell a good story,' she said quietly. 'Have you ever thought of taking people on tours, I mean professionally?'

He glanced across at her. 'We did think about it once, when we were first married. We were so full of ideas. We planned on opening a guest house and running battlefield tours on horseback.'

'What happened?' She sensed his unwillingness to go on, to cast a shadow on the afternoon. 'You don't have to tell me, Alistair. Sorry, I don't mean to pry.'

He looked across at her again. 'No, it's okay.' He took a deep breath. 'It took a few years to register as a guide and set up the business. Plans had been passed to build on the farm. By the time it was all coming together, Marilie had a breakdown. She couldn't come to terms with not being able to conceive. She blamed me. Hated herself. I decided to shelve the whole business and keep things simple. And then she was killed. And the nightmare began. I had nothing left. I mean, I had no reserves to take on anything new. Or anyone.'

'And then I come and push you around,' said Hannah.

'No,' he said, wanting the remorse in her eyes gone. 'Then eight years passed and I should have got over my mistrust of strangers. And women.' He lowered his voice to a mutter, 'And especially strange women.' He smiled, keeping his eyes on the road but feeling her surprised glance.

'Hey!' she objected, poking him in the arm. 'I heard that. I'm well-versed in men, you know.' His sardonic look had her laughing. 'I mean, I've had years of managing my aggravating bloody brother.'

Alistair liked the tone of this banter better. 'What's your brother's story?'

'Joseph? He's older than me. He has a brilliant mind and is the rising star in his archaeology department at Cambridge. He's been the golden boy in our family since he was born. Of course he crawled, walked, talked, and began reading way before other children. My parents call him gifted.'

'And he's not?'

'He is very bright, but I think his giftedness is more along the lines of making people love him. It's much easier to be successful if everybody thinks you're amazing. I am disappointingly average, and my mother hasn't ever really known what to do with me.' He glanced across at her to gauge her mood and met her eyes. She was smiling; she had taken on this picture of herself.

'Let me get this straight,' said Alistair. 'You speak at least two languages fluently, maybe more?' He glanced across at her and saw her nod. 'More? What else?'

Hannah kept her eyes on the road and said lightly, 'I picked up some French and a bit of German. A smattering of Dutch, but that doesn't really count – it's so close to Afrikaans. Nothing extraordinary.'

'But you can converse in them?' She nodded. 'Read them?' She nodded again, and he burst out laughing. 'Hannah! You are completely nuts! Add to that, you're doing your PhD at a prestigious university. You move on your own to a strange town, pick up a new business, and within days you have a legion of fans throughout the town, my parents among them. This is in no way average on any front.'

Hannah looked at him in surprise. 'I am bunking out on my PhD; I'm flying by the seat of my pants in the shop; and "fan" is a strong word. But that aside, it's the nicest thing anyone has ever said to me.'

He glanced from the road and took in her bemused smile, thinking it was a sorry indictment of the people in her life. 'And Joseph's position at the moment?'

Hannah shook her head. 'I'm not entirely sure – he says he's taking a break for a few weeks and can help us with our investigation into the Goshen camp. Are you free to meet and talk about a way forward?'

Alistair noted she had made the investigation sound like a team effort. He wasn't sure what he thought about that. It made him more than the reluctant landowner he actually was. On the other hand, it would mean time with her.

'My sister arrives this weekend from Cape Town. She's on leave over Christmas, but I'm around.'

They pulled up outside the bookshop and Alistair walked Hannah to her gate.

'Thank you for the lift home,' she said with a smile. 'And for the afternoon. It was wonderful. All of it.'

He caught her arm as she turned to open the gate, arresting her movement. 'Hannah.' His hand slipped down her arm. He held his breath at the feel of her skin beneath his hand.

She looked at their hands joined. 'We managed to get through a whole afternoon without fighting,' she said lightly.

He knew what he wanted to say, but it was an act of will to speak the words out loud. 'Hannah … I'd like to see more of you.'

She looked up and raised an eyebrow, amused. He laughed out loud, grateful the tension had snapped.

'I didn't mean that exactly, though what man wouldn't? I meant, I want to spend more time with you. I enjoyed this afternoon. So much.'

At that moment, Joseph opened the door, calling out, 'Alistair, you coming in?'

'Bloody Joseph,' muttered Hannah as their hands separated.

Alistair raised his hand in a wave to Joseph and gave Hannah a rueful smile. 'I'll rather go.'

'How about meeting Monday morning, here?'

'Come to the farm, then we can walk the site. Ten o'clock?'

Hannah nodded and he stepped away from her, walking around the car to his door.

CHAPTER SIXTEEN

The farm phone was ringing when Alistair pulled up at his house. He didn't hurry, thinking that, if it was important, the person would call back. But it kept ringing. He picked it up eventually. 'Goshen Farm.' There was silence on the line. 'Hello?'

A whispered voice, close in his ear, 'I know you did it.'

Alistair put the phone down immediately. It rang again and he picked it up, but only held the phone to his ear, not saying anything.

'You did it. You did it. She's dead and you did it.'

He jammed his finger onto the switch hook, cutting the call. The menace of that 'You, You, You' sent a racing shiver along his arms. He put the receiver down on the table next to the phone and jumped at the loud knock on the front door behind him.

His father poked his head around the door. 'Your mum has dinner ready. She says there's enough if you want to come over.' Registering the shock Alistair knew was on his face, Neil said, 'You okay?'

'I just got a call. You know, threatening, like before.'

'But it's been years! Why now?' Neil's face clouded with anger.

'Because I might be finding out what it's like to be happy again. Of course something would start now.'

'Alistair!' Neil said sharply. 'The universe is not out to get you. This is a person. A messed-up person, yes, but your life coming right at last has no bearing on it.'

He pushed his hand into his hair. 'I know, Dad. It's just so perfectly timed.'

'Put caller ID on again, like the cops told you to do before.'

Alistair tugged on the hair gripped in his fist. 'It'll be the same. A private number. Untraceable. And we know who it is, don't we?'

'But we can't prove it.'

'No, we can't. Come, Dad, let's go eat.'

The table at the cottage was laid and Sarah ladled thick stew into bowls. Her crusty bread sat on a board, cut into thick slices for dipping into the stew. They sat and Neil said grace, Alistair taking comfort in the routine he had known his whole life. When they began to eat, Neil put his utensils down and looked across at Sarah, concern etched on his face. 'Alistair had a call tonight, like before.'

Sarah took a moment to understand, and then stared wide-eyed at Alistair. 'After all these years? Why would she start again?'

Alistair covered her hand with his large one. 'Esme is unhinged, Mum. The day Marilie died, something clicked out of place. Hoping she'd get over her daughter's death might have been too much to ask.'

'No, you never recover from losing a child, but clinging on to the idea that you killed Marilie is insane!'

'Exactly,' said Alistair. 'And the least I can do is weather a few phone calls. I might not have killed Marilie, but I was responsible for her. Esme expected me – as I did – to protect her daughter. I failed in the worst possible way.'

Neil slammed his hand on the table, making Sarah jump in her seat. 'Rubbish!' he said. 'You cannot protect anyone from harm in this world. Bad stuff happens in spite of you. There are no guarantees. We go by the grace of God, all of us! To think you can protect yourself, your wife, or your children is beyond arrogance – it's blasphemy.' After a moment, Neil collected himself. He picked up his fork and began to eat again. Alistair and Sarah followed, but the chink of utensils on bowls was loud in the silence which hung over the table.

'Well, Alistair,' Sarah said, trying hard to restore the balance between them, 'how was your day at Surrender Hill?'

'Good,' he said softly. 'The story came back to me easily, which was a relief. It's been so many years since I told it to people. It reminded me how much I loved doing it.'

'Maybe we should look at those plans again,' said Neil. 'It was a sound concept for a business.'

Alistair looked across the table at his father. 'What about the guest house?'

'Building is a pain in the arse, but we can do it. The books look good this year, don't they? We could hire a manager when it's done. Leliehoek is growing its tourism industry – maybe we should think about taking a piece of that pie.'

'There's a lot going on right now, Neil,' said Sarah. 'Let's see how this camp investigation turns out first. It might be a boon for a guest house, or it might not get off the ground at all.' She turned to Alistair. 'What's the news of Hannah's brother?'

'He's here in Leliehoek. We're meeting to talk about a way forward.'

'Remember your sister arrives this weekend.'

Neil took another slice of bread and reached for the butter. Alistair watched him change his mind at Sarah's fierce glare and dunk the bread, unbuttered, into his stew. 'Suzanne would also be interested in the camp story – maybe she should tag along.'

Alistair didn't like the thought of Suzanne being anywhere near Joseph. 'Let me handle the meeting first, see where it's going.' He collected the plates and stood, pushing his chair back to take the dishes to the kitchen.

His mother called from behind him. 'There's a rhubarb crumble on the table and a jug of custard. Please bring them through.'

Alistair smiled at the thought of his father. Sarah made the crumble for Alistair because she knew how much he loved it. She deliberately ignored her husband's grimacing face across the table. Alistair loved that their relationship exhibited these small wars; loved even more that Neil submitted to her with good humour, allowing the small victories which made Sarah feel she was in charge.

Alistair knew that his father's strength, when you met it, was iron-clad. That, when it came down to the line, Neil was the backbone of the family. He had seen it on the day Marilie was killed. His father, sitting in the driveway, holding Alistair's face together while he quietly organised the scene. Staff were sent running to call emergency services and bring blankets for Alistair. Sarah was made busy packing a hospital bag for Alistair, grooms dispatched to catch the horse and restore order in the stable. Neil had held Alistair in his arms on the driveway for the whole time it took the ambulance to arrive, allowing him to keep hold of Marilie's body for as long as possible.

When her parents had arrived at the hospital, Neil had shielded Alistair from their grief and their rage. Alistair knew he would not have come through the trauma without his father carrying him. He owed him his life.

He had said as much one day in the shed while they were working on a tractor. Neil had simply looked at him and said, 'You are my son, whom I love.' Alistair had choked on the thick tears which had risen with those words, and Neil had squeezed his shoulder, then bent down to continue working.

Now, Alistair returned to the dining room, touching his dad's shoulder as he passed. Neil looked up and grimaced at the sight of the desert. 'My most favourite pudding, Sarah, you shouldn't have. You really shouldn't have.'

Sarah tapped him on the hand with her serving spoon. 'This house does not revolve around you, Neil.'

But everyone, except perhaps Neil himself, knew it did.

CHAPTER SEVENTEEN

Hannah and Joseph were met by Alistair's dogs in full force on Monday morning. Their barking and jostling had Hannah hanging onto her car's wing mirror for balance. Joseph knelt down to put his arms around the two Labradors and was knocked flat onto his bottom by Grant. Laughing, Hannah watched as he attempted to bat the dog's profuse licking away with his hands, but it was only Alistair's stern command which had the dogs sitting obediently next to Joseph. Alistair couldn't help grinning at Joseph and the three dogs lined up in the dirt. He offered Joseph a hand up and pulled him to his feet.

Joseph dusted himself off and held out his hand again to Alistair. 'We haven't met properly. I'm Joseph Harrison.'

As Alistair gripped his hand, Hannah could see him assess her brother. She hoped he would see Joseph like she did, completely secure in himself and completely likeable. What some might consider arrogance was actually self-assurance and good humour. In allowing himself to gambol about with three exuberant dogs, Joseph couldn't have endeared himself to Alistair in a better way.

'Come in,' said Alistair, gesturing to the front steps, and following Hannah and Joseph inside. 'Go straight into the kitchen – we can sit there.'

Hannah passed what she glimpsed was a lounge, then entered a room which had been remodelled as an open-plan kitchen-dining room. It had been decorated in formal greys and blacks, a modern minimalist style. The windows were empty of blinds or curtains, the walls blank, apart from the odd starkly painted canvas, unframed. Hannah wasn't convinced the style suited the old house or Alistair at all. The black granite kitchen counters were clear, no piles of papers or smudged recipe books, no dumped handbags. Empty.

'Wow,' said Joseph, coming into the room. 'Who tidies for you? I could do with someone like that in my house.'

'You don't have a house,' said Hannah.

'Someone to follow me around then and pick up after me,' said Joseph cheerfully.

Alistair avoided Hannah's gaze. 'My wife had the house done. She wasn't the homey type, though, and we always had someone cooking for us. Now I eat with my parents a lot. Still, it's a waste of such an enormous kitchen. Please.' Alistair gestured to the plain dark wood table. Hannah and Joseph settled there and he put the kettle on the hob, taking three mugs from a cupboard. 'Tea or coffee? I can use a plunger if you'd prefer.'

Hannah smiled. 'I got into trouble several times overseas, asking if I could make coffee with a plunger. People thought I was about to whip out the old toilet plunger.'

Alistair's mouth pulled up at the corner.

'I'd love a decent cup of coffee,' said Joseph. 'Hannah's place has every possible type of tea, most of them disgusting, but neither of us can figure out the coffee machine.'

'I've taken to drinking my coffee at Kathryn's,' said Hannah.

'Better than this will be, no doubt,' said Alistair, slanting a smile at Hannah.

Hannah pulled Rachel's journal and her own notebook from her bag.

'So this is the famous journal,' said Alistair, reaching for it across the table. He began turning the pages gently, scanning the tightly cramped writing. 'How do you read this?'

'Hannah is a language master,' said Joseph. 'The Afrikaans department had high hopes for her until the English department grabbed her for her PhD – you could say another Anglo-Boer War was fought over her,' he said, laughing as he poked her in the shoulder.

'How do you know all that?' said Hannah, poking him back, surprised he had been keeping track of her life.

'I have eyes and ears everywhere,' said Joseph.

She poked him again. 'You have women in universities everywhere, you mean, who would tell you anything to stay in your favour.'

'They have their uses,' said Joseph, returning the poke with a grin.

'So,' Alistair gestured at the journal, 'where do we go from here?'

'Right,' said Joseph, clearing his throat and putting on a serious face. Hannah shook her head at him, wondering if they would ever relate to each other as adults.

'Right,' said Hannah, taking over and opening her notebook. 'We have the journal written by Rachel Badenhorst. When I visited Silwerfontein, I found photographs of her and her family, and a marriage register including her parents and her brother. Wolf's wedding took place after the war, and his grave is in the cemetery in town. And then,' she paused, not sure how Joseph and Alistair would react, 'there are Kobie's stories about Goshen.'

Alistair lifted his eyes from the journal to her, one eyebrow raised. 'You can't base an excavation on ghost stories.'

Joseph linked his hands on the table and began tapping his thumb thoughtfully. 'The paranormal and archaeology have always been linked. When you're dealing with the dead, it's obvious that people's fascination with the paranormal will be fed. What are the stories?'

'Kobie's been on the farm his whole life,' Hannah said. 'He speaks of the smell of sewage or the smell of smoke when there's no fire. He says he's heard keening on the wind. Says he and his sister have seen two different women in Boer clothes. I believe he's telling the truth — at least, he believes it's true.'

'It's complete nonsense,' said Alistair strongly. Hannah looked down at her hands on the table, feeling her heart shrink a little, and glad she hadn't mentioned her own experience on the plateau.

'There are some archaeologists who are into "ghost science".' Joseph punctuated the words with his fingers. 'I'm more pragmatic than that. Chances are that stories of the camps have been passed down the generations in some form or other, and placed a sense of expectation in Kobie's mind, whether he remembers hearing the stories or not.' He smiled at Alistair's frown. 'We mustn't discount stories – they might have begun in reality. Besides, a few ghosts here and there are very helpful for funding.' He winked at Hannah before continuing, 'Why this specific site on Goshen? What do you call it? The plateau?'

Hannah began thoughtfully, 'When I first asked Alistair's mother, she just assumed I was talking about the plateau. Kobie's stories are based up there, and then, when I went up with Alistair, I saw the line of gum trees which Rachel references in her journal.'

Joseph's interest sharpened. 'What trees?'

'She describes how the camp children planted a windbreak. A line of gums stands on the plateau, with no other apparent purpose.'

Joseph turned to Alistair, who was looking down at his hands on the table, a frown drawing his brows down. 'What do you think, Alistair? About the plateau's being the site?'

'It's a creepy place, for no reason that I ever knew before now. The trees? I don't know. Anybody could have planted them, I suppose, down the years.'

Joseph must have heard Hannah's intake of breath, because he turned to her and said, 'No, Han, it's good to have a devil's advocate. It means we can't make assumptions without looking at all the angles. And sometimes,' he shrugged, 'struggling with something produces more exciting results than what was simple and obvious.'

'I don't mean to be rude,' said Alistair, 'but are you the right person to be doing this investigation? I mean, shouldn't we be getting a South African War historian to do it? Do you know enough about the period to run a project like this?'

Joseph laughed. 'Good question! Historians and archaeologists are two different beasts. Archaeologists use scientific evidence. There are archaeological processes which we follow, and our conclusions are based on what we find, rather than the archival record. An historian cannot run a dig. I've been doing a bit of phoning around in the last few days. There is only one archaeologist working on camp excavations in South

Africa. He's a goldmine of information, and was very interested in part-nering with me to look at this site. He's overseas at the moment. He's going to do some teaching there, so he can't get back for a while. Are you happy for me to work with him but be the hands on the ground?'

Alistair nodded, but the look on his face told Hannah he was feeling this snowball was rolling already and there was little he could do now to stop it.

'Besides,' said Joseph, 'this is all presuming there is anything to find.' He winked again at Hannah, who had looked up sharply.

She felt a bubble of excitement begin to build in her as she stared at her brother with new eyes. She had always assumed he was so far above her in intellect and success that he would never credit her for anything of her own. But now, sitting here, perhaps she had misjudged him. He was taking her seriously. 'Where to now?' she said.

'I think we need to take a two-pronged approach. One is the site, which is my domain, and the other is the recorded evidence. Hannah, that journal is key, so you need to make copies, perhaps translate it so that we lesser mortals can read it. It needs to be combed for any detail, no matter how small. References to time, physical landmarks, food, water supply, fuel, shelter, anything we might find remnants of. And then you will need to go further afield to the archives to find any con-nections with the official record.' He paused to take in their reactions. Hannah was smiling, almost vibrating with excitement, but Alistair, with his arms folded in front of him, had a frown of worry creasing his face. 'Are you ready for this?' Joseph said.

Alistair's 'No' collided with Hannah's 'Yes!'

'All right, then,' said Joseph, his brows raised, 'shall we go see the site?'

The Hilux bounced as they climbed the hill behind the house. Alistair's dogs ran with the pickup, Grant keeping up with the vehicle and the two Labs managing to lumber behind. Hannah sat in the middle, re-membering her first ride in the truck with Alistair, painfully holding herself away from him. Now, she relaxed and let the rolling of the vehi-cle slide her between her brother and Alistair. At one point, he changed into lowest gear and his hand shifted to her leg to hold her in place as the truck ground over a particularly steep, rocky section of road. Her insides clenched at the feel of his hard hand on her skin, but it was gone too soon, both hands gripping the steering wheel and Alistair looking straight ahead as if nothing had happened.

There was no doubt, she was attracted to him. The few times they had touched, by accident or that moment on the pavement outside her house, her reaction had been visceral. A physical tug which sat deep but made no sense to pursue. Too much emotional baggage on both sides to wade through. She hadn't allowed herself to think about it. And shouldn't now.

Todd had set the pace of their relationship from their very first meeting. He had been handsome in a smooth, trendy sort of way, and his charisma had pulled her into following him. She had never questioned why she had enmeshed herself in his life or exactly what it was that she liked about him. They were a couple from the moment they met. She had fitted herself around him, never asking herself if it was what she wanted. She went with the flow, drifting along rather than purposely choosing him.

Now there was Alistair. And a slow pull towards a man who stood damaged but stood nonetheless. A man for whom opening his heart before her took great courage. But was she up to the responsibility? Was she ready for the intensity she was sure would come with getting involved with Alistair? Her heart skittered and shrank at the thought.

Joseph hopped out to open the fence gate, waiting a few moments for the dogs to catch up before closing it and hopping back in the truck. The plateau looked innocuous in the sunlight. The grass shone gold in the sun and not a blade stirred. Joseph climbed out of the pickup and stretched his arms high above his head. He turned a full circle. 'It's pretty remote for a camp,' he said. 'Most were along railway lines or adjacent to garrisons.'

'Does that mean it's unlikely to have been one?' said Hannah.

'It means it doesn't follow the pattern, but that's not evidence in itself.' He turned to Alistair. 'Are you aware of a blockhouse on the farm or a garrison?'

Alistair shook his head. 'All I know is that my mother's house was built after the war, but, as you say, that doesn't mean there wasn't anything before that.'

'Kobie's family have lived on the farm since the war, so those dwellings or at least the site of the dwellings might be older,' said Hannah, looking at the wind pump and remembering her fright. The pump stood tall and silver in the bright morning, its blades still.

Joseph followed her gaze. 'And the pump?'

'Rachel speaks of a well,' said Hannah. 'That's a discrepancy with the journal.'

'Not necessarily,' said Alistair. 'Wind pumps were around during the war, but they only became common on farms later – this one could have been put in on a well site.'

Joseph nodded. 'Rachel's speaking of a well is also more in line with the fact that the British were all about keeping their costs to the minimum. It was a hugely expensive war, and the army was under enormous pressure from home to keep costs down. They wouldn't have spent money on engineering for a camp.'

'The British,' Alistair added, 'made do with whatever infrastructure was in place. That proved to be one of their biggest problems. Having to feed and supply such a huge force was almost impossible. They resorted to pillaging whatever they could from the farms they crossed.'

'Rachel speaks of that – they stripped her farm of everything. And shot all the livestock. Why would they do that? When they needed horses and food?'

Alistair shook his head and shrugged. 'I think it came down to the British commanders on the ground. If they couldn't manage to drive the stock away and care for it, they annihilated everything so that the Boers couldn't use it.'

'It seems so barbaric, and for people who considered themselves civilised!'

'Remember, they were trying to end the war as quickly as possible. They just grossly underestimated the Boers' endurance – that of both the men and the women.'

Joseph walked down the line of trees, his eyes on the ground. When he came to the end, he turned at a ninety-degree angle and walked in another line until he was standing two hundred metres away from the pickup, where the ground began falling away. He then walked the edge of the plateau parallel to the line of trees. Halfway along, he stopped, squatted to the ground, and began shouting across the plateau to Hannah and Alistair.

When they reached him, he was kneeling on the ground, peering at an object lying half-buried. He looked up as they approached. 'Our first find!' he said.

'Already?' Hannah knelt next to him. 'Josey, you are the luckiest bastard.'

'That's our mother you're talking about.' Joseph grinned at her. 'Don't lift it,' he said quickly as she reached out. 'We might have to do a survey of this whole site, which means mapping every inch with GIS before we can dig up anything.'

Alistair crouched down next to them. 'It's a ration tin,' he said.

'Yes, it is!' said Joseph triumphantly. 'And it might just be the beginning of a very interesting project.'

'What does this mean?' said Hannah, her face flushed with excitement.

'It means,' said Alistair dryly, 'that someone had a British army ration tin.'

'Don't mock me!' said Hannah crossly.

'But it is all we can deduce from just one tin,' said Joseph. 'Those ration tins would have been distributed all over the country. Wherever a British soldier went, you could conceivably find a ration tin.'

'Oh,' said Hannah, somewhat deflated.

'Don't worry,' said Joseph, his eyes smiling at Hannah. 'What it does say is that this is a good site to pursue further. The Boer camps were fed with these tins. If this was indeed a camp, we will find plenty more of these.' He stood and began to walk back towards the pickup.

'What about the tin?' called Hannah, still crouching.

Joseph turned and threw her a smile. 'It's been here for over a hundred years – it will still be here when we come back. Come on, I'm starving.'

Hannah turned to Alistair who was still bent over the tin. 'Is it just me, or is my brother exceptionally annoying?'

'It's just you,' said Alistair, not looking up, even when Hannah huffed an irritated sigh. 'It's amazing to think,' he said, 'that this tin was opened and the contents eaten by someone so long ago. A hungry homesick soldier, or a starving Boer child. It might have meant life to someone, maybe even your Rachel.' He looked up and caught Hannah's gaze.

She felt a surge of emotion for him, this man who was so rational and yet could be transported by a tin lying in the veld, moved to feel compassion for people so long ago. He stood and pulled her up to stand next to him, then looked around the plateau.

'I feel the responsibility quite heavily. Whatever this place was, perhaps it's waited long enough to have its story told.'

She touched his arm. 'Strange that events could line up, my coming to Leliehoek, finding the journal, meeting you, Joseph's coming. It's a crazy coincidence.'

'My parents don't believe in coincidence – they would say it was planned.'

'Do you believe in God?' she asked.

'Yes, I do,' he answered slowly, looking down at her. 'It's difficult to be a farmer, so dependent on the land and the weather, and not believe in God. But I've been so angry—' He stopped, perhaps not sure of how he wanted to continue.

'Hey!' Joseph's voice carried over the plateau. 'I'm chewing on the tyres over here.'

Alistair smiled ruefully. 'Let's go feed your brother.'

Half an hour later, they were back in Alistair's austere kitchen. 'There's not a lot to work with,' said Hannah, standing in front of an enormous double-door chrome fridge.

'Sorry, I'll go across to the cottage and beg,' Alistair said. He returned with his arms loaded with packs of cold meat, cheese, a loaf of bread, and salad.

Joseph helped him unload onto the table. 'What's the salad for?'

'For me, you Neanderthal,' said Hannah, elbowing him out the way, and tipping the lettuce into a bowl.

'You say that like it's an insult,' said Joseph, grinning. She ignored him, threw some cherry tomatoes into the bowl, and headed outside to Alistair's kitchen garden, returning with a handful of fresh basil and coriander, their sharp scent wafting in the door with her.

They were soon sitting at the kitchen table tucking into thick triangles of toasted ham-and-cheese sandwiches.

'Heaven,' said Joseph, popping the last crust into his mouth.

'I don't think I've ever seen anyone eat that fast,' said Alistair to Hannah. 'Is that normal?'

'Nothing about Joseph is normal,' she said.

'Enough of the chit-chat,' said Joseph, getting up to put his plate in the sink. 'We need to talk about a plan of action.'

'You're the boss now,' said Alistair. 'What do we need to do?'

'Hannah, like we said earlier, you take the journal. We need copies and details, and as much about the camp as you can find from the archives in Bloemfontein.' He turned to Alistair. 'You have historical experience and probably more background knowledge on the South African War than I do. You take the area's history. Try to find out about all the action that took place here – if there were garrisons stationed close by, if there were blockhouses.'

Alistair nodded. 'I know the archives quite well. I've just never thought to look for that kind of detail.'

'That's the problem with historical research – you only find what you're looking for. Archaeologists dig up things we never dreamt we'd find. That's the beauty of it.' The smugness of his words was tempered by the passion in his voice. 'Can you get hold of aerial photographs of the plateau?'

Alistair nodded again. 'I've got some pretty recent photographs.'

'And older ones?' said Joseph, opening the fridge and peering inside.

'Try to get pictures of the ground as far back as you can. We might see things in the older pictures we can't see now.'

Hannah watched him choose a Coke and pull the tab on the can. 'Make yourself at home, Joseph,' she said.

'I love the Free State,' said Joseph. 'People are so hospitable.' He ignored Hannah's snort and continued after a short pause. 'I'll start putting a team together. Then we can begin mapping the site whenever we're ready.'

'What about permits?' said Alistair, watching Hannah. She felt his gaze and the slow heat which prickled at her neck, rising to her face. She began to clear the table around Joseph, who had settled back into his chair. Alistair stood to help her and they moved around each other without making eye contact.

Joseph took a sip from his Coke. 'Any actual excavation will need permission from SAHRA, South Africa's heritage agency. When we have some idea of what we're looking at, we can put together a proposal and apply for permission.'

'Permission for what?' said a voice behind Joseph's back.

He twisted in his chair to face a girl leaning in the doorway behind him. Her clear hazel eyes were looking at him with interest and he choked on his Coke. As he spluttered and coughed, she leant forwards and whacked him hard on the back. Hannah watched as he struggled to regain his composure, a state he was rarely, if ever, in.

'Suzanne, this is Hannah and her brother, Joseph,' said Alistair, standing upright from stacking the dishwasher.

Hannah smiled at Suzanne, taking in her deep red hair which was pulled back from her face in a messy ponytail. Her baggy tracksuit pants and overly large T-shirt did nothing to hide the fact that she was gorgeous. For once, Joseph was speechless, and Hannah filled his awkward silence: 'I was hoping for some tea. Do you want some, Suzanne?'

'Not for me, thanks. Alistair said you're here to investigate a concentration camp?' She pulled out a chair next to Joseph, dislodging his feet. He shuffled his chair up a bit to make room for her.

'Yes,' he said, sitting more upright in his chair and clearing his throat.

Alistair took mugs from a cupboard. 'Joseph, how are we going to afford the project? We'll need help to do the slog work, won't we?'

Joseph cleared his throat again. 'Yes.'

They all looked at him, waiting for him to elucidate.

'I've got … uh … connections at UCT.'

Hannah rolled her eyes at Alistair; he responded with a small smile.

Joseph continued, 'I'll see if I can get some students up after Christmas. They will still have six weeks of holiday left – we could do lot in that time.'

'And the costs?' said Alistair.

'Let me talk to some people in Cambridge – there's bound to be some funding somewhere for a project like this. The South African War still garners a lot of interest in the UK.'

'Interesting,' said Suzanne quietly, her intelligent eyes taking stock of the three people in the kitchen.

Joseph swung his full attention towards her, as sure now and as intense as a lighthouse beam. 'Tell me your story, lovely Suzanne.'

It was Hannah's turn to splutter into her cup, and Alistair reached a hand across her chair to thump the flat of his hand on her back, all the while not taking his eyes off Joseph. Hannah, recovering, recognised a glitter in Alistair's eye.

But Suzanne rose from her chair. 'Nothing compelling about my story, I'm afraid,' she said. 'Nice to meet you.' She smiled at Hannah, barely giving Joseph a glance beyond what was polite, then pushed her chair in and disappeared out the kitchen door, leaving Joseph speechless and Alistair grinning into his tea.

'She's not your type, Josey,' said Hannah, reaching across and patting his hand.

'I have a type?'

'Your pattern of twenty years leans more towards the glamorous, ambitious, attached variety.'

He scratched his chin. 'Patterns can change.'

'She takes her work seriously,' cut in Alistair, 'and she doesn't play games.'

'Sounds like a warning, Mr Barlow.' Joseph grinned.

'Consider it a caution,' said Alistair carefully. 'She's still my little sister.'

'As Hannah is mine.'

'Oh stop it, you two. I can't bear the hum of testosterone!' Hannah dumped her mug in the sink and marched down the passage. 'I'll be at the car, Joseph,' she called over her shoulder.

She could still discern their voices as she left the kitchen.

'That put us in our place!' Joseph was saying, pushing his chair back. 'We might have to ally ourselves to survive this project.'

'Indeed,' said Alistair. And then Hannah could hear no more.

Later that evening, Hannah sat at her laptop, notebook beside her, to begin researching the archives. She saw what Joseph had meant when he said you had to know what to look for. Eventually, she figured out the index system and began to search for documents. She would have to go to Bloemfontein in person to read them, but at least she could find the references from her computer. After an hour of hunting, she had found nothing about the Goshen camp, no matter what permutations she tried. There were, however, many references to the Winburg and Harrismith camps, including reams of death notices. A trip to Bloemfontein was clearly needed in the next week or so.

She closed her laptop, feeling the fatigue set in after a long day and the up-down of emotion.

Joseph looked up from his laptop across the table. 'Going to bed?'

'I'm exhausted,' she said, looking over his shoulder to see him scrolling through a Google search page. The name typed into the search box was Suzanne Barlow.

'Come on, Josey.' Hannah leant over his shoulder to peer at the pages he was now browsing. 'It was pretty clear she wasn't interested.'

He ignored Hannah, engrossed in his reading. 'Did you know that she's a doctor at Red Cross Children's Hospital? She doesn't look old enough to be out of school, let alone specialising in paediatric anaesthetics. And she's beautiful.'

'Josey, please don't cause trouble here. I'm finding my feet and the Barlows have been a big part of that. Not to mention the dig – we can't mess that up.'

Joseph twisted to look at his sister, her hand brushing the hair off her forehead and her eyes tired and concerned. He relented, pushed his chair back, and surprised her by enveloping her in a big hug, squeezing the breath out of her. 'Okay, you win. I'll leave her alone. But' – he pulled back to look down into Hannah's face, grinning – 'if she approaches me, the deal's off.'

'Agreed,' said Hannah, thinking of Suzanne's breezy imperviousness to Joseph earlier that day.

Joseph moved backwards to perch on the edge of the table. 'Clearly the same rules don't apply to you though.'

'What do you mean?'

He tilted his head to the side with a look of mock disbelief. 'Come on, Hannah, there were moments today when I thought Alistair would gobble you up whole. And,' he continued, seeing her about to fob him off, 'don't pretend you don't know what I'm talking about.'

Hannah leant back against the sink and sighed. 'I don't actually know what to tell you. There's a spark between us, that's for sure – we nearly killed each other when we first met. But now,' she paused, pulling her cheek between her teeth, 'I suppose we're friends.'

Joseph snorted.

'Joseph, it's complicated. He's been mourning his wife for eight years – I'm not convinced he's over that. And I'm—'

'You're happy,' finished Joseph, his words making Hannah look quickly up at him. 'For the first time in … I can't actually ever remember seeing you this strong and independent and happy.'

She nodded. 'That's exactly it. And I'm not sure I'm ready to give that up … be consumed again by another man.'

'You're making the assumption that Alistair is like Todd. There is no comparison, Hannah.'

'How do you know that?' She turned to the sink.

'I only met Todd a few times, but I pitched him from the first as a narcissistic arsehole.' Hannah looked over her shoulder at her brother, her brows raised as he continued, 'And yes, I am the king of narcissistic arseholes, so I know another when I see one.'

'Just your saying that,' she said, 'removes you from the category.'

'Thank you,' he said, bowing slightly. He rubbed a hand over his stubbly cheek. 'I like Alistair. There's a rawness to him, a grainy integrity. Put it this way, I would – ten times over – rather have you with a damaged farmer than a slippery, lying bastard of a politician.'

Hannah smiled at him, reaching out to squeeze his arm. 'Thanks, Josey. But, to be honest, I can't see it working out. I've never even been on a proper date in my life, let alone handled a relationship with someone so fragile. It would be better to keep my distance, I think.'

'Better for whom?'

'For everyone, surely. This Leliehoek bubble I'm in won't last forever. I will have to return to my life eventually.' She smiled sadly, drying her hands on a tea towel.

'This could be your life, Hannah.'

'In my dreams,' she said, raising her hand in a goodnight wave. 'See you in the morning.'

He reached forwards to close his laptop, and she caught a glimpse of Suzanne's profile picture. 'In my dreams too,' he said softly to himself as he shut the lid on her.

August 1901, Goshen Camp, Orange River Colony

Dear Wolf

I used to think I was connected to you by some invisible thread. We used to know what the other was thinking. We used to finish each other's sentences. I thought I would know if something happened to you, but I have felt nothing of the kind. Maybe that means you are still alive. Maybe I would know for sure if you were dead. I cling on to this. I imagine the three of you riding free. I picture you crouched over a cooking fire, trying to make my bread. I see you browned by the sun, your eyes full of life. You are not like the beaten, hollow Boers I see driving wagons for the British. The hendsoppers. I can't let you be.

Winter this year is the worst I can remember. Is it because we are sleeping on the ground in these makeshift shelters? Or is it really terribly, terribly cold? Snow has lain thick on the ground for days now, and most of us are without shoes. My big feet have grown even bigger since I came here. I wore my old shoes until they were so painful to put on, I could not bear it any longer. Now I wish I had held on to them, even if to just half slip on so that I could walk in the snow. Our feet are bound in rags. Even rags are precious here.

I have seen such cleverness in this camp, though. Andries and Helena were married in May, and her mother made new dresses from scraps. Old dresses and cloth cut into something new. I hope I can do the same when this is over – reconfigure myself into something new and beautiful – because right now I am only scrap. Too ill-fitting and tatty to be appealing to anyone.

The dresses were beautiful, ingenious in their design. Ma Maria cut those precious fabrics to fit the girls perfectly, and they could have walked into town with their heads held high. The wedding party gathered for a photograph, standing proud in their wedding finery.

Yes, life goes on here. Even in the bitter cold, amidst the death and the grieving. I sometimes wish it didn't. I sometimes despise the laughter and chatter, the children playing in the stones. I want the world to stand still and acknowledge my despair.

I have heard nothing of the others. I beg for news from anyone new to camp, even from the soldiers who come from the blockhouse. They sneer at me. They say the commandos are gone; they say they have run away and left us. But I know that is not true.

I try not to think of the others at all. If they are in a camp like this, I can't pretend that everything is well with them. I won't write their names in case the words draw pictures in my head. But I can't help Lizzie and Kristina visiting me at night when I'm asleep. They crawl into bed with me like they used to at home. But their bodies are no longer soft and warm, their breath sweet on my face. They are bony and cold. I wake with such gut-wrenching fear and then I feel the ground hard and cold below my blankets, my own knobbly spine and hips and shoulders never finding a soft place. I tell myself it was just this discomfort that made me dream so.

Come for me, Wolf.

CHAPTER EIGHTEEN

Hannah spent every spare moment to translate the journal. She had made good progress, but every time she delved back into Rachel's story, she felt an urgency to find out what had happened to the family. As if finding the Badenhorsts would save Rachel from the terrible anxiety and fear the girl had lived with in the camp. Hannah had arranged with Barbara and planned to go to the Bloemfontein archives that week.

Joseph too had made progress, pulling strings at the University of Cape Town; Hannah didn't want to know exactly what strings. A team of students were going to arrive at Goshen after Christmas, and Sarah had insisted on managing the logistics. Where usually they would set up camp at the site, she was planning to put them up in one of the sheds behind the main house. She had the shed swept clean, and Neil supervised the installation of basic wooden partitions to divide the enormous space into two dormitories, a rustic ablution area, and a living space. A gas stove and ancient fridge had already been installed, and Sarah was on the hunt in the district for folding chairs and mattresses. She and Joseph were getting on famously, his charm set to full blast, with Sarah enjoying every minute.

Joseph had told Neil that, if he had been around forty years previously, Neil wouldn't have stood a chance with Sarah. Neil, secretly flattered, had replied it was a good thing Joseph hadn't been around then. That finding Joseph's remains buried on the plateau would have confused the dig mightily. Joseph found this hilarious. As a result, he had made himself at home on Goshen, and was coming and going as he pleased within days. Hannah juggled marvelling at his brazenness and being thoroughly irritated she couldn't muster the same unabashed assurance.

Leliehoek had filled up for the holidays and the shop was seeing more business than Hannah had thought possible in a small town. Anticipating the holidaymakers and knowing the kinds of books she herself liked to read on holiday, she had ordered a range of paperback bestsellers which had sold remarkably well. She had also experimented with books which might be good Christmas gifts and found, to her surprise, that she had been right. A selection of classic children's books had flown off the shelves, as had a selection of new South African War books and coffee table books of the area. She was thrilled with her December turnover, knowing it would carry the shop through its quieter months.

Kathryn, on the other hand, completely run off her feet, was wishing the holidays over, or so she told Hannah when they had the chance to have a quick coffee. Kathryn had even roped Douglas in to wait tables but had discovered he was more hindrance than help. He chatted so much to the patrons that they stayed far too long, and she couldn't turn the tables over fast enough. Eventually, as Christmas drew closer, he apologetically asked if he could be excused to prepare his Christmas services and Kathryn had to pretend she was disappointed. Christmas itself was always tough for Kathryn. She was exhausted by the time it arrived and then had to muster the energy to put on the best possible day for her kids. Doing it alone was all the more difficult. Every year, she packed a hamper to send to Durban, and filled it with food and a set of new clothes. She included photographs of the children and art they had produced. Every year, Kathryn confided in Hannah, she wondered if her husband would even open the box, let alone recognise the love which was packed into it. In the beginning, she had hoped it would bring him home, but as the years passed, she began to hope it would not. She had let go of the dream they could reconcile, and it was a logical progression from there that she should begin to think about divorce. But she was not quite ready yet.

* * *

Alistair, meanwhile, was immersed in researching the history of the area. Canvassing the farmers in the district for any scrap of information, he had gathered that most farms had been razed and left desolate, the families relocated to camps in Winburg, Harrismith, or even further afield. He heard about heirloom rifles and pianos, Bibles and furniture that had been dug from their hiding places after the war.

Alistair had spent a long time with Mrs Venter, an elderly lady who had lived her whole life in the area. She was the fifth generation of Van Rooyens on the family farm. It was now run down, her children not interested in or capable of restoring it. Alistair sat with her in her creaking lounge, the ceilings sagging and the plaster cracking off the stone. The house had been rebuilt after the South African War, the heavy stones moved up a small slope to a new site. She led Alistair out of the house to a sheep kraal, a rondavel shelter standing in the middle. 'Under that mud plaster is stone,' she said in her reedy voice, pointing at the rondavel. 'That is the dwelling where the elderly grandparents lived when everyone else fled the farm. The only building left standing after the British came through. They burnt everything else. The men were off on commando, and the women and children hid in a big cave in those hills.' She turned and pointed to the steep sandstone faces behind the house. 'There was much movement by both sides after Surrender Hill, and from that cave you can see the whole valley. Those crafty women developed a signal system with mirrors to warn the Boers when the British were coming. Ha! Teach them to burn our farm!' A sadness shadowed her face, and she suddenly looked tired, her ninety-five years heavy on her. 'I hope that whoever buys this place doesn't knock down that old rondavel. It's seen some things in its time.'

Alistair felt an overwhelming urge to bundle this feisty old woman up in a big hug and tell her that he would buy and fix her farm. What a disgrace that her children could let her down, pursue their own ends in Johannesburg, and leave her to fret about her home. But this was happening all over the Free State. It was a tragic but common story. People from the cities would come, snap up this place for a song, and renovate the life out of it. It would stand empty for weeks while they alternated between their beach and berg holiday houses.

Mrs Venter had walked him to his car, a little crossbreed dog at her feet, and stood on her tiptoes to receive his soft kiss on her cheek. She patted him on his. 'You're a good boy, Alistair.' He drove off, concerned about leaving her alone on such a big place, and thinking he must talk to his parents. Something had to be done for her.

A week later he had concluded that, despite the wealth of anecdotal information, there was little detailed knowledge of the British army in the area. He realised he would have to look in the archives to find more official documentation.

When he called the bookshop one morning, it was Barbara who answered.

'Hannah's just busy with a customer.' He could hear her hand muffle the receiver before she said, 'Alistair, may I take a message and she'll call you right back?'

'Um, yes. I wanted to know if she was still going up to Bloemfontein this week.' He paused, feeling awkward, knowing that the speculation would hit the streets of Leliehoek in a matter of minutes. 'Tomorrow? I was wanting to tag along – would she mind?'

Alistair could hear Barbara's smile across the phone line. 'I'm standing in for her tomorrow. Why don't you pick her up early, say six o'clock?'

Alistair wasn't sure how Hannah would deal with the arrangements being made on her behalf, but he wanted to end the call as quickly as possible. 'Fine. Thanks, Barbara. Goodbye.'

Barbara replaced the phone in its cradle.

'What did he want?' said Hannah, returning to the desk and beginning to ring up a sale.

Barbara took the books on the counter and packed them into a brown paper carrier bag. 'He phoned to say he'd drive you to Bloem tomorrow.'

'What? I don't need to be driven to Bloem. I'm perfectly capable of driving myself.'

'Of course you are.' Barbara's attempt to sound soothing was undermined by her grin. 'But why be a feminist when you can be chauffeured?'

Hannah harrumphed in reply.

'He's picking you up at six. Put something nice on.'

Scowling, Hannah returned her attention to the computer while a still-grinning Barbara handed the parcel to the bemused customer.

The following morning, Alistair pulled up outside Hannah's gate as she stepped out onto the deck. She'd chosen a soft skirt that came to her knees, and a light cardigan over a strappy vest top. Wearing just the barest of make-up, she had left her hair loose to fall to her shoulders. She hoped he wouldn't notice her efforts. He held the door for her and, as he walked around the front of the truck to the driver's door, she saw him smile and lightly tap the bonnet of the car. Dammit, he had noticed. She tucked her skirt under her legs and pulled the cardigan closed over her chest, not meeting his eye.

It was only when they had left Leliehoek behind that she turned to him. 'Why did you want to come with me?'

He glanced across at her, perhaps trying to read her mood. 'I have some things to look up at the archives too, so I thought we might as well travel together.'

'Oh.'

'I want to find out where the blockhouses were built in our area. The anecdotal information I've found so far is more to do with Boer farms and the camps than the British army's positions.'

'I suppose that would make sense if Leliehoek farmers are mostly Boer descendants. Aren't there still blockhouses which remain?'

'Not in our area, it would seem. Maybe the Boers demolished them when they returned to their farms.'

'I certainly would,' said Hannah, thinking of the families returning to devastated farms and burnt-out homesteads. 'I wouldn't want any reminder of what the war had done to my home.'

'And building materials would also have been in short supply,' said Alistair. 'Corrugated-iron sheets and bricks would've been very useful in rebuilding. If we can establish where the blockhouse line ran, then it might explain why a camp was built on Goshen, so far from the railway.' He glanced at Hannah, who had relaxed as the conversation had shifted away from themselves. 'What is your agenda for today?' he asked.

'I need to find out what happened to the Badenhorst family. I know it doesn't have particular bearing on the Goshen camp, because they were sent to another one, but not knowing is gnawing at me.' Hannah propped her forehead into the cup of her hand, her elbow leaning on the window frame. 'Imagine being separated from your family and having to spend at least two years in a camp, not knowing where they were or if they were still alive. Rachel's despair is driving me crazy. I can't bear it. What if she never found out?'

Alistair smiled at her, his eyes gentle. 'It's rather lovely actually. You care deeply for her and want to help. That it's over a hundred years down the line is inconsequential.'

As they approached Bethlehem, Hannah watched the mountains of the eastern Free State fall away and the land begin to flatten out, stretching to the horizon.

'Did you know,' said Alistair, raising a smile from Hannah, 'Bethlehem got its name from the Hebrew?'

Hannah laughed. 'No! I'd never have guessed.'

Alistair persisted, now grinning. 'It means, "House of Bread",' he gestured out the window, 'and, as you can see, it makes a lot sense.'

In every direction stretched vast fields of wheat, and Hannah smiled at him. 'I actually did not know that.'

It was nine o'clock when they reached Bloemfontein, the Free State's bustling capital. The archives were housed in an unprepossessing house on the university campus. It sat on Badenhorst Street which struck Hannah as a promising coincidence. Alistair parked outside and pressed the gate intercom. They were buzzed through and followed signs to the reading room. An impeccably dressed lady worked behind the desk and looked up as they approached. Her hair was braided in intricate patterns over her scalp. She stood to explain the reading-room procedure, handing them request forms.

Hannah and Alistair sat at adjacent tables and began to fill in the forms from the notes they had made from their online searches. When they handed them to the lady, she disappeared through a door behind the counter. Twenty minutes later, she returned, pushing a wooden trolley, the shelves loaded with brown cardboard box files. She left the trolley between their tables and returned to her desk.

Hannah opened one box at a time, sifting through the documents in each. When she came to the boxes of death notices from Winburg Refugee Camp, she reached for her notebook and settled in to read them at length. With a mix of horror and fascination, she ran her finger down each page, eyes scanning the columns. Too many of the dead were small children.

She found Rachel's youngest sister, little Lizzie, first. Elizabeth Badenhorst, dead in June 1901 from diphtheria. Rachel's ma, Aletta, died a month later, from typhoid. Beautiful, wild Kristina at the end of 1901 from measles. And Oupa Jakob in the winter of 1902. Hannah's throat caught as she took in the implications of this loss. Rachel's sisters, her mother, her grandfather – all gone while she sat on Goshen, longing for them, fearing for their lives and wishing for the day when they would be reunited on the farm. She looked again at the dates she'd scrawled, and her heart twisted at the thought of gentle, wise Oupa Jakob, nursing the last of his girls alone, until Kristina too was dead. Those last six months of his life must've been desolate.

Hannah sat back in her chair, her heart sore in her chest. She had expected to find that one or two of the family had been lost at Winburg. But all? She thought of the photographs in the album at Silwerfontein, of the little girls in their best dresses. Their faces without the formality of the adults' capturred, their eyes alive, and bodies just before they were cast into motion once again. And Ma. Firm, capable, fiery Ma, who couldn't save her children in the end.

She thought of Wolf's wedding portrait from after the war, his solemn face and distant gaze. No wonder he couldn't summon any lightness on his wedding day. He had returned from commando to find the house destroyed and empty, the women of his family gone.

Alistair looked up from the piles of papers on his table, seeing Hannah's face.

'You found them.'

She nodded. 'All dead.' She looked back down at the papers. 'I can't actually believe it. All of them? That leaves only the two sons and their father.'

'And Rachel,' said Alistair.

'And Rachel,' she repeated. 'Although, who knows for how much longer. I mean, I only found Wolf's grave. What if he was the sole survivor? How terribly tragic.'

Hannah felt Alistair's sympathy and took comfort in his gentle, 'Sorry, Hannah.' He paused for a bit, watching her. 'Do you want to go?'

She nodded and gathered up the files, replacing them on the trolley.

Outside, the midday heat was heavy on her skin, the seats in the baking-hot Toyota burning the backs of her legs. Rolling down the window only marginally helped. She could feel Alistair's eyes on her.

'Are you hungry?' he said. 'I'm going to need some food before we head home.'

'Can we get a take-away?' she said, not feeling like being in Bloem any longer. 'I'd like to be back before the end of the day.'

They were quiet while Alistair negotiated his way around the campus. Hannah rolled her discovery around in her mind. Fumbling with her sense of loss. They found a cafeteria, which in term-time would have been packed with students, but now was largely empty except for a few staff members. Alistair insisted on paying and they carried their salad wraps and icy cold Cokes back to the car. Alistair unwrapped the wax paper and demolished his in five big bites, then started the engine, his cooldrink sitting between his thighs where he could reach it. Hannah felt slightly nauseous, and tried to force a few mouthfuls down before rewrapping the paper and putting it in her bag.

'You okay?' asked Alistair, glancing between her and the road. Hannah nodded but looked out her window rather than answer. 'Finding the Badenhorsts really knocked you, didn't it?'

She nodded again, feeling tears prick her eyes. All she had discovered that morning threatened to overwhelm her and she drew a deep breath. *Come on, Hannah*, she told herself. *Pull yourself together. Just until you get home.*

Alistair looked across at her again. 'I found some helpful stuff this morning.'

She knew he was trying to distract her. Pulling a tissue from her bag, she blew her nose and turned towards him. 'Sorry, I didn't even ask. Were you done? Did you want to leave just then?'

His smile was gentle as he said, 'I can come back if I need to.' A moment passed while he negotiated his way through an intersection. 'So, it turns out that the blockhouse line split at Bethlehem. One line followed the road down towards Fouriesburg and the other ran across to Harrismith.' He looked at her, clearly expecting to see understanding dawn across her face, but she remained blank. He sighed. 'Goshen sits right in the middle. If, as Rachel says, they were growing food for the troops, it would have been perfectly placed. Those blockhouses were manned by British infantry – at least seven men, but sometimes double that. They were built about a kilometre apart, in sight of one another, and joined by barbed wire. That's a lot of blockhouses. And a hell of a lot of men to feed.'

Hannah lay her head back against the headrest and smiled at him. 'You almost sound excited.'

He kept his eyes front but smiled. 'Okay. Go ahead.'

'Go ahead with what?'

'You know you want to.'

She scrunched her brows. 'Want to what?'

'You've been dying, from the first time we met, to put me in my place.' He swung one arm wide. 'Go ahead. *I told you so. I told you it was true. I told you this was real. I told you this was gripping.* Come on.'

'No. It doesn't have the same effect. You can't tell me to tell you so. There's no satisfaction in being prompted. I need to wait for my own "na-na-na-na-na" moment.'

He shot her an amused glance. 'Fine.'

'Fine,' she said, shutting her eyes but allowing a grin to play on her lips.

She must have fallen asleep, because she awoke with Alistair's hand on her shoulder, not shaking her awake but running down her arm, softly. She sat up, pushing her hair off her face. Alistair came around to her side of the pickup, opening her door, but she stayed in her seat.

'You okay?' he said.

'I feel a bit ridiculous. Like Rachel's waiting in there for me. When I open her journal again, she'll be there, still longing for them, still hoping they're okay, and now I know the truth. It's awful. Even just a touch of her grief is so heavy. I can't deal with it. I don't want to deal with someone else's grief.'

When she glanced up at him, he was still holding the door open for her, but his face had closed. 'I'm sorry,' she said quickly, 'I didn't mean you ...'

He stepped away onto the curb, pulling the door wide, and she climbed out, feeling drained and inadequate.

She let him open the gate for her and escort her up the steps to the deck. Joseph was sprawled on a lounger there.

'My favourite farmer,' he said, swinging his legs to the side and reaching up a hand for Alistair to shake. 'Productive day?'

'Revealing,' said Alistair.

Hannah stepped towards the French door. 'I think I'm going to lie down for a bit. Thanks for driving me, Alistair.' She disappeared inside, leaving Joseph staring after her.

'Is she okay?' she could hear him ask Alistair.

She had scrubbed her face clean and was tying her hair back in front of the bathroom mirror, when she looked up to find Joseph lounging against the doorframe. 'What happened up there that has both of you acting so weirdly?'

She ignored him.

'What happened?'

'Nothing.'

'Alistair says you found out the Badenhorsts all died in a camp.'

'Yes.' She stepped past him, and he followed her back into the kitchen where she picked up her keys off the counter.

'I thought you weren't feeling well,' he said.

As she walked out onto the deck, she said over her shoulder, 'I'm just going across to Kathryn's. I'll be back for supper. Maybe you could make some for a change.'

'You don't know my cooking,' he called after her. 'You'll have to take your chances.' But she didn't respond, walking quickly out the gate and disappearing around the corner.

Hannah found Kathryn serving her last table. A family were enjoying coffees and pretty milkshakes, the children shrieking in delight at the tall plastic glasses, piled with marshmallows and sprinkles. Hannah pulled out a bar stool at the counter and asked Maisie for a pot of tea. She soon had a pot covered in a pink-and-grey crocheted tea cosy which she found immensely comforting. Kathryn came up behind her and, placing a hand on her shoulder, spoke across the counter to Maisie, 'Please take over that table – they want double fudge cupcakes all round.' She pulled out another stool, still with her hand on Hannah's shoulder, and sat down. The gentleness communicated through Kathryn's touch brought hot tears to Hannah's eyes.

'I've been thinking about you today, hon,' said Kathryn. 'Something to do with Alistair and Marilie?'

Hannah turned swimming eyes to Kathryn. 'How do you do that? When I first arrived, you spoke like this too – like you know stuff without being told. Are you clairvoyant or something?'

Kathryn laughed and shook her head. 'Nooo!' She stood up on the rungs of her stool and reached over for another cup, pouring herself tea from Hannah's pot. She said matter-of-factly, 'It's Holy Spirit stuff. I've learnt to listen to him, but I want to hear this story from you.'

A part of Hannah's brain wondered at her own lack of surprise or suspicion of something so weird, but deeper than that was the fact that she trusted Kathryn completely. 'Alistair and I went to Bloemfontein to do some research today. It was all going so well, and then I found out that Rachel's sisters, her mother, and her grandfather died in the Win-burg camp. I just felt so desolate afterwards.' She shook her head. 'I can't explain it. Then I shot my mouth off to Alistair, saying I can't deal with someone else's grief, that it feels like too much. He shut down after that.' Kathryn tutted, making Hannah bridle. 'What? You think I was insensitive too? Don't you think he should be over her by now? Eight years, Kathryn!'

Kathryn put her hand on Hannah's arm to draw her attention fully. 'It's not just the loss of his wife he had to get over, Hannah. Alistair carries the scars of that day on his face, and no doubt scars of that day in his mind for the rest of his life. He lost his life as he knew it. Esme has attacked him over and over. The press picked up the story because Marilie was so well known in sports circles. People came crawling all over the farm, looking for where it happened, for the blood stain on the driveway.' Kathryn caught Hannah's raised brows. 'No, really, they did. Which is why he is so wary of strangers on the farm. That he is allowing this dig at all is a miracle, and perhaps testament to how much he feels for you.'

Hannah shook her head, not wanting to deal with that added load of emotion.

'Hannah, he is a kind, gentle, damaged man who deserves to live again. Don't step away from him.'

'I'm not strong enough to deal with all of it.'

'Who said you aren't strong?' Kathryn's voice had sharpened.

'Todd ... my mother ... me.' Hannah twisted her hands in her lap.

'Stop it this instant!'

Hannah looked up in surprise at her friend's fierce face. Kathryn was oblivious to the curious glances from the occupied table, her eyes flashing. 'You haven't even begun to discover the depths of your strength, but you will. You have made a new start here. It could be a new life. Don't run away now, at the first obstacle. Why do you think you have such a connection with Rachel? Because she was strong like you, a survivor like you. You'll see.' Kathryn settled back down and Hannah thought of a bird unruffling its feathers.

'More tea?' Kathryn asked, as if her mini tirade had never happened. Hannah shook her head.

'Are we still on for Christmas day?' said Kathryn, moving behind the counter and reaching for their cups.

'Um, yes. Do you mind if Joseph joins us?'

'No, you must bring him. Douglas is also coming.'

Hannah got to her feet, tucking the bar stool back under the counter. 'What can I bring, Kathryn?'

'How about some Christmas crackers? The kids love them. And chocolates for the table, maybe?'

'That doesn't sound like much,'

'It's that or nothing – your choice,' Kathryn called from the kitchen at the back.

'Mean and bossy,' muttered Hannah.

'I heard that!' She appeared again, grinning.

'Can you believe it's Christmas Eve tomorrow already?'

'I can't wait. I close this place tomorrow at lunchtime. And then two days of bliss.'

'Two days of cooking up a storm at home, you mean,' said Hannah with a wry smile.

'Who said I was cooking? Didn't I tell you we have toasted sandwiches for Christmas lunch?'

Hannah picked up her keys and turned for the door. 'That would be fine with me. It's you who would never allow it.' She could hear Kathryn's burble of laughter as she walked down the front steps.

As she ambled back to the shop, Hannah was lost in thought. Kathryn's words came back to her. She didn't know her strength. She had never flexed that muscle. But then, the thought of Alistair's complexity frightened her. If she wasn't strong enough to deal with him and his past, she certainly wasn't strong enough to manage the fallout which would certainly come when she left him.

* * *

24 December 1901, Goshen Camp, Orange River Colony

Dear Wolf,

I am dreading Christmas in the camp, ashamed I complained about last Christmas at all. I didn't know then how bad things were going to get. We were on Silwerfontein. We roasted chickens and potatoes. We pulled beans from the garden, and glossed carrots with honey. And then you surprised us. The girls sang for us at the pianoforte, Lizzie's lisp and earnest eyes making us smile. Oupa Jakob scooped her up and danced her around the room, her little feet swinging as she threw her head back in delight.

Kristina was the star, though, wasn't she? I wonder if, after the war, she might explore music further? It seems the only thing she feels passionately about, the only discipline she will sit under. She would certainly draw a crowd with her singing, even now, untrained. And Pa took Ma in his arms and they danced on the stoep in the dark, with the music floating through the lit windows. It added a headiness to the night, the joy of being together after so many months apart. It is a dangerous dream now.

I think, if I ever leave this place, I will always remember this December 1901. It has changed my picture of December, but it is right to remember the great loss this month. So many have died – the worst month I have seen. We have not been able to dig graves fast enough.

People don't stop dying because it's Christmas. I am the bearer of their names and perhaps I, more than anyone else in the camp, realise how many we have lost. Because I keep count and write their names, the lists haunt me. People know they must come and report a death to me, and they do. Sometimes a mother comes, the grief and horror slack on her face. Sometimes it's a child, telling me his sister or mother or granny is dead. Sometimes they are so little, I have to wheedle out their name. Sometimes the child doesn't know what their mama's name is. The worst for me, though – and perhaps because I fear this for myself – is when someone notices a body in a neighbouring shelter. It might have been lying there for a few days but because they were alone or the last of their family, nobody was there at their passing. This fills me with dread, because it will happen to me. More than anything I want to know that I am loved.

Am I?

CHAPTER NINETEEN

Christmas day dawned with an intense Free State blue sky. Hannah could see it would be fiercely hot later. She walked through to the kitchen, finding Joseph nursing a cup of coffee at the table. Reaching for a mug, she flicked the kettle back on to boil.

'I think I might go across to the church this morning,' she said.

Joseph looked up in surprise. 'What for?'

'It's Christmas day, Josey!'

'Yes, and have you ever been to church on Christmas day before?'

'No, but so what? I think I'd like to try it.'

'Hannah, it's not a new flavour of ice cream. You kind of have to believe in God to go to church. Just as a bare minimum.' Amusement was thick in his voice.

'Laugh all you like. It might be fun. And who knows, I might meet him there.'

'Who? Alistair?'

'No, you muppet, God! I might meet God at church.'

'Riiight,' said Joseph, earning himself a soft clip to the head.

Hannah, not sure what one should wear to church, eventually pulled on a gypsy top with a denim skirt which almost reached her knees. She twisted her hair into a loose bun at the nape of her neck and pulled on simple sandals.

The sun was already hot on her neck, even at eight in the morning, as she crossed the square, ducking into the deep shade of the plane trees. Cars were parked on the verges outside St Luke's, and smartly dressed people streamed through the lychgate into the arched doorway of the church. Douglas stood at the door, looking strangely comfortable in a long white robe and white-and-gold embroidered stole, its two ends hanging in front to mid-calf.

His face lit in a smile when he saw her. 'Hannah!' he said, pulling her into a big hug.

'Douglas, you look … different.'

'Weird, hey?' he said cheerfully; then, drawing closer, he whispered loudly, 'But you would never know I only have my underpants on underneath this robe.' He winked at her shocked intake of breath, and she had to smother her laughter as he turned to greet a staid-looking couple behind her.

The service was a surprise. The church was full of holidaymakers and local families. Little children, dressed in their new Christmas outfits, snuck up the aisle and hung on the communion rail while Douglas led traditional Christmas carols. After the singing, Douglas began to tell the nativity story by enacting a play on the fly. He pulled members of the congregation up to the front, furnishing them with donkey ears and shepherds' crooks. He charmed the women in the church by turning some into angels, complete with halos and wings. Even a frail ninety-year-old lady was pulled into the fun, garlanded with tinsel and told she was gorgeous. Douglas called a mother from the back, where she was jiggling a baby and trying to be unobtrusive. He pulled a blue sheet around her, turning her into a shy Madonna, and the story came alive. The laughter and strong sense of family were intoxicating. Hannah's memories of the posh London cocktail parties, designer trees, and elaborate gifts fell away. She felt like she was experiencing Christmas for the first time.

Neil and Sarah caught up with her outside afterwards. Neil tucked her into his side with one arm and kept hold of her while they chatted about the service. Alistair exited the church with Suzanne on one side and a pretty woman, who looked so like Sarah, Hannah thought she must be another sister, on the other. They came over, and Sarah introduced Hannah to Gen, who had arrived the day before. She was small and immaculately dressed in a pastel shift dress with flats to match, her hair falling in glossy waves to her shoulders. You couldn't get two more different sisters. Suzanne, her beautiful face clear of make-up and red hair pulled into her habitual looped ponytail, had put on a faded-blue cotton sundress for the occasion. Hannah wondered how much Sarah had had to do with that. Yet, with no effort or self-awareness, Suzanne still managed to look like a model off a summer shoot.

Alistair kept to the background of the family chatter, his hands shoved deep into his pockets, listening and smiling at the bubbling interactions of Gen and his mother, but looking at the ground as he did so. He glanced up as his mother spoke. 'Hannah, we always hold a picnic braai down at the river on Boxing Day,' said Sarah. 'We would love you and Joseph to come.'

'That sounds wonderful,' said Hannah, thinking of the alternative of sitting at home with Joseph and her laptop.

'Good. Come at twelve o'clock.'

'Can I bring something?'

'Heavens, no,' said Gen rolling her eyes. 'The ladies of the district will bring every possible version of three-bean salad.'

Suzanne laughed. 'And the men bring enough meat to put the whole district into cardiac arrest.'

Sarah patted Hannah's arm. 'Ignore them. It's a fun day, and it would be good to have you there.'

Neil, his arm still around Hannah's shoulders, gave her a squeeze. 'You're part of Leliehoek now, whether you like three-bean salad or not.'

She smiled up at him. 'Good thing I do, then.'

The rest of Christmas Day continued in a similar vein. Lunch with Kathryn's family was noisy, chaotic, and morphed from the afternoon into the early evening. Everyone was in and out of the enormous old-fashioned pool behind Kathryn's house. Wet footprints sizzled on hot paving, and damp swimming costumes left dark patches on the ancient canvas folding chairs. They sipped pretty coloured cordials with ice and fresh mint leaves crushed into the glasses, holding their hands over the tops to keep the bees out. The day smelt of zinc sun cream and honey-glazed gammon. By the time Joseph and Hannah drove home, they felt like they would never need to eat again.

When they pulled up outside Hannah's gate, Joseph hauled himself out of the car and said, 'There's certainly something to be said for spending Christmas with Christians.'

Hannah pulled her bag onto her shoulder. 'It's not much fun being an atheist, is it?'

Joseph laughed, walking up the path to the house. 'Tell that to Mum and Dad.'

'Oh, Joseph.' Hannah's voice shifted to imitate the clipped tone of her mother. 'Can't you see that the meta-discourse of religion is tied to the insecurity of self?' Joseph snorted and shook his head.

'Maybe we should phone them, today of all days,' said Hannah, feeling a nudge of guilt at mocking them.

'Go right ahead. I would rather the day not end with Mum's hounding me about getting back to work and some professor of anthropology she wants to set me up with.'

'Come on, Josey, sounds perfect for you.'

'Been there,' he said callously. 'What did you say the other day? Glamourous, sophisticated, ambitious, but this time, amazingly, unattached. She is perfect for me. But my tastes seem to have changed.'

Hannah thumped him on the arm. 'Recently changed? Like, this week changed? Remember our deal, Joseph Harrison, especially as we'll see Suzanne tomorrow.'

He grinned at her as he rubbed his arm and wandered off to shower.

When they arrived at Goshen the next day, they followed a line of cars making their way to park in a field next to the river. Trestle tables, covered in white cloths, had been set out in the shade of willow and poplar trees that grew along the banks. Already, bowls of salad and loaves of homemade bread were accumulating on the tables. People were sinking bottles of wine and cans of beer into zinc tubs filled with ice. The fires sparked and crackled in rustic half drums. Groups of men gathered around the braais, cold beers grasped in large calloused hands. Joseph made his way over and Neil introduced him around. Hannah, watching her brother relax in the company of these men, shook her head. He looked like he had been born in the district, already laughing at the jokes and throwing in his own stories.

She saw Kathryn and Douglas arrive. One of the twins was riding on Douglas's shoulders, the other holding Kathryn's hand. They looked like a family. Hannah wondered how long it would take Kathryn to relent. She moved over to them as Kathryn began to unpack a basket onto a dessert table. 'How come you were allowed to bring something? Sarah wouldn't let me.'

'She said no to me too,' said Kathryn with a grin. Out of the basket came two pecan nut pies and a tray of mince pies, the pastry lids decorated with delicate pastry snowflakes and dusted with sugar. Hannah reached for one and had her hand sharply smacked. Kathryn threw a light gauze net over the desserts and turned to Douglas. 'How about you bring Hannah and me a drink?' He bowed low in mock subservience, and left laughing as Kathryn lightly kicked him on the backside.

They found themselves two striped deck chairs in the shade and collapsed into them. Douglas returned shortly and delivered chilled bottles of cider before ambling over to the braais to join the men. Before long, Suzanne and Gen had joined the women, stretching out on picnic rugs laid on the grass. Gen's fiancé, Glen, had arrived that morning from Johannesburg. He settled himself on the rug with the girls and fished out his phone, madly tapping away at it while the conversation drifted around him. He was a good-looking man with designer stubble and gym-toned arms reaching out of a tight white t-shirt. Skinny orange trousers were rolled up at the ankles, revealing white sneakers without socks. Hannah couldn't help wondering how this city man would fit in with the Barlows. She couldn't imagine Neil or Alistair shunning him, but did they have anything in common?

Resting her head back into the canvas, she listened to the 'poor father' call of the ring-necked doves. At the braais, Alistair was heaving metal grids onto the drums and giving them a good scour with a wire brush. He stood back and brushed his hair out of his eyes, leaving a black smear on his skin. She smiled and he glanced over at her, as if aware of her gaze, his mouth curving tentatively in response. He lifted a hand in a small wave and she felt her stomach turn over, but with what emotion she wasn't sure. She needed to apologise to him. Kathryn was right. It had taken a great deal of courage for him to reach out again after all he'd been through. Maybe a bit of light romance was what they both needed to get back on their feet. Maybe then she could return to Cape Town with the confidence to start her own life there.

A movement caught her eye and she turned her head to see a large BMW park at the edge of the picnic. Karl de Jager stepped out of the driver's door and moved around to open the door for his wife. Hannah sucked in her breath when she saw Esme, in high-heeled sandals, pick her way over to the tables and deposit a small foil-covered plate on the table. Her white shorts rode high on her thighs, revealing shapely but overly tanned legs. A tight red vest exposed a bony chest and brown, stringy arms. Hannah felt sorry for her, a woman trying so hard to hold on to her past, yet so brittle, as if she could fracture at any moment.

She watched Esme perch on the edge of a chair and try to follow the older women's conversation. Karl hovered over her for a while, and then moved over to the braais, where he was handed a beer and a pair of braai tongs. He was soon fully immersed in the group.

'Poor woman …' Kathryn was also watching Esme fluff her peroxided fringe with her fingers and then pull a lipstick from her bag, turning her lips a stark red.

'How can Sarah and Neil still include her in days like this after what she did to Alistair?' said Hannah.

Kathryn sighed. 'Karl is from one of the longest-standing farming families still on their farm. They've been on Silwerfontein for over a hundred years or something like that. The community love him.'

Hannah looked again at Esme. 'She doesn't fit in, does she?'

'From what I hear, she never has really. Karl was completely infatuated with her. Imagine what she must have looked like forty years ago?'

Gen followed their gaze across the lawn. 'As a little girl, I remember thinking she was just like my Barbies, long blonde hair, thin, tanned. Always in heels. I thought she was amazing. No doubt the men in the district shared my opinion then too.'

Suzanne, lying on her back in the shade, raised herself to lean on her elbows. 'Amazing to look at, maybe, but I think most men are practical at heart. Farmers need wives to be partners, almost extensions of their own bodies. A wife who is not interested in or capable of driving a truck, taking a new lamb into their house, getting up before dawn, or managing farm books is not ideal.'

'Not that farm wives have to be frumps,' said Gen sharply, tucking a blow-dried wing of hair behind one ear.

'Your mum is a good example of ideal, isn't she?' said Hannah, smiling at the two sisters.

'Yes,' said Suzanne, looking thoughtfully at Hannah. 'We just hope that Alistair finds a good wife and has some children, because Mum's qualities were split between, rather than passed on to, us girls. Neither of us would manage this farm like she does.'

At that moment, Sarah, casually but impeccably dressed in beige linen trousers and a fitted white T-shirt, clapped her hands and called everyone to lunch. The tables by now were groaning with food. Hannah picked up a paper plate which had been set into a basket holder. She chose a lamb chop, trying not to think of the lambs she had seen in the fields alongside the house, and a small piece of spicy boerewors. The selection of salads was overwhelming, and she was grateful she hadn't brought anything. Nothing she knew how to make would have looked at home on this table.

She took her plate back to her deck chair. Alistair came up behind her. 'Kathryn, Hannah? May I get you something to drink?'

'Another cider please, hon,' said Kathryn grinning up at him. He turned enquiring eyes to Hannah.

'Um, some kind of juice?'

Alistair smiled at her. 'I'll be right back.'

Returning a few minutes later, he handed her a tall glass of lemon juice, the ice cubes chinking as he passed it down to her. 'It's my mum's famous lemon syrup.'

Hannah took a sip. Cool, tart, and sweet – perfect for the day. But then Sarah never seemed to get things wrong.

He came back with a plate of food for himself and settled next to

Douglas on the edge of a blanket. Joseph plonked himself down beside Suzanne, and proceeded to regale them all with antics from his travels, even managing to draw trendy Glen away from his phone as he followed Joseph's stories with amusement.

'So, while some are theorising about complicated burial practices, the rest of us are thinking, what sensible prehistoric person would squeeze themselves down a pitch-black, tiny tunnel, stretched into a superman pose. Not a chance! It makes much more sense that it's a case of Darwinian survival of the cleverest. The first idiot squeezed down the tunnel to see where it went and couldn't come out. The second idiot squeezed down the tunnel to see where the first idiot went, and couldn't get out either. And so on, a whole heap of their bones lying at the bottom for thousands of years, until some brilliant archaeologists discover them and decide it's evidence of high-functioning human-like behaviour.'

Douglas grinned. 'It is human-like, just not so much high-functioning.'

Hannah watched Suzanne, comfortable with the light-hearted conversation, throwing the odd dry remark which revealed her quiet wit. Her complete obliviousness to Joseph's attention intrigued Hannah. She didn't ignore him, but she showed none of the breathy awareness most women fell into around her brother. Joseph's eyes constantly flicked to her, though, trying to gauge her responses, and Hannah could see this was completely new to him. He was, in fact, mystified. She grinned to herself, thinking that, perhaps, for the first time, Joseph might actually have to work very hard for a woman. And, in the end, he might not win. It would be groundbreaking, perhaps even heartbreaking. But then Joseph swore he didn't have a heart. Interesting times ahead, she thought.

Soon, a cricket game started up on the grass. Joseph and Neil elected themselves captains and pulled people onto their sides. Even a few elderly men joined in the game, declaring that the youngsters would have to run between the wickets for them. People drew their chairs into the shade and turned to watch the fun. Hannah was coerced by Joseph to take up the bat, and she surprised even herself by still being able to smack the ball over the fielders' heads.

'Woohoo!' yelled Kathryn from the sidelines. 'You've been holding out on us, Hannah Harrison!'

'First team at her school, you know. The only girl in the squad!' shouted Joseph from the other end of the wicket. 'Watch out, Neil, she'll win this single-handedly!'

'Sounds like insider trading to me,' called Glen from the boundary. He had put on a fedora-style hat and looked keen, if rather out of place.

Hannah's run of luck ended with a brilliant ball from Neil, which thumped the improvised wickets behind her. She lifted her bat in salute to much applause from the spectators, and Neil came jogging over to her, slinging his arm around her shoulders. 'What a smashing girl you are!' Hannah grinned up at him, loving the open admiration on his face and thinking she'd never received this from either of her own parents.

Back in the shade, she poured herself more lemon juice and held the glass to her flushed face, sinking into a chair beside Sarah. 'My goodness, that's the way to Neil's heart,' said Sarah, smiling at her. 'For some men, it's good cooking, but Neil is a cricket fanatic. You will have him as a fan forever.'

'It's mutual,' said Hannah, watching him resume bowling to Joseph. Alistair had taken up as wicket keeper, and he crouched behind Joseph, sniping remarks.

Joseph eventually turned to him, laughing. 'You can be rude to me after the game, but I need to concentrate right now.'

'He's our secret psychological weapon,' called Neil.

'You don't need any more weapons, Neil. Your bowling is quite enough!' said Joseph.

Dessert was served. Hannah helped herself to an ice-cream cone and wandered down to the river. The willows bent low to the water and the chatter from the picnic faded as she skidded down a small bank and found herself a large flat rock to sit on. Finishing her cone, she dipped her bare feet into the water, gasping at the temperature, but still lowered her feet to the stones at the bottom so that the clear water reached her calves. Dragonflies buzzed on the surface of the pool and the sudden sharp kik-kik-kik of a kingfisher broke the stillness, giving her a start. A footstep behind her had her turning her head quickly, and she saw Alistair hop down a set of rough stone steps she had missed earlier.

'May I join you?' He kept his distance until she nodded, and then settled next to her, his boots drawn up to the edge of the rock, long arms looped around his legs.

'The water's lovely,' she said, looking across at him. He smiled and began unlacing his boots, stuffing his socks into the boots and throwing each one behind him up the bank. He winced as he immersed one foot at a time into the water. 'Lovely when you get used to it, I mean,' she said grinning.

'I'm relieved you're feeling better. I was worried about you the other day.'

'I know, I'm sorry. I behaved badly.'

'I understand now how much Rachel means to you.'

Hannah reached across and took his hand. She laced her fingers through his and raised their linked hands to her mouth. As her lips grazed his knuckles, she heard his breath hitch, his grip on her fingers tightening. She looked up to meet his gaze, his eyes deep and dark. She pulled her feet from the water and knelt on the rock alongside him, bringing her mouth within inches of his, until she could feel his breath, quicker now, on her lips. As his eyes searched hers, she saw the fear there and the questions. An intensity and a vulnerability that made her heart contract and stalled her intention. The pause was enough for him to pull away and let go her hand.

'Hannah. Can we talk about this? I'm sorry. I don't know ... I haven't ... I'm not ...'

She swallowed a wash of guilt. What was she doing playing with this poor man? Alistair couldn't do light romance if he tried. Maybe he could have once, but certainly not now. She looked across the quiet pool. 'It's okay. I understand if you don't want to.'

He laughed, a low bitter sound as he pulled his feet onto the rock. 'Don't want to? Are you mad? I couldn't want anything more. But it's not that simple any more. There's this fear, gut-wrenching. I can't help it. It paralyses me, and I'm so scared it will never go away.' He pushed his hand into his hair. Hannah recognised the gesture for weariness. He went on, 'When you arrived, I found myself thinking, for the first time, about you rather than Marilie. You got into my head. It felt like I'd been set free from her ... but it's not over yet.'

Hannah dropped her chin to her knees. 'You mean, just now, when we were ... you were thinking of her?'

'No, Hannah! Dammit! I just can't get this out right.' He scrubbed his face with his hands and then looked directly at her. 'No. I mean, I second-guess myself all the time. I read a hesitation as unwillingness. A frown as disgust. Hannah, I've lost my nerve.'

She nodded. Neither spoke for a while, and she wondered how to sidle round the silence.

Alistair swallowed loudly and then said, with a rasp in his voice, 'Hannah, would you try kiss me again?'

Her throat tightened at his courage. Scared to meet his eyes this time, she twisted her body to sit cross-legged in front of him. She took both his hands in hers, felt his fingers clench and then relax as she studied them. Using the resistance of his arms to pull herself onto her knees before him, her gaze slid to his neck, sunburnt above his collar, to his jaw, then his mouth. She felt her pulse begin to quicken and lightly touched her lips to that scarred mouth, feeling the ridges of smooth skin pulled crooked. Her lips softened and opened, and he gasped, his hands releasing hers to anchor her hips in front of him. His tongue tangled with hers and grew more demanding. She drew a sharp breath when his mouth moved to her jaw, to her ear, and the words were spoken against her skin: 'I've wanted you like this since the moment I saw you.' His hands pushed up under her shirt, rough against the skin of her back.

She threaded her fingers into his hair, pulling his head close as he moved his mouth to her neck, the pressure of his teeth making her gasp. 'Alistair ...' Her whisper snapped the tension, and he leant the top of his head against her collarbone, breathing unevenly. She drew another breath, still stroking her fingers through his hair. 'I don't think this a good idea. I mean, right now. The whole district is sitting fifty metres away.'

'Sorry,' said Alistair. Then: 'I'm not really sorry,' and she smiled into his hair.

Hannah kissed him softly on the forehead and sat back on her knees. She watched him get to his feet, move up the slope to retrieve his shoes, sitting back down next to her to lace his boots. When he was standing, he reached out a hand to pull her to her feet and into his arms once more. His mouth this time was soft. A kiss on her smiling lips, a kiss on her cheek, and a gentle nip on her ear which made her draw a sharp breath. He stepped away from her and turned to haul her the short distance up the riverbank. When they were back on the grass, he kept hold of her hand, and Hannah felt her heart contract again.

CHAPTER TWENTY

They walked hand in hand towards the others. Hannah saw Esme register their approach with shock, her hand reaching up to grasp her throat, her eyes stricken. Alistair dropped Hannah's hand as if scalded, as Esme stumbled from her chair, through the startled people still lounging on the grass, towards her car. Small, agonised yelps came from her mouth, an animal in distress. She scrambled into the front seat of the car and slammed the door closed. Sarah hurried over to the car, tried to open the door, then spoke through the window, but Esme sat immobilised. Her face like stone staring blankly forwards. Alistair quickly moved off to find Karl, leaving Hannah uncertain and guilty. Her hands hung at her sides, feeling horribly empty.

Karl touched Sarah on the shoulder and spoke quietly to her. She squeezed his arm, looking so full of pity that Hannah felt a lump in her throat. He walked around the car, pulling his keys from his pocket, his face weary and suddenly drawn. As they reversed and drove off, Esme still stared ahead, frozen.

The mood of the day had splintered, and people began taking their leave of Sarah and Neil. Hannah moved to the tables to help Suzanne and Kathryn as they covered dishes with plastic wrap, loading crates with glasses. Hannah shook out a black rubbish bag and began to collect paper plates and crumpled serviettes. She always found the aftermath of a party depressing, but this was horrible. She felt responsible for its terrible end.

As if reading her mind, Kathryn pulled her into a side hug, saying, 'It's not your fault.' Hannah threw her a sarcastic scowl. 'Okay, you could have timed your reappearance a bit better.' Kathryn's mouth spread in a grin. 'And maybe tried to hide that great big hickey starting on your neck.'

Hannah's hand flew to her neck. She had completely forgotten Alistair's teeth on her skin. She groaned, 'How could this have happened? I'm such a terrible person.'

Suzanne came up alongside them, taking the black bag from Hannah. 'Any girl who gets my brother playing cricket and kissing her senseless gets my vote as the best thing that's happened to him in a long time.'

'I should go,' said Hannah, looking for her bag under the deck chair.

'Please don't,' said Alistair's voice from behind her. 'Don't let Esme ruin more than she has already.' He watched as Hannah pulled a light cardigan from her bag, tying it into a knot around her neck. 'Sorry about that,' he said. 'I wasn't thinking.' He smiled. 'I seem to be doing that a lot around you.'

'Too late to cover it up now. Everybody's seen it, Hannah,' said Douglas, coming over to Kathryn with one sleeping twin against his shoulder and giving Hannah a wink. Hannah groaned and hid her face in her hands.

They watched Douglas and Kathryn drive away. By the time the field had been cleared, the light was fading. Hannah walked up to the house with Gen, the zinc tubs stacked together between them and each woman gripping a handle.

Gen was furious. 'What was Mum thinking, inviting Karl and Esme! Alistair will never come out of mourning if he constantly has to be under Esme's judgement. Mum and Dad are too forgiving.'

'I didn't think there was such a thing for Christians,' said Hannah quietly.

'What?' Gen looked at her sharply.

'Being too forgiving, I mean. Aren't Christians supposed to forgive seventy times seven or something like that?'

'You're talking to the wrong daughter.'

Hannah glanced curiously at her.

'Let's just say I've strayed from the fold. When I told Mum that Glen and I had moved in together, I thought she was going to fall down dead from the shock.'

'What did she say?' Hannah couldn't imagine Sarah shaken.

'She managed to recover, and now she tries very hard with Glen, but I know that my two worlds don't really mix. I've chosen his world, and will just have to make sorties across the border every now and then,' she said, her mouth curving in a small smile.

'It might be different when you have kids. I can't imagine your parents being content with occasional sorties where their grandchildren are concerned.'

Gen was quiet for a few moments. 'We've decided not to have children.' Her resolute face made Hannah wonder how much of that decision was really Gen. 'Please don't say anything though, Hannah. Mum doesn't know yet.'

Hannah nodded, and they were quiet as they walked the last few yards to the main house.

Sarah was presiding over Alistair's kitchen, turning leftovers into another meal.

'Mum, we aren't going to eat again, are we?' said Gen.

'You'll see, as soon as I put this out, people will be hungry again.'

She set Hannah to work laying the large kitchen table. By the time Alistair and Neil had come in from the sheds, the table was groaning yet again.

'Don't wait for Glen,' said Gen, 'he's busy with something.' Hannah caught a glance between Neil and Sarah, Sarah shaking her head at him to stop him saying something.

Alistair chose the seat next to Hannah and handed her a plate. She couldn't believe she was helping herself to more food after the lunch they'd had, but chose cold slices of steak and salad, adding a piece of crusty bread. Alistair's thigh brushed hers under the table, and his hand came to rest on her leg just under the hem of her skirt, his calloused palm bringing a hum of response along her skin. He ate with a fork in his right hand, not looking at her and contributing to conversation as if nothing else were going on, but the warmth of his fingers on her thigh, just lightly brushing her skin, distracted her completely.

The farmhouse phone rang and Gen left the table to answer it. She had her back to the room and shortly replaced the receiver, returning to her seat to continue eating.

'Who was it, Gen?' asked her mother.

'Nobody. They just hung up.'

Alistair stiffened beside Hannah, withdrawing his hand and putting his fork down on his plate. The phone rang again. Hannah watched, confused, as Neil pushed his chair back and picked up the handset, depressed the switch hook with his forefinger, and put the receiver on the counter, leaving it off the hook. He turned back to his chair. 'Let's not allow phone calls to disturb our supper,' he said. 'Sweetheart, remember our old rule that nobody answers the phone during meals?'

'I remember the rule that nobody should phone after eight o'clock,' said Gen putting her fork down. 'Al, do you remember Pietie Rossouw who was so desperately in love with Suzanne? He tried to phone her once after eight and got Dad on the line.'

'Poor guy was too frightened to talk to her ever again, even at school,' said Alistair.

'What did you say to him, Dad?' said Suzanne mildly.

'I just told him that if he wanted to consort with my daughter in the middle of the night, he'd have to get through me and my shotgun.'

'Consort! He was only twelve, Dad,' said Gen, laughing.

'It worked, didn't it? He's in his thirties now, married with three kids, and he still speaks to me with his cap in his hand and calls me "Mr Barlow, Sir". I like that,' said Neil, grinning at his daughters.

Sarah stood to collect plates and Joseph jumped up to help, leaning across to Neil. 'May I take your plate, Mr Barlow, Sir?' causing everyone around the table to collapse laughing.

Neil slapped Joseph on the back. 'You're a fast learner, boy. Which daughter would you like to have?'

'Hey!' said Gen. 'I'm not on the market!'

'More's the pity,' whispered Neil to Joseph and got his foot stamped on by Sarah.

Coffee and left-over pecan pie followed, and it was late when Alistair pulled Hannah away from drying dishes, into the garden. He led her out of the light pouring from the windows, into the shadow of an oak which grew on the corner of the house. He slipped his arms around her waist, pulling her onto her tiptoes. Angling his face down to hers, they touched foreheads. 'I like seeing you in my kitchen with my family. I find myself wanting you there more and more.'

'In your kitchen? Maybe barefoot? Pregnant?' she said, a tease in her voice.

'It came out wrong,' he said, laughing against her cheek, and then his voice softened as his breath tickled her ear, making her shiver. 'But maybe that's exactly what I want.'

Her stomach clenched into a knot. 'Alistair, I can't think beyond a few weeks or months. Living in Leliehoek is a dream for me – and I know that I'm going to have to wake up at some point. What will you do when this ends?'

He put her at an arm's length. 'What do you mean? I thought after today … I thought you wanted to be with me?'

Hannah sighed. 'I did … I do. But I'm not thinking about getting married! We kissed, Alistair. That's all. Besides, I can't be a farmer's wife. I couldn't do what your mother does. I don't know the first thing about farms. I can barely put a salad together, let alone put on a feast for the whole district. Suzanne said today that a farmer needs a partner for a wife – how could I ever be that to you? Like Marilie was.'

He dropped his hands from her. 'Marilie was never a partner, not how you think, anyway. She and I lived alongside each other, like railway tracks. Perfectly parallel. Her horses and her showjumping were her total focus. To be honest, the dream of a guest house and tours? It was my dream, and she got excited about the horse trail part of it.' He leant against the trunk of the oak, the silence stretching for a long moment. Then he said, 'When you … when you say you couldn't be a farmer's wife? Do you mean you don't think you're capable?' He paused, before saying in a rush, 'Or that you actually don't want to be one?'

'Why does it matter? Alistair, we've only kissed once! Why are we talking about getting married?'

'You really are asking that? You have that little insight?'

'Maybe I'm not as clever as you. It doesn't give you the right to insult me!'

'Hannah! What are you talking about? Not as clever as me? You're one of the most intelligent, bat-shit crazy people I've ever met. How can you not know how big your brain is? How talented you are? You could run rings around me in any field. If I could just have a few minutes with the people who beat the belief out of you ...'

He moved away from her out of the shadow of the oak. In the light spilling from inside, she could see his hands clasped around his head, which was thrown back to look upwards at the night sky. 'You drive me nuts. You know that?' He was quiet for a moment before he turned to face her, 'I'm not saying I want to marry you, okay? If our relationship doesn't work out, I'll deal with it. But I'm not interested in a fling with you. Do you understand that? Otherwise we're wasting our time. And my heart is on the line here, Hannah. It's in a pretty sorry smashed-up state as it is. I don't think I could handle getting more involved with you than I already am, knowing it won't go anywhere.'

Joseph's voice cut into the darkness: 'Hannah? You out there? Ready to go?'

Hannah stepped forwards to take Alistair's hands in hers. 'Give me a little time to think,' she said. His back was still to the light, and she couldn't see his expression, but felt his disappointment.

As she moved towards the house, he tugged at her hand. 'Hannah? Thanks for being honest. It's important.'

Kobie leant his head against the mud-plastered wall. The ancient stool had stood outside his doorway for as long as he could remember. It was worn smooth with the weight and slide of many, many bodies doing what he did now. Sitting in the cool of an evening, a cigarette pinched between his fingers. The stars were bright tonight against a deep navy-blue sky, the moon just a silver sliver hanging low above the horizon so the farm was dark below it. His gaze was drawn to the hill behind the house and suddenly he sat up, his body rigid. A fire lit on the edge of the plateau, and then another and another, until the top of the hill glowed with the scattered, small blazes. Small smudges of orange against the black night. The smell of distant smoke reached his flared nostrils. Kobie's heart jolted. Fire on the farm could be a disaster, even in the middle of summer. There was a drill for this. Alistair needed to know. The water tankers had to be hitched up, the workers roused, the neighbours called. Before he could call to his daughter, just as suddenly as he had seen them, the fires disappeared. With them vanished a sound Kobie only registered when it was gone. The sound of people. That low indistinct hum of humanity.

He pressed his left hand into his eyes, pinching the bridge of his nose, but when he looked again, the hill was a black absence against the brighter sky. The night, once more cool and quiet. The skin of his arms and neck rose in a shiver, but he leant back against the wall and brought the stub of his cigarette to his lips, drawing deeply, his eyes not leaving the hillside.

January 1902, Goshen Camp, Orange River Colony

Dearest Wolf,

We heard a good story. A trader came into camp and brought the news that Christmas day was a triumph for General De Wet at Groenkop. He overran a Khaki camp and captured over two hundred men! Were you there? So close as the crow flies, just a wagon ride away. Did you feast from the captured wagons and drink to your success? Did you think of us at all?

Life in the camp carries on, such as it is. People continue to arrive. Some have been forced by their circumstances simply to walk in. Their homes have been demolished, their crops and livestock looted or destroyed. Their last hope of survival is to work in the camp for food. I look at them with such judgement. I know what the Lord says about judging others, but, Wolf, what I wouldn't give to walk out of here! I swear I would scrape a life for myself in a cave in the mountains if I could. I've had enough of the death and the work and the months of being hungry. The feeling that I'm walking circles in a desert, getting nowhere and achieving nothing. Oh, to have space. To wash myself clean with no one watching. I would indeed turn my eyes to the hills. Relish the solitude, the distance from other people's grief. It has become too much for me.

The cemetery is full. There is no more space on the flat ground, and people have begun to disinter the old graves, burying the first body deeper so that there's room above it. It is done quietly; the British are terrified of disease and would no doubt halt the practice immediately. But what is to be done? There is no more room.

Yours,
Rachel

CHAPTER TWENTY-ONE

The students began arriving in the week after Christmas, most in small cars loaded with sleeping bags and pillows. Sarah soon realised that her anxiety about their accommodation was in vain. That they had a roof over their heads was a luxury for them. They were full of praise for her arrangements. Alistair gave the group the use of a spare farm pickup and two quad bikes so they could get from the homestead to the site. It wasn't long before a routine emerged. Joseph held a meeting every morning, and ran through the work that needed to be done, getting feedback from the day before and setting the students to new tasks.

They spent the morning on site, coming back down for lunch. Alistair had to get used to seeing bodies on mattresses, fast asleep in the shade of the farmyard oaks. They were back on site for the afternoon, working until the light dimmed. The strum of a guitar and floating laughter carried across to the main house in the evenings. The farm felt alive, like it hadn't been in years. And yet he was in turmoil. The dig would come to an end. Joseph would wrap up his investigation and go back to Cambridge. What would be left to keep Hannah in Leliehoek? Would she leave? He had said he would cope if their relationship did not work out, but he felt that he was already in too deep. The thought of going back to empty days spent at his desk, with only his dogs for company, was too awful to contemplate.

Alistair found himself venturing out if he saw Joseph's car to sit and drink a beer with him, talking or simply sitting, listening to the joking, teasing banter that emanated from the shed.

It was clear that with a group of students mixed together over a couple of weeks came politics. Alistair saw the interest that more than one girl had in Joseph. Despite the opportunities, Joseph showed nothing but professional interest in the students. He was friendly, but kept himself apart, preferring to hang out with Alistair in the evenings, perhaps in the hope that Suzanne might join them.

'Are you still driving across to Hannah's to sleep?' said Alistair on one such evening.

'Ja,' Joseph said, leaning his head back into Alistair's couch. 'Let's just say it would complicate things if I started sleeping in the shed. I don't feel like fending off – and he used his fingers to punctuate – '"sleep walkers" in the middle of the night.'

Alistair grinned. 'So you've noticed the attention?'

'You'd have to be dead not to notice! Those girls have the subtlety of a jack hammer.'

'I've got two spare rooms here if you want one,' said Alistair, leaning forwards to mute the sound of the TV as the rugby game came to half-time and an advert segment began.

Joseph turned his head to Alistair. 'Hey, thanks. I'll take you up on that. I still want to be at Hannah's every now and then, but it'll make getting to the site so much easier.'

'No problem. Tina, my housekeeper, will be delighted to fuss over someone.'

'Being fussed over sounds awesome. I certainly don't get that at Hannah's.'

The camp investigation moved slowly forwards, helped by the student labour force. Alistair had managed to source aerial photographs going back a few decades, and Joseph brought Hannah to the farm one afternoon to talk through their progress.

Joseph spread the photographs over the kitchen table. 'You can see in these, even over thirty years, that the basic look hasn't changed as much as one might expect, even after fires have been through. Can you see these areas?' He pointed to patches on the photographs. 'These areas are clearer and the vegetation is sparser, growing lower than say here,' he said, gesturing to other places, 'which looks like compacted ground.'

'Couldn't it be naturally shallow, maybe stone just below the surface?' said Alistair.

Joseph shook his head. 'And be this regularly spaced? I doubt it.'

'What would have compacted it?' said Hannah, holding her hair to one side as she pored over the photographs.

'If you had to set up a tent or a shelter on open stony ground, what would you do first?'

'Clear the stones,' said Alistair.

'And that's what these people would have done. Nobody's going to sleep for two years with stones under their bedding. Also, just the act of living in a space, the foot traffic, the weight of bodies and possessions, would compact the ground over time. Then, when the camp is dissolved, the tents gone, and the veld regrows, the vegetation growing on those compacted spots will be more stunted than in other places.'

'It's fascinating, Josey.' Hannah looked up at him with a smile.

He grinned back at her. 'There's something else you can see on these pictures. Look here.' His finger marked a number of spots. Hannah and Alistair both stared at the picture, then looked at him blankly. 'Make that, something only I can see,' Joseph said with a wink. 'I think this area may have been a cemetery. I can count at least twelve obvious places which look like low, long cairns of rock. But these are too even in size simply to be random piles of stones. I reckon that if we examine this place' – he circled a wide area on the photo – 'we're going to find graves.'

'Twelve graves sound way too few to be a camp cemetery, especially how Rachel describes it,' said Hannah.

'I can identify at least twelve cairns on the photos,' said Joseph, standing up and stretching his arms behind him. 'We might find more on the ground, and then some graves might not be marked with stones. We just don't know at the moment, but we have twelve graves as a start. That's significant, Hannah.'

'What are you busy with at the moment?' said Alistair.

'We're using GIS and mapping the site. It's terribly tedious, but we have to do it. With so many workers, it shouldn't take too long, but we're systematically combing the surface of the site and marking anything we find on our GIS grid without removing the item.'

'Have you found anything yet?' said Hannah. 'Apart from our ration tin, I wouldn't think much would be left on the surface after a hundred or so years.'

'More than you would think, especially on a site so remote. The surface has hardly been touched, even by animals. Your ghosts have been doing a really good job keeping everything away.'

'They're not my ghosts,' muttered Hannah, earning a fleeting smile from Alistair.

'So far,' continued Joseph, picking up a notebook from the counter behind him, 'we've found some shards of glass, part of a hoe, a tiny earring, a piece of what looks like crate strapping, and some odd bits of leather – one piece might be some plaited rope. Oh, and the best so far, a ration tin with a handle ingeniously hammered on to it.' He looked up proudly.

'It doesn't sound like much, Josey,' said Hannah, and Alistair could see his face fall somewhat. He wondered if perhaps Joseph's confidence had some weak points after all. Or was it that, in getting to know him, Joseph was becoming easier to read? That the easy-going, unshakeable surface had always been just that, a thin veneer for strangers?

'It doesn't seem like much to you maybe,' said Joseph, 'but to an archaeologist, that's really good.'

'Why is the ration tin important?' said Alistair.

'It tells us that they didn't have much crockery, if they had to improvise cups from ration tins. When we have all the official permits lined up, we'll be able to examine the artefacts more closely, research each one to find out what it is and where it came from. Just think, determining whether a shard of glass comes from a medicine bottle or a whisky bottle tells us something significant about the camp, doesn't it? And this is just the surface scatter!' he said.

'How is the official side of things coming along?' said Alistair. 'Do you need any more help with it?'

'No, your part is done. I've finished most of the application. I just need to include the artefacts from the surface survey. We should finish that this week. I thought I would go in person to SAHRA. Nothing speeds up an application like someone hanging around, waiting for it. I'm good at sitting politely in people's offices until they do the paperwork to get rid of me.'

'I can just see you doing that,' said Hannah, shaking her head.

'Any progress on your side?' said Joseph.

'No, not since Bloemfontein. I'd like to go through to Winburg at some point to see the family's graves, but that's more of a personal pilgrimage than pertinent to the camp. I've got a strong feeling there's more in Gisela's cottage.' Joseph looked confused and Hannah went on, 'You know, Karl's mother had a little house on Silwerfontein? I want to go through that house again, look at the album, the Bible, everything. I think I missed something there. Anyway, it's pointless even talking about it, because there's no way any of us will get access there now. Not after the picnic.'

'Please don't even try, Hannah,' said Alistair, his stomach clenching at the thought of Hannah meeting Esme again.

'What about the journal, Hannah? Are you finished?' said Joseph, still focused on the camp.

'Almost. I have one last section to do, then I can make copies and give you each one. Maybe when you read it you'll see why I've grown so attached to Rachel.' Alistair reached over to touch her arm, then dropped his hand. Watching her in his kitchen, looking so relaxed, he felt his heart contract, like new scar tissue pulling. He was still waiting for her to make a decision. Every day that passed without her coming to see him hurt. As much as he wanted to give in, just sink into something easy just to be with her, his heart couldn't risk it.

'And you, Alistair, anything new?' said Joseph.

'I told you about the blockhouse lines. From what I've managed to find out, there was a hang of a lot of British and Boer movement after Surrender Hill. The British camped down the Fouriesburg road, then they camped right near us here, probably mopping up problems. Then they moved out of the area and set up command centres in Bethlehem and Ficksburg. At that point, the mobile remnants of the commandos came out of the woodwork and moved through here a lot. The blockhouse lines stopped large-scale movement and sabotage of the bridges and railway lines. But they couldn't stop small units of Boers cutting their barbed wire or simply pulling their fence posts out the ground and riding underneath them.'

'In a nutshell?' said Joseph.

'Sorry, I get carried away with this stuff.' Alistair's smile was rueful. 'In a nutshell, I can find no reference to a camp here, but I can't find a reason why there shouldn't have been one. There were enough civilians in the area to warrant a refugee camp, and enough soldiers in the area to warrant the camp's growing food for them.'

'That'll do,' said Joseph, gathering the photographs into a pile and slipping them into a folder.

'Something which has been bothering me,' said Hannah. 'Why send Rachel's family all the way to Winburg and send her to Goshen? Surely other families in the area would have been sent to Goshen too, and people would have heard about it?'

'From the stories I've heard,' said Alistair, 'camp allocations were pretty random. One Leliehoek family was split and some sent all the way to Heilbron. That's miles from here. Another thing I've noticed is that the only way details like that are still known today is because some-one kept a journal. Most modern families wouldn't know which camp their great-great-great-granny was in, or perhaps even care.'

'So,' continued Hannah, 'some families might well have been sent to Goshen but not kept a written record to pass on.'

'Or not survived,' added Alistair. They were quiet for a few seconds.

'On that cheery note,' said Joseph, 'let's adjourn. Hannah, I'll take you back to town?'

'Actually, I'm having dinner in town with Kathryn and Suzanne, so I'll catch a lift when Suzanne's ready, thanks, Jose.'

'No problem. I'm going to take a ride up the hill and make sure my reprobate team pack up properly for the night. See you, Han.' She raised her hand in a goodbye as he left through the back door.

Hannah sat across from Alistair, wondering what to say. He held her gaze for a few moments.

'I'm not going to beg, you know,' he said.

'What do you mean?' she said, hoping confusion would cover her guilt.

'You know what I mean, Hannah. The ball is in your court this time.' He pushed out his chair and waited for her to do the same. 'I'll walk you over to Suzanne.'

She followed him through the garden towards the cottage, wishing she could make the awkwardness between them dissipate. It was another clear Free State summer day, the skies cobalt, and Sarah's garden awash with colour and alive with the hum of bees. Hannah wanted to grab Alistair's hand and pull him onto the lawn to lie there and look at the sky, but followed him silently instead. When they came to Sarah's back door, he opened it for her. 'I've got work to do in my office.' He left her there feeling frustrated and disappointed in herself.

Suzanne borrowed Sarah's Ford to drive them back into town, and they stopped at the bookshop for Hannah to change. Soon they were sitting on the deck of the bistro with Kathryn, enjoying glasses of crisp white wine as the sun disappeared over the mountains above Leliehoek.

White daisies and scented geraniums tumbled out of tubs along the edges of the deck, and every time a waitress brushed past, the sharp lemony scent carried over the table. Hurricane lamps were lit as the light faded, the citronella oil adding to the scent-filled air.

Kathryn leant forwards on the table. 'Hannah, you have to end the suspense. I can't bear it any more. What on earth is going on with Alistair? It all looked so promising at the picnic, and now? You're both buried in your houses.'

Hannah looked down at her glass, running her finger around the base. 'I don't know what to do. He says he's not interested in a fling. That marriage has to be a possibility, and nothing less will do. For Pete's sake, we've only kissed once. It's madness.' She looked up and saw the other two girls staring at her. 'Why are you looking at me like I'm the crazy one?'

'Because that is the daftest thing I've ever heard.' Kathryn shook her head as she saw Hannah nod in agreement. 'Not Alistair, you nutcase –

you! Don't you see that he doesn't want to mess with you? It's romantic and honourable and sweet, and I can't believe you're sitting here feeling sorry for yourself!'

Hannah, stung, drew herself up a little. 'I don't know how to deal with it. I've never begun a relationship thinking of marriage. I've kind of been telling myself I might never get married—'

Suzanne quietly interjected, 'Have you been hurt before?'

'No ... yes,' she paused. 'Todd was my only other significant relationship. We were together for nearly ten years, lived together for most of that. He bought me a ring and called me his fiancée, but he said it was because we needed to clarify our relationship for his colleagues.'

'Charming!' said Kathryn, causing Hannah to look at her in surprise.

She became thoughtful. 'It actually doesn't sound so nice, does it? I suppose I always just let him take control. I followed him wherever he went, dressed as he expected, socialised with the right people. I never took initiative. Until I found a woman in my bathtub.'

'Ouch,' said Suzanne, taking a sip from her glass.

'Alistair says the ball's in my court. The awful thing is that I feel like my feet are planted in cement, like I can't physically get myself across the court to reach the ball.' She sat back in her chair. 'And even if I wanted to marry him, I would be an absolutely useless farmer's wife. I've only lived in Cape Town and London. I have no experience of the country at all. It would be a disaster.'

'You seem to be managing country life perfectly fine,' said Kathryn. 'In fact, I would go further and say you're blossoming.'

'And,' added Suzanne, 'you only get experience by doing something. Yes, my mother is a model farmer's wife, but she has been one for forty years! More importantly, my parents love you. That carries more weight than a lifetime in the platteland. Actually, my mother would dance on the table if she knew we were having this conversation.'

'Which she absolutely can never know, Suzanne!'

Suzanne put her hands up in a gesture of surrender. 'Of course. It all stays right here.'

Their meals arrived and they tucked into slices of fillet with chips, and salad picked from the bistro garden.

'Speaking of your parents,' said Kathryn, 'I picked up some concern about Gen and Glen at the picnic.' She snorted, making the others look up from their meals as she lifted a napkin to her mouth. 'Sorry, Gen and Glen? Even their names! Like a nursery rhyme.'

'You know that his surname is Wren, right?' said Suzanne smiling. 'Yep, Gen and Glen Wren.'

'I liked him,' said Hannah. 'Not that I got to talk to him much, but he seemed like a nice guy.'

'He is a nice guy,' said Suzanne. 'I'm just not convinced he's the right guy for Gen. Already, they spend the bare minimum of time on the farm. I'm worried he'll draw her away completely.'

Hannah thought of her conversation with Gen about children. Suzanne was right to be concerned, but she kept quiet.

'What can you do? They're engaged and planning a huge society wedding in Joburg,' continued Suzanne.

'Not on the farm?' said Kathryn, shocked. 'How's your mother handling that?'

'Gen said it's too far for their friends to travel.' Suzanne rolled her eyes, but there was concern on her face. 'Mum doesn't know about it yet.'

'Although,' said Hannah, 'a big wedding on the farm would raise that awkward thing of the De Jagers. Imagine Esme pulling a stunt at Gen's wedding? Gen would never forgive your mum.'

Suzanne shook her head. 'Gen thinks in black and white. She finds Esme creepy and cannot understand how other people make allowances for her. Esme gives me the creeps too, but she's a very ill woman. You can't shut her out for that.'

Kathryn leant back in her chair, cradling her wine glass on her stomach. 'The thing is, though, she's also dangerous. We know she torments Alistair. My impression is that she's becoming more unstable, not less.'

Hannah's skin lifted in a shiver, and she pulled her cardigan off the back of her chair and around her shoulders. Glancing at her watch, she saw the hands shift to half-past eight. The next moment, the lights went out.

'Damn, I forgot there was load-shedding tonight,' said Kathryn, 'Eight-thirty to ten-thirty.' A few seconds later, the restaurant generator kicked in, and fairy lights flickered and came on again. 'What these power cuts do to my fridges in the shop, I hate to know. I have a recurring nightmare that one morning I'll come in and find my shop swimming in melted ice cream and mousse cake.'

'Speaking of nightmares, Hannah,' said Suzanne, 'Mum says you spoke to Kobie about the plateau. What did he tell you?'

'What's this?' said Kathryn.

'There's an old guy who's lived on Goshen his whole life, and his mother and grandmother before him,' said Hannah. 'Sarah suggested I ask him if he knew anything about the camp.'

'And did he?'

'Not as such, but he's experienced strange things up on the plateau. Seen women dressed in Boer clothes, smelt smoke or sewage, heard keening. Did you ever hear these stories, Suzanne?'

'No, Mum never told us. I suppose she didn't want to frighten us as kids, but I saw something once.'

'What?' both Hannah and Kathryn said in unison, sitting forwards in their chairs.

Suzanne smiled at their response. 'I was home on holiday from university, dealing with some stuff … Anyway, I rode up to the plateau on my own, just for some space. I don't know why I did – I've always found it unsettling there. I got to the gate, and my horse wouldn't ride through. He was a bit silly sometimes. I thought he was just acting up, so I got off and tethered him to the fence post. Kept going on foot. As I crested the slope, I saw, down at the other end of the plateau, two women digging a hole. One was standing in the hole, hip deep, and one was on the edge. I thought they must be workers doing something for my dad. But, for some reason, something unnerved me, and I turned before they saw me, went quickly back to my horse, who was trying to get away from the post. He nearly threw me off when I eventually managed to mount. We bolted home.'

'And?' said Hannah. 'Were they workers?'

'This is the weird part. When I got home, I realised they had been dressed in old-fashioned clothes. Their heads were covered and they wore dresses to their ankles. I know some women labourers still wear dresses, you know, over trousers? But this was different, long sleeves and cinched-in waists. And then I went with my dad the next day in his pickup. There was no hole. He didn't know what I was talking about.'

'So freaky!' said Kathryn, enthralled.

'What's your take on ghosts, Kathryn? You're into spiritual stuff,' said Hannah.

'I'm not sure.' Kathryn tipped her head to one side. 'I certainly believe in the spiritual realm. You can't be religious and not believe that there are other realities out there. But I'm no expert. I don't understand why only some people see them, or why some people might get stuck after they die and reappear.'

Hannah took a sip of wine. 'I've been raised in an atheist household – all this kind of stuff has always been termed nonsense. Then I come up here and meet rational people, like you' – Hannah gestured to Suzanne – 'who have stories like that. I don't understand.' She paused for a moment. 'And then a crazy part of me wants to ask you about the hole they were digging.'

Suzanne laughed. 'What about the hole?'

'How big was it?'

'Maybe a metre and a half? And narrow.'

'Could it have been a grave?'

'I suppose so,' said Suzanne. 'Why?'

'Because Joseph said he thinks he's identified the cemetery. If your hole is in the same place he's identified, it just adds another whole level of weirdness to this story.'

They sat for another hour, sipping Amarula Dom Pedros for dessert, enjoying the soft evening air. They kept the conversation light, trying to steer away from any topic which might unsettle them now that it was time to make their way home.

They parted in front of the bistro, Kathryn and Suzanne getting into their cars.

'I can drop you at your gate, Hannah,' called Kathryn.

'And drive me twenty metres round the corner? No, I'll be fine.'

They waved and Hannah walked down the front end of the block, passing the shop gate. The power hadn't come back on yet, and the street was darker than Hannah had expected. Feeling silly, but wishing she'd taken up Kathryn's offer, she quickened her pace. At the best of times, the dark unnerved her, but the talk of ghosts and scary Esme added a layer of anxiety, and her heart pounded a beat in her ears. As she rounded the corner, she noticed a car parked across the road which hadn't been there when she'd left. It had a Free State number plate but its windows were black, revealing nothing. She hurried in through her gate, taking the steps two at a time, key ready in her hand. As she reached forwards to unlock, a figure rose from a chair in the shadows. Hannah screamed. In two strides, the figure had grabbed her. She kicked out, connecting with bone, adrenalin pumping through every inch of her. She wrestled the iron grip on her, about to scream again when she realised the figure was saying, 'Hannah! Stop it, Hannah!' Todd's voice. She twisted away from his hands, her heart stuttering. Her fingers rattled the key as she opened the kitchen door.

Once inside she managed, with shaking fingers, to find her stash of candles and set some on the kitchen counter. As she lit the last one, the lights came on, blinding her. 'Bloody power cuts!'

'You sit,' said Todd, still rubbing his shin. 'I'll sort out some coffee. Have you been drinking?'

'Just a few glasses of wine with supper,' she said, then wondered why she was explaining to him. He took charge of her kitchen, figuring out the unfathomable coffee machine in seconds and setting a cup of very strong coffee in front of her. She hated black coffee, but he had always insisted that milk and sugar ruin the flavour. Now she hated herself for obediently sipping it. He studied her small house without comment. She glanced around the kitchen and saw what he was seeing. Her

ProNutro bowl in the sink from breakfast, Patchy's food bowl on the counter. A jersey and bag heaped on the chair. Books piled next to her computer on the table. General disorder. The familiar feeling of inadequacy came slinking back.

'What are you doing here, Hannah?'

'What do you mean?' Hannah folded her arms across her lap.

'I mean this concentration camp nonsense.'

'It's not nonsense,' she said, feeling childish.

'Hannah,' he said smoothly, persuasively, 'I can't have you digging up Afrikaner Nationalism in the current climate.'

'What are you talking about?'

He sighed. 'Hannah, don't you know anything that's going on? We're in a political crisis. The opposition is having a field day with our leadership. We simply do not need someone digging up the past, and such a loaded past right now.'

'Are you talking about the ANC party's not needing controversy or not needing you?'

Todd's eyes hardened. 'Do you have any idea how this looks? I've worked my arse off to build my reputation and credentials with a black party, and now my fucking fiancée is making headlines with old Afrikaner propaganda!'

Hannah slammed her mug down on the table, noting his horror at the hot coffee spilling onto the wood. She pushed her chair away from the table. 'Firstly, I am not your fiancée, Todd, fucking or otherwise. And secondly, nobody knows about this dig, so what the hell are you going on about?'

He pulled his leather attaché case from below the table. She had bought it for him in Italy. Spent a fortune on it – just before she found out he was sleeping with someone else. He unclipped the flap, hauled a newspaper from it, and threw it across the table so that it skidded in front of her. The paper was folded to an inside page but the headline was bold, 'South African War Concentration Camp Found on Free State Farm'. Below the headline was a picture of Hannah and Joseph on site, looking across the plateau.

'Where did this story come from?' said Hannah, horrified, thinking about Alistair.

'I'm glad you grasp the seriousness of this,' said Todd. 'The best thing is for you to come back to Cape Town. As long as you aren't here, I should be able to distance myself from it. Leave Joseph to do his thing.'

'It's also my thing, Todd.'

'Hannah,' his voice returned to the smooth tone, 'your parents are sick with worry. Your department head is wondering where you are. I've even heard talk of a junior lectureship in the offing … If you come back with me, I can arrange it. Hannah, I care about you.' He moved over to her and slid his hands around her waist, pulling her hips closer. The familiar smell of him hit her nostrils, expensive aftershave, laundered cotton. He lowered his face to her neck and she felt his tongue on her skin.

Hannah felt the drift into passivity, like an insect being drawn into a swirl of water to a drain. 'What do you know about archaeology anyway, Hannah? Why not stick to your strengths? Come. In the morning, I'll help you pack. We can drive back together.'

'I have a job, Todd, I can't just walk out.'

He lifted his head and his handsome face was suddenly ugly. 'It's a shop assistant job. How hard can it be to give notice?'

Hannah wished she could summon the guts to push him away, fire the words to tell him to get out, but they simply wouldn't come. She couldn't tell Alistair that she wanted to be with him and now she couldn't tell this … this bully to get out of her life. What was wrong with her?

Just then, keys sounded in the lock, and Joseph pushed the door open.

'I thought you were staying on the farm,' said Hannah with relief, extracting herself from Todd.

'I changed my mind.' Joseph's gaze came to rest on Todd, whose mouth was curved in a self-satisfied smile. 'It's been a while, Todd. What are you doing here?' It wasn't often that Hannah saw Joseph unfriendly, but now it rolled off him.

'Isn't it obvious?' said Todd, snagging a strand of Hannah's hair and bringing it to his lips.

'Did you come to apologise?' said Joseph, still standing.

Todd curved his other hand around Hannah's hips. 'Apologise for what?' She looked nervously at Joseph but his stare was only for Todd.

'I don't know, for being an arrogant, unfaithful prick, perhaps?'

Todd pushed Hannah away. 'Just hang on—'

'Joseph, enough,' said Hannah. Joseph raised his hands in mock apology, and turned to the sink, pouring himself a glass of water.

'Are you heading back tonight, Todd?' said Joseph with his back to the room.

Todd looked across at Hannah. 'No, I was thinking of staying a few days, actually.'

Joseph turned and leant against the sink. 'There's a small hotel down the road. I can show you where it is now, if you like. Unfortunately, this place is pretty cramped with Hannah and me here,' he smiled, not looking in the least apologetic.

Todd stood and picked up his attaché case, leaving the newspaper on the table. 'I'll find it myself, thanks. Hannah?' he raised his brows at her. 'I'll see you tomorrow?'

Joseph opened the door for him and shut it firmly, locking it before Todd was even off the deck. He turned back into the room to see Hannah scrubbing her face with her hands.

'What the hell is he doing here?'

'The dig has somehow made it into the paper – look.' She passed the paper over to him. 'How did the press find out about it? Joseph, it was a condition of Alistair's that it stays out the media.'

'I'm not worried about Alistair,' said Joseph sitting down at the table and examining the article. 'Why is Todd the Sod here?'

'He says we're digging up old Nationalist propaganda and it's going to ruin his career with the ANC.'

'Good.'

'No, Joseph, not good. What if he causes trouble? He'll be able to pull all sorts of party strings – what if he sabotages our application?'

'And the bastard wouldn't think twice. Damn! Maybe I shouldn't have been so rude.'

'Ya think?'

'Did he actually threaten you?' said Joseph, looking up at her.

'No, he wants me to pack up and go back to Cape Town with him.' Hannah stared at her hands on the table.

'With him, with him?'

She felt terribly tired. 'I don't know, Josey. He's a bully, I see that. But he did have a point. What am I doing here? I don't know anything about archaeology or running a shop or being a farmer's wife for that matter.'

'Whoa.' Joseph leant back in his chair. 'You've got ahead of me, a farmer's wife? When did that happen?'

She stood and pushed in her chair, smiling sadly at him. 'Nothing's happened, that's the problem. I'm exhausted, Jose. I'm going to bed.' She left him sitting at the table, staring at the paper.

Hannah slept fitfully. She awoke with a headache and somebody's words ringing in her head … *You haven't even begun to discover your strength.* Pushing them from her mind, she had a shower. Then, feeling marginally better, she went through to the kitchen where Joseph was standing at the sink, finishing his coffee.

'Morning, Sunshine,' he said, turning as she came in. She felt the farthest thing from sunny, and muttered under her breath as she put the kettle back on to boil.

'I think I know who our leak is,' said Joseph, putting his mug in the sink. 'I think one of the students took this picture. I'll interrogate her this morning.'

'Why do you think she did it?'

'I don't think she's malicious, just not the sharpest. I laid out the rules before we started, and no media contact was one of them. But this girl is permanently on her phone – she probably didn't think that Facebook counts as media. It would just take one journalist friend to ask her some questions and there we are, Hannah and Joseph, famous at last.'

Hannah smiled at his effort to cheer her up. 'Have a good day, Han. I'll call you later to check what the Sod is doing. If he's still around, I'll come back here tonight.'

'Joseph, you don't have to hover, you know. I am a grown-up. I should be able to look after myself.'

'You are perfectly able to look after yourself; it's just more fun this way.'

'You just love a pissing contest.'

'Oh, you know me so well.' He grinned, stopping at her chair on his way out and bending to plant a kiss on the top of her head.

'Not so well, apparently. I had no idea you were sweet, Joseph Harrison.'

He threw her a smile over his shoulder as he left.

CHAPTER TWENTY-TWO

Hannah opened the shop at eight o'clock, glad for the routine to distract her from her thoughts. It was quiet, and she managed to catch up on admin she'd let slide over the busy Christmas period. Barbara came in at nine and they worked companionably. Hannah felt herself relax, the only demand being that of her admin systems, and she found creating order there therapeutic.

At ten o'clock, the doorbell tinkled and she looked up to see Todd come in, followed by Moses Motala, the mayor. Moses smiled kindly at Hannah, nodding his head in greeting. Hannah's stomach immediately cramped. Todd had a familiar, triumphant smirk on his face.

Barbara, taking one look at Hannah's face, whispered that she would deal with the shop. 'Take them into the reading room. I'll be right here if you need me.'

Hannah nodded gratefully and led the men across the passage. Todd sat down immediately, setting his attaché case on the table like a lawyer about to interview a witness. Moses remained standing, waiting for Hannah to take a seat before he pulled out a chair for himself.

Todd launched into a monologue about the ANC party's vision for a united South Africa, about the dangers of divisive history, and how pursuing a dig like this, resurrecting the concentration camp narrative, would be contrary to the cause of nation building. When he at last stopped and turned to Moses, he was puffed up with satisfaction.

'Moses is, as you know, a senior ANC party member in the Free State. He has much political clout in the area, and I brought him here to convince you that continuing is not an option. What if Leliehoek becomes the centre of something ugly? What if this turns the communities against each other? If this dig upsets the tenuous balance between blacks and whites again? In fact, Moses has enough connections with SAHRA to halt the process altogether, if it be in the country's best interests.'

Moses had been sitting quietly, listening intently, and now he cleared his throat. 'I understand your concerns, comrade.' Hannah's heart plummeted. 'I came here today to hear you out. I have been the mayor of Leliehoek for a long time now. I know this town.' He looked at Hannah becoming smaller and smaller in her chair. 'Comrade, your concerns sound noble, but I think Leliehoek can handle this fine.'

'What?' Todd sat forward in surprise, opening his mouth to disagree, but Moses held his hand up.

'Since you called me last night, I've done some phoning around my-self. This community has long since grasped difference, like a stinging nettle, you know? We've got used to the sting now. If nothing else, the exposure and tourism potential of this dig could be good for us. I do have connections with SAHRA, but, Hannah, I think I might lend my support to this dig, rather than my opposition.'

Todd drew a sharp breath and was about to launch forth another time, but Moses held his hand up again. 'And I also know the ANC. I have been a member since I was eighteen, before 1994. Believe me, I know about tensions and divides.' He paused for a moment, and then said gently to Todd, 'Look to your own position in the ANC, comrade. If there is any threat at all, it would be for you, not for the party or the country for that matter.'

Moses pushed his chair out and Hannah saw him to the door, where he shook her hand and thanked her for the meeting. When she returned, Todd was sitting slumped in his chair and Hannah felt a moment's pity for him. He had spent years building his political reputation; it would be unfortunate if it came crashing down around him. But then, Todd was a politician through and through. She doubted whether he would stay down for long. She couldn't imagine his allegiance to the ANC was based on anything more than convenience. If things were to sour there, he would no doubt find a place in another party, no matter how ideologically different the alternative might be.

He looked up and she cringed at the malice in his eyes. Before he could say anything, the shop phone rang, and Hannah jumped to escape and answer it, relieved Barbara was busy with a customer.

'Leliehoek Books.' There was silence on the other end. 'Hello?'

Nothing.

She put the phone down and, as she moved back to the reading room, the phone in her house began to ring. She darted down the passage to answer it. 'Hello?'

Nothing.

Hannah replaced the receiver slowly and returned to the shop. Just as she pulled the passage door closed behind her, the shop phone began to ring again. She heard Barbara answer it: 'Leliehoek Books. Hello? Hello?'

Hannah walked through to Barbara, took the receiver from her, and, putting her finger on her lips, placed the receiver on the desk without hanging up. Whoever was doing this could damn well pay for a long call. If she didn't hang up, then the caller couldn't call out again. Walking back through to the house, Hannah also took her home phone off the hook.

By the time she got back to the reading room, Todd was standing at the window. 'Even the phones don't work in this shithole.'

'Todd, I've got work to do. It's better if you go.'

'I'm waiting for you to pack up and come back to Cape Town. I'll sit here all week until you do.' The stubborn set of his jaw made him look petulant. 'You know I'm right. You know that you're not cut out for this dump – you're a city girl. You'll never cope out here once the novelty wears off. You belong in Cape Town. The galleries, the restaurants, the wine estates, the parties. You love it there!'

'No,' said Hannah quietly, 'you love it there. You've never asked if I do.'

'Stop being so fucking melodramatic – your friends are there, Hannah, and most importantly, your work!'

'Actually, my friends are here and my work is here.'

'Work? In this crappy little shop? When you could be lecturing at UCT? You've got to be fucking joking.'

'I'm happy here, Todd,' she said softly.

'No, you're not.'

He wasn't listening and she gave up.

'I've got an errand to run.' Backing out the room, she stuck her head into the shop. 'I have to get out of here,' she whispered to Barbara, who clearly had been straining her ears to catch every word. 'Ignore him.' Hannah indicated with her head to the reading room. 'Hopefully he'll go away.'

Barbara rolled her eyes. 'At least get me something from Kathryn's as compensation.'

Hannah crossed the square to Kathryn's and found Douglas sitting at the counter, sipping hot chocolate. He was dressed in a formal black shirt, a white collar at his throat.

'You look very sombre this morning, Hannah,' he said cheerfully. 'Perhaps you should've taken the funeral instead of me.'

'A funeral? Oh, sorry, Douglas, that must've been hard for you.'

'Not at all,' he said, grinning. 'She was ninety-seven in the shade and had been on her deathbed at least seven times in the last year. The family was getting fed up with racing from all over the country to say goodbye, only for the old duck to make a miraculous recovery. She had them exactly where she wanted them! Marvellous old bird.'

Hannah smiled at him, envying his buoyancy.

Kathryn came through from the back. 'Hannah, can I get you something?'

'Um, yes, something to take back to Barbara. I left her with Todd.'

Kathryn's eyes widened. 'Todd's here?'

'Who's Todd?' said Douglas.

'Hannah's ex-fiancé from Cape Town.' She turned back to Hannah. 'What does he want?'

'He wants me to go back with him. He wants me away from the dig – says it will ruin his political career with the ANC.'

'Do you care?' said Douglas, watching Hannah carefully.

'I don't care for him any more. And he feels nothing for me. No doubt his supermodel girlfriend is waiting for him at home. It's all

about his position on the ladder. I gather being a white man in a pre-
dominantly black party is tenuous. Any threat could topple him.'

'Especially old Afrikaner history?' said Kathryn.

'It's made him rather ugly.'

'Tell him to bugger off,' said Kathryn, busying herself with packing
shiny apple Danishes into a pink cardboard box for Barbara.

'I want to.' Hannah perched on a stool pulled up to the counter, resting her head in her hands. 'Something about him always paralysed me.
It still does, even now that everything is over. He turns me into this
little girl who takes instructions. I can't bear it.'

'Is he a churchgoer?' said Douglas.

'No. He can't handle any power higher than himself.'

'That says a lot,' said Douglas, standing. 'Would you like me to help
get rid of him?'

'Shouldn't I be doing it myself? I'm so pathetic.'

'Hey!' Heat flared in Kathryn's eyes. 'This is what he does to you.
Makes you feel pathetic, and you are not! You need him gone. Out of
your life. It doesn't matter how.' She reached across the counter to grip
Hannah's arm. 'What's that proverb, Douglas? Like a dog returns to its
vomit, so a fool returns to his foolishness.'

'That's disgusting,' said Hannah. 'It's in the Bible?'

Douglas grinned at her wide eyes. 'Kathryn's right. This man is toxic.
Let's get him away from you so you don't have to revert to being someone you despise. Feeling compelled to eat your own vomit.'

'Sies, man, you two,' said Hannah, but she already felt lighter.

Douglas pulled Hannah off her stool. 'Kathryn, you got a knobki-
erie? An axe? How about a butcher knife? No? Oh well.' And then,
crowing in his favourite Southern accent, 'We'll just have to lean on the
power of the Almighty!'

Kathryn laughing, called after him, 'You are the most idioti—'

'But you love me!' he yelled back.

Hannah became more and more apprehensive as they approached the
shop. She pushed the door open, and Douglas gestured for her to go to

Barbara as he entered the reading room, leaving the door open. Hannah and Barbara positioned themselves at the desk where they had a clear view across the passage. Hannah stood frozen to the spot at the computer, feeling heat pound in her face at the shame of her friends being caught up in this but also leaning in to hear what Douglas was going to say. She needn't have bothered, because Douglas pulled out his sermon voice, and it rang clearly through the shop. Hannah slid into the passage and flipped the shop sign to 'Closed'.

Todd was sitting in one of the reading-room armchairs, one ankle on the other knee, idly flipping through a magazine. He looked up in surprise when Douglas came in, his face beaming.

'At last we meet, Todd. I have heard so much about you from Hannah.' Douglas sat down in the opposite chair, leant forward, and shook Todd's hand vigorously. 'I have got to know Hannah so well in the past months. She's involved in our church activities, and I have come to appreciate her as a fine woman who is really growing in her faith. Praise the Lord.'

Hannah could see that Todd was so taken aback by the zealous force of Douglas, he was rendered speechless.

'And when I heard just now that her fiancé was here to fetch her, I thought this indeed was the Lord at work. I had to come across to meet the man who wants to take Hannah to wed. How wonderfully we are made. Are we not?'

Todd shifted in his chair. 'Um, I'm not sure you understand—'

'You are so right! Of course we do not understand the majesty of the Lord – how could we? Todd' – Douglas looked seriously at Todd and gripped his arm – 'our little community is holding a humble Bible study this afternoon. Will you come and lead us in our study of Lamentations? Hannah has told me of your incisive mind and authority. Your input would be enlightening.'

Todd opened his mouth to speak, but Douglas filled the gap: 'And then! Then we could hold a simple ceremony of matrimony for you and Hannah. She is an honourable woman who does not set much store on the trappings of the world – I'm sure you know this already. She would be delighted with a small wedding, just the Bible study group to witness your troth. I will call our organist right this minute.' He took his phone from his pocket and began tapping at the keys.

Todd interjected quickly: 'I'm afraid that won't be possible.' He looked at the door. 'I have a flight out of Bloemfontein this afternoon,' he said, glancing at his watch. 'I will need to leave ... very soon.'

'Oh dear,' said Douglas settling in, 'maybe another time.' He called over his shoulder, 'Barbara, how about some tea?'

Barbara grinned at Hannah and hurried down the passage to put the kettle on.

Now that Douglas was clearly not going anywhere, Todd stood awkwardly for a few moments and then picked up his case.

'Travel well,' called Douglas cheerfully.

Hannah opened the door for Todd and walked him down the steps to the pavement.

'This isn't over, Hannah.' His eyes were mean.

'Actually, Todd, it is over. Completely and utterly over. Please don't contact me again.'

'I said in the beginning and I'll say it again now, Hannah. You're a quitter. You won't stick at this, just like all the other things you've started and then baled at the first hurdle.'

'You're wrong.'

He laughed. 'Oh really? If I'm so wrong, why not come with me now and we can patch things up between us? Give it another go, hey, Hannah?'

'And be the woman you cheat on for the rest of my life? Why would I?'

'Because you're not capable of more, Hannah. I'm the best opportunity you'll have because I know you. Hell, I made you. No one else would put up with your dithering, your flakiness.'

'Go to hell, Todd.'

'Fine.' He shrugged. 'You know where to find me. I'll be there to take you in when this' – he gestured a circle to the town square – 'this fucking fantasy is too much for you to bear.'

She stood as he walked to his rental car and waited until he disappeared around the square.

Hannah climbed slowly up the steps. So he was gone. It's what she wanted. So why was she feeling so beaten? Breathing in a long, deep breath, she pushed open the shop door. Barbara and Douglas were sitting in the reading room, a tray of tea and the box of apple Danishes between them.

'You, my girl,' said Barbara, 'need a cup of tea.'

Hannah smiled and sank into a chair just as the doorbell tinkled and Alistair peered round the door.

'Alistair!' called Douglas. 'Come on in, we've been having fun and games and now we're having Danishes.'

'I've just come by to drop this off for my mum.' He came in and put an envelope on the table next to Hannah. 'It's money for the book you brought her the other day?'

Hannah smiled up at him. 'Oh, she needn't have done that – it was a gift.'

He smiled briefly back and looked to Douglas. 'What's this about fun and games?'

'We've just managed to see off Hannah's fiancé, Todd. Marvellous performance on my part, hey, Barbara?'

Hannah didn't hear the reply; she was watching Alistair. His mouth smiled, but she could see his brain trying to catch up, his face desperately covering his confusion. Hannah could feel him withdraw from her and she wanted so much to shout, 'Stop!', freeze the scene, make it rewind to a few moments before when she could have met him outside, told him herself, ended this awful slow-motion unfolding of her past for him.

But Alistair left a few minutes later with Douglas, who was still going on about Todd. Alistair said goodbye, but didn't look at Hannah, and she felt the cut deeply.

'Barbara, why are relationships such minefields?' she asked, dropping her head on the table.

'There'd be no thrill if there was no danger, sweetheart.' Barbara squeezed Hannah's shoulder as she left with the tea tray.

'No thrill sounds rather nice right now,' said Hannah to the empty room.

CHAPTER TWENTY-THREE

Hannah saw nothing of Alistair for two weeks. He didn't come near the shop, and when she visited the Goshen site with Joseph, there was no sign of him. Her guilt and relief intermingled. If he despised her so much that he didn't want to see her, it certainly resolved the issue of their relationship. She didn't know how to deal with her sense of loss, though. She had glimpsed a connection with him which had been so fragile but beautiful too. Spider-web like. The only thing she knew how to do was shut off. She immersed herself in finishing the journal instead.

The last sections of Rachel's journal were terribly sad for Hannah to read. Rachel's mother and little sisters were all dead, and Rachel still didn't know.

> March 1902, Goshen Camp, Orange River Colony
>
> Dear Wolf,
>
> I have not written for so long. As the weather cools again and autumn approaches, we are hard at work harvesting the crops. There seem to be more and more British moving across the veld. The more soldiers, the more mouths to feed, and the more we are expected to grow. The camp rules remain the same: if we work, we can buy food at a fair price. If we refuse to work, we'll have to pay double. Work or starve – those are our choices.
>
> Fewer people are coming into the camp at last. It is as if the war is getting tired now, running out of fuel. It can't be bothered to bring more misery down onto the

land. It is merely limping along, waiting for an end. I feel the same. No newcomers, but people are still dying here. The number of strong, well people is getting smaller. The load of work for us who can still bend to the fields is getting heavier. We see little of the doctor. He came one day with some visiting nurses. The women wore smart uniforms. Their white aprons and white veils looked so beautiful, so remarkably clean, we could only stare at them, our faces vacant and dull. A man took photographs of them and us, a record of their presence in the camp, but we have not seen them again.

The Methodist Episcopal minister, Reverend Charlie, has been several times to see us. He tells us the British have swarmed over this country like locusts. That the Boers left in the hills are bravely fighting, but that it is surely a lost cause now. The 'Bittereindes', he called them. And bitter indeed is the thought of you fighting for us while we feed the enemy.

Please don't forget me here, Wolf. I want to go home. I want to see Oupa Jakob. I will be a good girl for Ma. I will never again complain about my share of the work. I will play with Lizzie and Kristina, whatever they want to play. I will never say I'm too busy again. I will never be angry with you again. I will never be jealous of your horses again. I'm sorry, Wolf.

The shrill ring of the phone pulled Hannah from the journal and, not thinking, she went to answer, grabbing a tissue from the box in the kitchen to blow her nose and hoping she could mask the choke in her voice.

'Hello?'

Nothing.

'Dammit!' She slammed the phone down, then took the receiver off the hook before it could ring again. The calls were coming every night now, numerous times, and she'd resorted to leaving her phone off the hook mostly, especially when she went to bed. There had been times in Cape Town when the family had experienced something similar. Hang-up calls or just breathing. Her mother had dismissed them as random or, at worst, a disgruntled student, unhappy with a term mark. Ignored, the calls usually stopped.

Pouring herself a glass of water at the kitchen sink, Hannah glimpsed her reflection in the black window. The dark hollowed her face, making her think of Esme. She was still the biggest obstacle to finding out more about Rachel. Hannah knew there was more at the Silwerfontein cottage, if only she could get to it.

She had seen Karl at the petrol station earlier that day, and had quickly crossed the street, coming to the window of his pickup and greeting him.

He'd smiled at her, but there was a hovering awkwardness. 'Esme is just in the supermarket – I can't stop to chat, sorry, man.'

'It's okay. Karl, I just want to ask you one thing, please.'

He'd looked through the front windscreen and nodded slightly.

'There was this girl, Rachel Badenhorst. She was part of your family during the South African War. We think she was sent to a concentration camp on Goshen. Most of the family were sent to Winburg and they died there. Have you ever heard of this before? Did your mother or grandparents tell you any stories? Is there anything at Silwerfontein which could tell me more about her?'

'That's more than one question, Hannah,' he had said gently, looking at his big hands on the steering wheel. 'I don't remember anything about that stuff. I wasn't interested when my mother tried to tell me about her research. It bored me. Look, Esme's my priority right now. She's too fragile to risk setting off. I can't get involved, sorry.' As he'd looked up at Hannah, the deep sorrow in his eyes had filled her with remorse.

'It's okay. I'm the one who's sorry. I don't mean to cause you or your family more pain.' She'd stepped away from the car with a smile of apology for Karl.

But her mind raced. Karl's mother had researched the family? It was all probably sitting in her little house, gathering dust. The revelation hung over Hannah as she returned to Rachel's journal.

> Reverend Charlie led us in prayer. He is so angry. He shouts at the Lord and pleads with Him, like the psalmists. He said that enough people have died here. He says he's going to write and protest to the Queen herself, if things do not change in this camp. He is so full of ire, so enraged, I believe he would do it too. But then he read Psalm 23 and the words rang out in the camp. This was no quiet balm for our pain. He read with ferocity. A declaration against the evil we have seen.
>
> *The* LORD *is my shepherd; I shall not want.*
>
> *He maketh me to lie down in green pastures: He leadeth me beside the still waters. He restoreth my soul: He leadeth me in the paths of righteousness for his name's sake. Yea, though I walk through the valley of the shadow of death, I will fear no evil: for thou art with me; thy rod and thy staff they comfort me.*
>
> For eternity, I will think of that psalm read like a battle cry against that camp. Declaring the Lord as our master, not the British. His rod and staff raised in defence of the helpless.

To Hannah's relief, Joseph, with the helpful intervention of Moses Motala, was making huge strides. He had networked and pulled together a group of researchers who were interested in pursuing their own work on the site. One archaeologist was interested especially in the use of fuels in the camp. She was a botanist and wanted to investigate the hearths and take samples of charcoal or ash to find out which plant materials had been used. In that open Free State landscape, there were few trees to be seen, so it was likely that, like in many camps, people had collected and burnt cakes of dung. The presence of dung would suggest livestock around the camp, and that would say much about the life of the camp inmates.

Joseph told Hannah he had identified the main living area, though there was little left of the camp dwellings. The hearth places were useful, and it seemed that some tents or shelters had had a cooking place directly outside. The team had found the odd utensil and the leg of a cast-iron cooking pot to confirm the idea.

One day, Hannah caught a lift up to the dig with one of the students. She found Joseph at the far end of the plateau, working on the section which he had confirmed as the cemetery. Most graves were unmarked, though a few seemed to have small cairns built across the graves. Students were marking off the graves with lines of string, pegging the strings into the hard ground with mallets.

'You're making great progress, Jose,' Hannah said, coming up behind him.

He spun around, pulling her into his side for a hug. 'Nice to see you up here. You've been scarce.'

'Just busy,' she said. 'How many are you up to?'

'We've estimated two hundred graves.'

Hannah let out a slow whistle. 'Two hundred people? In two years? That's awful, Jose.'

'We haven't begun to excavate yet. There might be more than one body in some of these. The number could be twice or even three times that.'

'Rachel describes that in December 1901, actually. It just hits home when you're standing here looking at the real scale of it. How many people do you think were in the camp?'

'Difficult to say without records. The standard measure is that ten per cent of the camp populations died. That would put this camp at two thousand people at a minimum. But I don't think this plateau camp could hold that many people. I would guess that, rather, the death rate was horrendously high.'

'Rachel speaks of measles and typhoid being the main killers,' said Hannah, breathing a deep sigh and looking over the site.

'I would imagine we could add exposure to that list, thinking of being up here in winter. And starvation.' Joseph kicked a stone at his feet. 'We haven't found nearly as many ration tins as we thought. Certainly no condensed milk tins, which we expected to find. And very little military detritus. There's something strange about this camp.'

'What do you mean?' asked Hannah.

'We know quite a bit about other Boer camps. There were soldiers around a lot, managing the everyday running of the camp. The inmates were given rations – meagre, but still, they were fed. Here, we've found the odd buckle and a few ammunition shells, but nothing like the number we should have found. And very few ration tins.' He bent to pick a grass stem, and twisted it in his hands.

'Maybe they were just very tidy and threw away all the old tins.' Hannah grinned at Joseph.

He looked back at her and smiled. 'You think you're being silly, but you could be right. We've got the rubbish heap still to excavate – that should tell us more about what they ate here, I suppose.'

The afternoon light was shifting to golden as Hannah had seen it do in this valley. It brushed the distant sandstone faces, the grass even greener against the orange stone.

'Did Suzanne come up to say goodbye this morning?' Hannah pulled away to see his face as he watched the students, measuring and making sure their lines were straight.

'Um, yes, she did. She told me the story of the women digging the hole up here.'

'And what did you make of it?'

'I'm not sure.' He seemed distracted. 'She said it was down this end of the plateau, but she was quite far away. She could have made a mistake. Her imagination perhaps filled in the rest.'

Hannah frowned. 'Come on, Joseph, she's hardly the type to make up ghost stories. You can't get more rational than Suzanne.'

He kept looking out over the plateau. 'No. Not an ounce of emotion there. But she's gone now.'

She touched him lightly on his arm. 'Sorry it didn't work out with her, Jose. I know you had feelings for her.'

He looked at her then. 'What? No, it's fine. She didn't get close enough for me to get my hopes up. So distant, even when we were talking. Like her heart had been cut off from her clever brain. I couldn't get near her. But then she so clearly loves and engages with her family. I kept wondering if something had happened to her – hurt her badly, you know?' His eyes searched Hannah's for a moment, and then he shrugged and smiled. 'It wasn't to be, I guess.'

Hannah had never seen that puzzled, lost look in his eyes. Her confident, capable star of a brother. She had guessed this might happen, and had thought it would be good for him to be on the receiving end for a change. Now, seeing his confusion, she felt an empathy for him that had her putting her arm around his waist and squeezing him to her. 'You're a good person, Joseph, under all the crap.'

'Right back at ya,' he said squeezing her back and lifting her off her feet until she yelped.

Alistair pushed his hand through his hair and tipped his head back onto the chair. He was sitting on his veranda, a beer propped on one knee. 'I don't know how long I can go on like this, Dad. I'm exhausted. The calls, the threats. I'm ready to move on, but it doesn't seem like I'm going to be allowed to.'

'I think the time has come to do something more formal about Esme, my boy.'

'What do you mean? What could we possibly do?'

'Maybe we need to talk to Michael about some kind of legal action.'

'How is that going to help? She can't be locked up … And wherever she goes, if she has access to a telephone, that's enough to make my life a misery.'

'Let me ask Michael about it.'

Alistair nodded, his eyes fatigued. He drained the last of his beer.

'At least come for supper,' said Neil. 'Your mother's made enough bolognaise to feed the whole district.'

'I don't think so, Dad. I'm not hungry tonight. Don't tell Mum about the calls carrying on – I don't want her to worry more.'

'I tell your mother everything, and then we both worry about it. That's just the way it is.' Neil hauled himself out of the deep chair, calling Jim Beam to follow him. Alistair could hear the little dog's claws skitter on the wooden floorboards.

He stared at the darkening view, the rock faces paling from orange to beige to ghostly grey. A baboon up in the cliffs barked a warning to something, its shout in the dark raising the hairs on Alistair's arms.

The ringing phone startled him. He sighed and then moved to answer it.

'I see it now,' the whisper rasped across the line. 'It was you and your whore. You killed my little girl. The slut wanted my girl out the way.'

'Esme, stop it! It was eight years ago. It was a horrible accident, but it's over. You need to let Marilie go.'

The whisper became reedy: 'I will never let this go until you pay for what you did! You murdered my beautiful girl and nobody will listen, not even Karl.' Her breath hitched in a sob. 'It's time I stop asking other people for justice. I've waited too long. You took my girl. Now I'm going to take yours.'

'Esme! Stop this madness!'

But the line was dead.

Alistair dialled Hannah's house. The phone was engaged, and her cellphone went straight to voicemail. He dialled Karl, and his phone rang and rang.

No, no, no. This can't be happening. Alistair raced through to the kitchen, sliding his keys from the counter and leaving the kitchen door open behind him as he sprinted for his pickup.

'Joseph?' he shouted as he ran, but the shed was quiet.

The familiar road seemed ten times longer than usual, and he pushed the accelerator to the floor. When he pulled up at Hannah's house, he threw the gate wide to clang against the fence, bounded up the stairs, and hammered on the French door. 'Hannah? Hannah?'

She came through with her hair wet on her shoulders, dressed in cotton pyjama trousers and a vest. She unlocked the door, anxiety drawing her brows down. 'What's happened? Are you okay?'

He pushed past her and went straight through to the phone in her passage, barking at her. 'Why is your phone off the hook?' Fear had turned to fury which coiled his insides.

'Why are you so angry? I took it off the hook earlier. I've been getting strange calls.'

His hands curled into fists at his sides. 'Why didn't you tell me?'

'You haven't been around. I assumed you didn't want to see me.'

He pushed his hand into his hair, watching her fold her arms across her chest in defence.

'Sorry ...'

Hannah moved to him and pulled his hand, leading him into the little lounge where she pushed him into the couch. 'Stay there.' She returned with two mugs and curled onto the end of the couch. He gripped both hands around the mug and sipped the sweet foamy Milo, thinking of his mum making it for him when he was a boy.

Hannah smiled hesitantly at him. 'My mum used to make this for me when I was little – one of the few motherly things she used to do.'

'Mine too.'

Hannah reached across, laying her hand lightly on his arm. 'Alistair, what happened tonight?'

He put his mug on the coffee table. 'It's Esme. She's been calling me too, silent calls, but I knew it was her. She did this before. And then tonight she called and told me she was going to get even. That I killed Marilie and nobody would believe her. That she was going to take it into her own hands. She threatened you, Hannah, and I panicked. Sorry I frightened you.' Hannah's brows drew down but there was no fear in her eyes, just concern.

'Something needs to be done about her now, Alistair.'

'I know. My dad said the same thing earlier today.'

'I don't know what, but I think it's gone beyond everyone tolerating and excusing her behaviour. Poor Karl – I feel so awful for him; it will be up to him to manage this. He'll be devastated when he hears what she's said. Maybe there's medication which can help her or time in a psychiatric clinic?'

Alistair leant his head back on the couch and stared at the ceiling. 'We have to actually be proactive though, no more sitting around because if someone …' He turned his head to the side and looked directly at Hannah, the thought of Esme's poison chasing her away doubling his stomach into a knot. 'If I let her get to you, I would never forgive myself.'

'You don't think she would physically try to hurt us, do you?'

He shook his head. 'No, I don't. She's always done things remotely, over the phone or in the press, stuff like that. But I would hate for her to sabotage you in some way.'

'She and Todd should team up,' said Hannah, slumping back into the couch, holding her mug on her stomach. Alistair's gaze still rested on her.

'I'm so sorry I didn't tell you about him, Alistair. I meant to a few times and then I just didn't want to bring him into my life here – I didn't want to contaminate what feels like a fresh start.'

'What happened with the two of you?'

She sighed. 'We got together in the first semester of university. I was bowled along with his life from there, never stopping to think about what I really wanted. I followed him to London, and then I came home with him because he wanted to pursue a career in politics. We got en-gaged because it looked better than just shacking up.' Hannah raised cool eyes to his. 'Looked better for his career, I mean. I don't think he ever intended marrying me. I found out the same year that he was sleeping with someone else. I don't know how many affairs he had had before her. I left him then.' She paused. 'He asked me to come back to him. Said we'd figure out an open relationship and – this is the worst part – I actually thought about it! I couldn't get any lower. I withdrew. Hated myself for being so pathetic for so long. And that was it – until a few weeks ago when he turned up at the shop and wanted me to leave Leliehoek.'

'Because you were getting up his nose?'

She nodded and Alistair shook his head. 'What an arrogant prick.'

Hannah smiled, clearly appreciating his summation of Todd. 'I'm sorry I hurt you, Alistair.'

He shook his head again. 'When I said the ball was in your court, I thought you had never considered marriage before, and just needed some time to think – and a bit of pressure maybe.' He gave a small smile. 'And then I find out you were engaged ... that you had wanted to marry someone once. You said yes before. And maybe now the problem was me. That's why I stayed away. I was waiting for you to come and explain. And you didn't.'

'I'm sorry.' She put her mug down and leant towards him, taking his face in her hands and turning him to her, her mouth meeting his in a soft kiss. Her damp hair swung around his face as his mouth opened, and his hands stroked up her back to pull her hair into one fist as his lips moved down her throat, kissing the spot gently where he had bruised her before.

Alistair tightened his grip around her, and he slid her down onto the couch under him, his body pressing her into the cushions and his breath coming faster. He slid one strap of her vest down her arm, the scent of vanilla strong in his nostrils. His mouth explored hers again, and then travelled across her collarbone, his tongue tasting the freshness of her just-showered skin. Hannah gasped and she adjusted, shifting her legs apart to cradle his body. Then he placed a soft kiss on the top of her breast, and laid his head on her chest, his breath still short, heart drumming against hers.

'I haven't changed my mind, Hannah. Unless this is for the long haul, I'm not going to sleep with you, no matter how much I want to. And I do.'

'Alistair, I don't know. I'm not—'

'Then I should probably go home.' But he stayed where he was.

She struggled to sit up, and he shifted off her.

'Maybe you should go,' she said. 'I don't want to fight. Not tonight.'

'I don't want to leave you here. Come back to the farm. You can stay at my mother's.'

'No, Alistair. I have an early start in the shop. I'll be fine.'

'Let me stay here.'

'You really think you'll stay on the couch?' She cocked one brow. 'Look, I don't mind. In fact, I'd relish you in my bed, but I don't want you to regret it in the morning.'

'I'm pretty sure I wouldn't regret it.' He smiled at her, rubbing a hand over his face. 'You're right. There's no way I could lie here with you in the next room. Damn my principles!'

She laughed. 'I really will be fine. I'll lock up and Joseph will probably come back here tonight anyway. He took the team to that new pub just out of town.'

Alistair went from room to room, checking the windows, and then picked up his keys. She walked him to the kitchen and he waited on the deck while she locked the door behind him.

He hesitated before turning the key in the ignition. Was he really giving up a night with Hannah?

He laid his forehead on the steering wheel. It would be so easy to knock on the door again. She'd let him in, smiling wryly, and he'd be lost. Really lost. Alistair knocked his forehead gently on the wheel and then sat up, turning the key and pushing the gear stick into first, before he could change his mind.

Kathryn ran a drying cloth over the white dinner plate, and slid it onto the wooden rack above her sink. She took a sip from her glass of wine. The house was quiet. She had a few minutes before her favourite home improvement show began. Some over-the-top renovating drama was exactly what she needed at the end of her day. She had pulled the plug and wiped the sink when she heard Matthew's little voice from the doorway: 'Mama?'

'Sweetheart, why are you awake?' Kathryn turned and saw her son, drowsy in the bright kitchen, his hair tousled and little face confused.

'Mama? The lady at the door said—'

'What lady at the door?' She pushed past Matthew and looked down the passage, but the door was locked, as she had left it. She turned back to Matthew, a frown creasing her brow as she knelt in front of him.

'Matthew,' she said, looking into his sleepy face, 'what lady? Did you have a dream, baby?'

He lifted puzzled eyes to her. 'She was at the door and she spoke Afrikaans like Ouma. She said, "Tell your mama that Hannah needs help."'

Kathryn's hands clenched on his arms. 'What did she look like, Matthew?'

Her blood ran cold as he answered, 'Mama, she was at the door. She had a long dress and a white dolly bonnet.'

CHAPTER TWENTY-FOUR

Hannah padded through the dark kitchen and took a glass from the drying rack. Alistair was an enigma to her Todd-trained brain. She'd had sex with Todd a few days after they had met. Her seventeen-year-old-virgin self had been willing enough, and she had always enjoyed sex, but now she wondered if it hadn't all been part of a pattern driven by what Todd wanted. Always what Todd wanted. Would it ever have occurred to him to deprive himself to wait for Hannah to come to a decision? Her life had been driven by other people. How sad, she thought now, as she filled her glass from the tap. She glanced up, and swallowed a scream. Instead of her own reflection in the black glass, she saw the hollow face of Esme. Esme's make-up had blurred in dark patches under dead eyes, and her hair, normally so sculpted, was flattened on one side, as if she had awoken from a deep sleep. Hannah's scalp crawled. Esme's gaze slid from hers and she moved sideways to the door, trying the door handle slowly. Hannah was rooted in shock. Esme lifted a handgun, large and ugly in her tiny white hand, and smashed a pane of glass in the door. Pushing her left hand through the shards, she slid the bolt open from the inside, her skin shredding into strips.

Hannah dropped down to the floor, her blood thumping in her ears, and crawled behind the kitchen table. Esme stepped through the kitchen door, her stringy arm white and strong in the half-light, raising the gun. The bullet, fired at where Hannah had been standing at the sink, splintered wood and glass. It cracked in Hannah's eardrums as she hid in the shadow of the table, not wanting to chance the gap into the passage. Another shot reverberated. The bullet struck the table above Hannah's head, exploding a vase on the tabletop. Water and shredded flowers sprayed across the kitchen. Hannah knew she had to move or die. She scrambled from her cover as Esme fired a third round. Hannah felt the force of the bullet like a baseball bat. Her leg collapsed beneath her as she reached the passage, her brain just registering a weight she had to pull to drag herself from the room. Flattening herself against the passage wall, she crouched down to pick up the heavy iron doorstop. She felt the world slow down. Motion seemed suspended to a slow, flashing flicker. It danced beneath a strobe light. The floorboards in the kitchen shifted and squeaked as Esme crossed the room towards her.

Hannah's senses, opening wide, tracked Esme's movement coming closer. A pungent waft of musky perfume hit Hannah's nostrils as Esme stepped through the door, and Hannah reared up, smashing the iron into Esme's kneecap. She heard the bone crack and shatter. With a tortured shriek, Esme's skull-like face contorted with pain. Her leg gave way and she crashed into the wall, the gun clattering to the floor and skidding away. Hannah collapsed, the iron gripped in her hands. The gun lay down the passage, a few metres looking like miles as Hannah's leg pulled downwards, a lead weight. Esme was curled into a foetal position in the doorway. She sobbed such deep, wretched gasps, her body had become a shuddering wreck.

'I can't bear it any more.' Esme's body convulsed in shivers, her voice that of a child. 'I can't bear the pain anymore.'

Using the low bookcase, Hannah hauled herself onto the chair next to the phone. It rang before she could reach for it, Kathryn's stricken voice on the other side.

'Hannah, what's happened?'

'I need help, Kathryn. I've been shot.'

'Stay on the line. Keep talking to me, Hannah. I'm calling for help on my cell.'

Hannah held the receiver to her ear. She could hear Kathryn on the other end giving directions to the shop. The sound of her voice drifted near and far, as if electric windows were moving up and down, blocking and revealing the sound. Pain began to throb. Boiling wax dropped on her thigh and stirred, driving and twisting into her flesh.

She glanced to the side, and realised with a thick slick of fear that Esme was gone from the doorway. Hannah didn't know how long she had been sitting there, the gun still heavy in her hand.

'Kathryn? I need to move. I'm putting the phone down.'

'Hannah? Wait, stay where you—'

She shifted forwards in the chair and stood, all her weight on her left leg, the right now numb, pyjama pants slimy with blood. Leaning heavily on the wall, she pulled herself around the doorframe and raised the gun, pointing into the dimness of the kitchen.

At first, Hannah thought Esme had gone. Then she glimpsed a crumpled body lying on the far side of the table. Light reflected off a spreading pool of black on the floor. Hannah used the support of the counter and then the backs of the chairs to get around the table. Esme was motionless, the blood pooling under her head, a deep slice pumping blood from her throat. A black-stained shard of glass lay on her chest. Hannah dropped to one knee next to her and pressed her hand to the wound, applying as much pressure as she could.

Esme looked at Hannah, her eyes clear for the first time since Hannah had met her. Hannah tried to tighten her grip on Esme's throat but her hand slid in the blood.

She had never prayed in her life, but from somewhere Rachel's psalm rose in her throat. She looked into Esme's lucid eyes and the Afrikaans words came: 'Die Here is my herder; niks sal my ontbreek nie. Hy laat my neerlê in groen weivelde; na waters waar rus is, lei Hy my heen. Hy verkwik my siel.'

Esme sighed, and her face relaxed, beauty stealing over her.

Hannah continued, not understanding where the words were coming from. Not for a second letting go of Esme's throat.

Rushing footsteps on the deck stairs brought Kathryn and two policemen into the kitchen. The room flooded with light, and Hannah realised she was soaked in blood.

'Hannah? Hannah,' Kathryn was kneeling next to her, 'the ambulance is on its way.'

'I'm not letting go, Kathryn. She's lost so much blood already.'

As one policemen pulled rubber gloves onto his hands, Hannah could hear another man's voice, commanding but growing more distant: 'Escalate to advanced life support, we have two injuries. Yes. A gunshot and another with a stab wound to the neck.'

Kathryn appeared with towels and the policeman knelt next to Hannah. He quickly folded a towel into a pad and, as Hannah released Esme's neck, he pressed the towel to the wound. Hannah slumped back against the cupboard, exhaustion washing over her now.

'Where are you hurt, Hannah?' Kathryn's voice was urgent but so far away.

Hannah's hand fluttered to her leg and then dropped back to the floor as she felt herself retreat. She felt the weight of a heavy quilt being tucked around her torso and a pressure on her leg, so painful she could only gasp before she passed out.

The ambulance had to come from Bethlehem, and another twenty minutes passed before Kathryn heard the roar of vehicles approaching. The paramedics stormed into the kitchen and took over the scene. One paramedic dropped to his knees next to Esme, telling the cop to keep pressing on the towel. He shook Esme's shoulders firmly, and leant down to find a pulse in her groin. Sitting back up, he bent over her to place his ear just above her mouth. 'How long have you been here?' he asked the cop.

'Thirty minutes.'

'Was she conscious when you arrived?'

'No.'

Placing his hands on either side of Esme's head, he rolled her head from side to side and then he sat back on his heels. He looked across to Kathryn. 'Are you related to this woman?' When Kathryn shook her head, the paramedic said to the policeman, 'She's dead. She's your case now.'

Kathryn drew in a shuddering breath. She was still pressing a towel to Hannah's leg. Hannah was drifting in and out of consciousness. The second paramedic felt for a pulse in Hannah's foot and then cut Hannah's pyjama pants, peeling the blood-soaked fabric from her leg. He worked quickly, taking Kathryn's place and applying a dressing to an ugly wound on the inside of Hannah's thigh. He inserted intravenous lines in both arms and looked up to Kathryn with a small smile. 'You've done well. Keeping her warm and putting pressure on this wound was the best possible thing.'

'Will she be okay?'

'She needs a surgeon as soon as possible. Looks like the bullet went in and out. It's a miracle it missed the femoral artery, but we don't know what it's done to the bone or tissue. Will you ride with us?'

Kathryn nodded as they shifted Hannah onto a stretcher and wheeled her out to the ambulance. She got to her feet, her legs stinging with pins and needles. Grabbing her bag from her car, she climbed into the ambulance. As they pulled away, she fished her phone out of her jeans pocket and messaged Joseph and Alistair.

Within a minute, she had Alistair on the phone. She could hear he was running as he said, 'Kathryn? What the hell happened?'

'I don't know … Alistair, Esme shot Hannah. I'm with her now in the ambulance. We're on the way to Bethlehem.' She could hear his breath catch in a sob. 'Alistair, I think she's okay. But you need to come.'

'I'm coming.' He took a deep breath. 'Kathryn? I should have stayed with her.'

Kathryn's eyes filled with tears at the sound of his voice, broken. 'Alistair, this is not your fault. You hear me? She's going to have a helluva story to tell us when she wakes up.'

'I'm coming. I'll catch up with you.' She heard his car engine start up.

'Don't be a hero and kill yourself on the road, okay? Just get there.'

He cut the call and she sat for a bit, then messaged Douglas, who was at her house with the twins. A second later, he replied, *Things fine here. Glad you're safe. Love you, Kathryn.* Her eyes filled again. She breathed deeply, sat up straight, and pulled herself together.

She could fall apart when she got home.

CHAPTER TWENTY-FIVE

Hannah woke through a thick fog. Her mouth was desperately dry, and she felt a throbbing in her leg that was hot and uncomfortable. Turning her head on the pillow, she saw Alistair. He had pulled a chair up to the bed, and his head was sunk in his hands. She reached out, an IV line in her hand pulling as she did. He looked up quickly and grabbed her hand, holding it between his two palms.

'Hi …' She smiled, her lips feeling dry and stretched.

'Hi yourself. Are you sore? The doctor said to call if you need more pain meds.'

'A bit. Alistair?' He looked up from her hands to her tired smile.

Placing her hand against his cheek, he turned his mouth to kiss her palm. 'I thought … In that moment when I spoke to Kathryn, I thought I'd lost you.' His voice choked. 'It doesn't matter what you say or if you don't … I love you, Hannah.'

Hannah's eyes filled, and all she could do was cup her hand to his cheek. He loved her. Emotion welled up, but words wouldn't come.

Alistair sat up and dashed the tears from his eyes, composing himself. Her silence seemed to have brought him crashing back. 'I don't mean to put any pressure on you. I just wanted you to know.'

She nodded and cleared her throat. 'Is it morning?'

He checked his watch. 'It's five-thirty in the morning. You went into surgery at one am.'

'And you haven't slept all night?'

'Don't worry about me – I'll sleep later. I wanted to see you wake up. Make sure that you did wake up … It sounds silly now.'

'No.' She linked her fingers through his.

He nodded, though she could see his eyes fill with tears again.

The door swung open and Joseph raced into the room. He skidded to a halt next to her bed, breathing harshly. 'Hannah! What happened? I'm such an idiot! I got carried away last night … Shit! I only turned on my phone forty minutes ago and then I raced here. Hannah! I should have come back to your place last night. Shit! Look at you. I'm so sorry!'

Hannah smiled at the jumbled barrage. 'Josey, it's fine.'

Alistair rose and pushed Joseph into his chair. Joseph leant towards Hannah. 'Shit, Hannah, I stuffed up so badly last night.'

'You didn't know what was going to happen. It wasn't your fault.'

'Still, I was feeling sorry for myself, drank too much, and let myself be persuaded by one of the girls … I only looked at my phone when I was trying to sneak out of her room.' He rubbed his hands over his face. 'I can't believe I let it happen and then I didn't pick up Kathryn's message from the ambulance.'

Hannah smiled at her brilliant brother, now hungover, anxious and full of remorse. Leliehoek had changed him too. She had never thought she could like him so much, and she found herself reaching for his hand, the tight squeeze of his grip moving her with a sudden flood of affection.

Joseph looked across at Alistair. 'What happened? I only know what Kathryn messaged me last night.'

'I don't know much more. We were all waiting for Hannah to wake up.' Alistair looked quickly at Hannah. 'But you don't have to say anything until you're ready. Maybe now is not the time.'

'I'm really okay, I promise.' She looked over the edge of the bed and managed to find the bed control, pressing a button to raise herself to more of a sitting position. 'I don't know if Esme was outside while you were there, Alistair, but a few minutes after you left, she was at the door. She was …' Hannah paused, looking for words. 'She was out of it, seemed drugged, her eyes glassy and her face completely expressionless. She looked dead.' Hannah frowned and drew a deep breath.

'You really don't have to do this now,' said Alistair, concern edging his words.

'She smashed a pane of glass in the door and unlocked it. Didn't seem to feel the glass cut her hand. Then she started shooting at me. A shot hit me and my leg collapsed, but I got out the kitchen somehow and hid in the passage, and then when she came through the door, I hit her with that damned doorstop.' Hannah's voice caught and she turned to Alistair. 'And then it was like my vision cleared for the first time, and I saw this scared little girl curled on the floor. Then Kathryn called ...' Hannah frowned in confusion. 'Like she knew something had happened. And she told me to stay on the phone. When I eventually looked around, Esme had disappeared, so I went back into the kitchen to find her and she had ...' Hannah's breath came in a sob. 'She'd cut her own throat and there was so much blood ... everywhere. A great big pool of it on the floor. I tried to stop it. She was still alive and she looked at me. So lucid and sane. Like I could see the real Esme for the first time, and she was so beautiful ...' Hannah's brows drew down. 'I said a psalm over her.' She looked up at Alistair. 'I don't know any psalms. Then Kathryn arrived with other people and I don't remember much, just voices and lights and a strong sweet smell, like the scent of lilies.' She raised her hand to her nose to smell her skin. 'It's gone ...'

Hannah looked across to Joseph, whose eyes were brimming with tears. He cleared his throat and swiped a hand across his eyes before turning to Alistair. 'Did she have surgery?'

'The bullet fractured her femur, but missed the femoral artery. She was exceptionally lucky. She would have been dead on the floor before Kathryn got there if the bullet had been a centimetre to the side.' Alistair shook his head, fatigue casting a pall over his features. 'The surgeon put in a titanium nail. She's got a long road ahead of her, but he said she'll recover full use of her leg by the end.'

Joseph let out a sigh. 'Thank God for that.' And, as Hannah turned her head to him, he added, 'And I really mean thank God this time. Shit, Hannah, there is more than one little miracle in that story and, before right now, I didn't believe in them.'

Hannah looked at Alistair. 'When can I go home?' She frowned, thinking of her little house, smashed and blood-soaked. 'I'm not sure I want to go back to the house right away.'

'You aren't allowed out of here for a while. The surgeon wants to keep an eye on you for a bit still, and then you're coming to Goshen.' He raised his hand to stop her protest. 'When my mother hears what happened, she will insist on your staying with her – and good luck in saying no to her. I think it's for the best, unless you want to go back to your parents in Cape Town?' Hannah shook her head, and Alistair let go the breath he had held for a second.

'What about the shop?'

'Your house is being cleaned up today and then I'll ask Barbara to stand in until you're ready to go back to work. You don't have to worry about anything. Just rest, okay?'

Hannah nodded. 'Alistair? Esme died, didn't she?' Alistair, taking her hand, nodded, and Hannah's eyes filled with tears for the first time. 'She was so terribly, terribly sad. For all her damage, she really just loved her child.'

Alistair visibly struggled to hold himself together and just managed a nod. Hannah squeezed his fingers; it was over. After eight horribly slow years, Alistair's torture was finally done.

Hannah settled into the cottage on Goshen and spent large portions of her days on the veranda. Sarah fussed over her and Neil brought her treats from town. Alistair's dogs adopted her and usually lay around her chair, making it tricky for her to manoeuvre herself on her crutches. Sarah insisted on chasing them away, but Hannah liked having the dogs near, and would welcome them sneaking back onto the veranda when Sarah had gone. Neil, Sarah, and Joseph took turns driving her to Bethlehem for physiotherapy appointments, and slowly she began to put weight on her leg, though she kept her crutches for support.

Kathryn came to see her, bringing her pink boxes of pastries until Hannah eventually had to ask her to stop. 'I'm doing no exercise and getting fat on all of these. You're not helping me,' she had said laughing. So Kathryn shifted to bringing smoothies, and they sat most afternoons looking out at the view, sipping from their oversized paper cups. She had told Hannah about Matthew's lady at the door, and Hannah often thought about her – wondered who she was and why she should care about Hannah.

She saw Alistair every day too. He joined them for lunch and dinner, and Hannah looked forward to seeing him, though they were never alone.

One afternoon at the lunch table, Alistair laid down his knife and fork and looked at Neil.

'Dad, I've been thinking a lot about the tour thing, and I've got an idea. You know I visited old Mrs Venter at the Van Rooyen place?'

Neil nodded at him and wiped his mouth with a napkin.

'I've been worrying about her all alone there … I want to put in an offer to buy the farm. Her children are useless. I think they'd jump at the money.' He paused when Neil sat back in his chair in surprise, and then said quickly, 'I know it sounds crazy, but it's an amazing setting, an original house from the war and, if we could restore it, it would make a perfect guest house. We wouldn't have to build on Goshen, and we would be helping her out too. We could put her in a cottage on the property so she doesn't have to leave. There are stables we could restore—'

Neil had raised his hand to stop Alistair. 'You've put a lot of thought into this. Have you run the numbers?'

'Yes. I think we could recoup costs from stock sales and the business over the next five years.'

Hannah watched as Neil turned to Sarah. 'What do you think?'

Alistair's mother smiled at him. 'I think you are the most thoughtful, generous, clever man. I'm so proud of you.'

Alistair reached across the table, covering her hand and squeezing it. Hannah could see tears springing to Sarah's eyes, but she covered up by turning to Hannah and saying brightly, 'What do you think about it?'

'You can't ask me something so important … I'm just a visitor here, Sarah,' Hannah said, glancing around, and then hurriedly buttering a slice of bread. She caught Neil's open mouth, about to contradict her, stopped by a quick shake of Alistair's head. Her thoughts scrambled.

Was Alistair withdrawing from her? She had thought he was simply giving her space, but maybe with Esme's death he was able to move forward. Maybe now he could do that without her. An unfamiliar fear blossomed in her, and she pushed it down. Wasn't this what she wanted? To be able to leave Alistair without breaking him? The meal left her disturbed, and she found herself restless for the first time since she had come to stay.

Karl came to Goshen to see Hannah. He walked in, an old broken man. His life in tatters, he wept, holding tightly to her hand. 'I'm so sorry, Hannah. I'm so sorry for what she did.' Hanah had stroked his hand with her thumb as he cried. Esme had been buried next to Marilie in the Dutch Reformed churchyard. The whole community had come to the funeral, for Karl's sake. Hannah thought of a great rock about to topple down a hillside being propped up and held by others.

Karl's nephew from Pretoria was coming to help him on the farm, he told her. 'It's all I have left, that farm. The Wilderness house is on the market. I never want to see that place again. Now I feel like I need to sink into the farm, that it will heal me somehow, you know?' Hannah nodded and thought of Wolf returning to Silwerfontein and probably feeling the same way.

A few days later, Sarah came to Hannah's room to tell her that Karl had phoned to ask her to help clear out Esme's things. 'It seems a bit soon, don't you think?' When Hannah shrugged, she sighed. 'Poor man. I feel so desperately sorry for him. He's insisting he wants to put the house in order, get on with farm business. His nephew, Pieter, arrives next weekend. Karl wants the house ready for him. Do you want to come across with me today?'

Hannah was quiet for a moment, trying to untwist the emotions knotting in her. A chance to look through Gisela's things in the Ou Huis, but then, was she ready for whatever she'd find? Could she deal with finding nothing? Deal with Rachel's story ending just where it was? She met Sarah's searching gaze. 'I think I will. I need a change of scenery.'

They drove over in the afternoon and Lena showed them into the large house. It was strangely decorated. Sarah saw Hannah's reaction as they walked in. 'Most of this is original Silwerfontein furniture. It's taken as a given that no one is allowed to get rid of it, but Esme hated it. Shame, she tried so hard to modernise the house.'

Hard angles, glass and chrome tables, and beige-leather lounge suites jostled for place with the heavy antiques – a sad expression of Esme's struggle with her life here, Hannah thought.

They found the main bedroom. It looked as if it had been decorated for a teenager. Pink paint and a white shaggy carpet met a wall of white-and-gold cupboards overflowing with clothes. Many outfits still had their tags attached, and when they opened the doors, they were hit with Esme's overpowering musky perfume. Hannah gagged. 'I think I'll go outside, Sarah. Do you mind?'

Sarah had her back to Hannah. 'Go ahead. I won't be too long. This is a recce visit really. I'll have to bring some helpers back with me to tackle all of this. I think we should send it all to a Joburg charity shop. We can't have people recognising her stuff in Leliehoek or even Bethlehem.'

Hannah moved slowly down the passage to the back door. She could hear Lena putting a tea tray together. Once she was outside, the sun was gloriously warm. She breathed deeply and caught the scent of honeysuckle drifting on a slight breeze. As she turned towards it, she saw that she had come out near to the little house where Karl's mother had lived. Manoeuvring her crutches down the path, she was about to climb the single step when Karl came around the corner. Hannah felt a pang of guilt that she was there, but Karl approached her with a smile.

'I'm here with Sarah,' she said, stumbling a bit on a paving stone. Karl steadied her elbow and helped her up onto the veranda. He leant against the balustrade. 'I've always loved this house. My ouma lived here. Then my mother moved in when Esme and I married. His face shadowed for a moment, and he drew a breath. 'It must be the oldest building on the farm, did you know that? It was the original homestead. The British burnt it down during the Boer War and then the family rebuilt it after. These stone walls saw a lot. Ten or fifteen years later, they built the main house.' He glanced at her, leaning on her crutches. 'After all that's happened, are you still interested in my family?'

She nodded and he pulled the key from his pocket, unlocking the door and standing aside for Hannah to go in first.

The house smelt exactly the same as it had those months back, dusty and closed up, but it was warm, the sun stretching on the carpet. Karl crossed the small sitting room and knelt at the display cabinet, opening the bottom drawer where Hannah had found the family Bible. 'My mother spent years researching her family. You might be interested in her writing.' He pulled out a black cardboard-covered notebook and a lever arch file which was labelled, 'Tax'. 'She collected all sorts of things, wrote off to the archives and got copies of documents. It filled her time in those last years and I was glad of it. I just was never interested in hearing about it.' He sat back on his heels, passing the file and note-book to Hannah. 'I regret that now. I miss her still. She was such a strong woman. My dad died when I was only ten, and she farmed by herself until I took over. I wish I had half her courage.'

Hannah smiled at him sadly. 'Karl, I'm sorry for my part in Esme's breakdown. It seems like I tipped her over the edge, pushing with this stuff.'

Karl hauled himself to his feet. 'She and my mother didn't get on. Esme had a troubled childhood, and I always wondered if she was abused by her own mother. She couldn't bear anything to do with the past. She cut herself off from her family completely, wouldn't even talk about them. And then, when Marilie died, she just shattered. I couldn't put the pieces back together.' He sighed, his arms hanging at his sides, the grief heavy on him. Then he pulled his shoulders back, straightening to his full height. 'You take as long as you need with those,' he said, pointing to the bundle under Hannah's arm.

Hannah settled herself at the dining-room table, stretching her injured leg to the side. She opened the notebook first and began to read Gisela's account of the Badenhorsts. Gisela wrote beautifully. Her Afrikaans narrative was easy and compelling. Hannah followed the story of the Badenhorst trekboers who had settled on Silwerfontein in the 1830s, bringing their baby, Jakob.

Hannah read carefully, not wanting to miss a single detail about Jakob's son, Danie, taking over the farm and marrying Aletta. They had four children by the time the war broke out. Hannah retraced and read the sentence again. Four children? No, there were five. Wolf, Rachel, Paul, Kristina, and Lizzie. Maybe it was a simple misprint. She kept reading. The British arrived, burnt the farm to the ground, and the family split between the camp in Winburg and the men on commando. Both girls, their mother, and Oupa Jakob died in the camp.

Paul, their younger son, was killed on commando. He had been riding behind his father on the same horse, escaping a British regiment, when sniper-fire wounded him in the side. His father caught him before he fell, and rode with him to safety, only to discover his son was already dead. Paul had been eleven years old. Hannah paused her reading. Another child dead? Rachel's brother now? Was there no end to the despair of this family?

At the end of the war, Danie and his eldest son Wolf returned to Silwerfontein to find their lives devastated. They were the sole survivors of the war. They had no livestock, no crops, no home, and no money. Danie had some kind of breakdown. He moved to his sister in Pretoria, leaving Wolf to scrape an existence off the land. Eight years later, Wolf married a local girl, Corlie, and their son, Daniel, Gisela's father, was born later that year.

Hannah sat back in her chair, confused and upset. Why was there no mention of Rachel? Did she die in the Goshen camp? She turned another page of Gisela's neat handwriting and skimmed down the next page, titled 'Memories of Ouma and Oupa'. Gisela described her grandparents who had lived with them at the homestead. Gisela remembered a strict matriarch who had ruled the house, and gentle Oupa Wolf, who had lived with an irrevocable sadness in him which even a little girl could sense.

Hannah turned the page and drew in a sharp breath. Gisela had pasted in a photocopied page, and Hannah immediately recognised Rachel's writing. The neat, cramped words skittered across the page just like in the journal, but this was a letter. It was dated 3 June 1939.

My dearest Wolf,

Please accept my sincere condolences on the passing of
Corlie, though I will not grieve her loss myself. As you
know, there was much bitterness between us, but I do
grieve for your loss and that of your children. She was a
strong woman and, if nothing else, I respected her.

Is it not time for us to lay our past down and become
friends again? At least friends, if we cannot be anything
more. I have missed you, Wolf, more than I can possibly
express. I have missed your children and long to see
them again. May I come home?

There has been so much loss and grief in our lives,
too much for one person to bear, and so I wish to be by
your side. I wish to share the rest of our days, to come
full circle and be back on Silwerfontein like it was in the
beginning. There is no one else to remember the beginning but you and me. Do you speak to your children of
the girls? Of Kristina and Lizzie? Of Paul? Should they
be forgotten, Wolf? Please let me come home. Let us
put right what was broken.

Always yours,
Rachel

There was another photocopied letter pasted opposite. December 1939.

Dearest Wolf,

I have had no reply from you, and hope that the post
has mislaid my previous letter. The thought that you
would ignore me is too painful. All these years apart I
justified because Corlie could not tolerate my being on
the farm, but now she is gone. Wolf, why can we not be
together again?

I know people would frown at our living together in
the house but, Wolf, we have lived through so much.

Survived so much. We have so little time left. Let us be together again.

I know you do not like thinking about those days, but I have to say this. When I was in the camp, I prayed every night that you would come and fetch me. I cried out to the Lord to keep you alive for me. And He did. When the camp closed and the soldiers told us to leave, the inmates looked at them bewildered. Where would they go? To what? But not me. I knew exactly where I was going. I reached the farm that afternoon. That day will be etched in my memory forever. I walked up the avenue of oaks which had remained the same and I half-expected the house to be just like it was. Seeing the blackened shell, empty of everything and everyone I had loved, brought my grief back, hot and full of rage. Until I saw you, lying as if asleep on the grass. Your horse, not familiar to me, grazed nearby. When I knelt next to you, you opened hollow eyes to mine and you said, 'You are all I have left, Rachel Badenhorst.'

We scrounged for food, digging up what potatoes were left, and picking the last of the self-sown vegetables. We had survived the worst of times, and now we had to fight to make our lives count. For the sake of the ones we had lost.

And then came the days of work. The years of building and ploughing until we fell into our bed exhausted. And slowly, slowly, we brought life back to the land and we brought life back to the house and you loved me. We were partners.

I forgave you for Corlie. Being near you was enough. And then you let her send me away and I have forgiven you that too. I hear you have a grandchild. I long to see Daniel's girl. Please let us make it right, Wolf.

Yours,
Rachel

Hannah felt wrung out. Rachel had survived the camp. Wolf had not come for her after all but she, in her determination, had made her way back to the farm and to him. Why had Wolf's wife driven her away? Hannah frowned, skimming back through the letters. The tone was almost lover-like. Was that it? Could Wolf and Rachel have had some kind of affair? A relationship between brother and sister would explain the separation and even perhaps Rachel's excision from the family records, but somehow it didn't fit. There was something Hannah was missing.

She pulled the lever arch file closer and opened it. Gisela had filed documents in plastic sleeves, and Hannah began paging through them. There was the missing page from the family Bible, the births and deaths register. She ran her finger down the list and found no Rachel Badenhorst recorded. The puzzle just seemed to be spiralling tighter and tighter, making Hannah more confused, the more she found out.

As she flipped the sleeve in the file, she saw, at the back of the register, a photograph lying with its back facing out. Scrawled on the back, in fountain pen ink, was 'Rachel and me, 1909'. Hannah slid her hand into the sleeve and manoeuvred the photo out of the plastic. Turning it over, her heart seemed to stop in her chest. Wolf sat on the step of this very house, his hair bright and his face sporting a short beard. His eyes laughed at the camera, mouth caught in mid-speech. There was a lightness to him not present in his wedding portrait. Hannah's focus shifted to the other person in the picture. She stood with one hand curled around the pillar of the stoep and the other set on her hip. A tall, striking black woman, her hair braided in a coil on the crown of her head. She held herself proudly, a smile on her lips and her gaze direct. She was beautiful.

Suddenly things fell into place. Rachel was not a Boer woman. She was a black woman. The missing records, the separate camp, her tragic relationship with Wolf, doomed by the awful history of South Africa. It all made sense. Hannah's mind reeled with the implications. But Rachel wrote as if she had been a member of the Badenhorst family. How had that happened in those rough days when black people had been considered savages? No white family could have formally adopted a black child then.

Hannah went back to Gisela's notebook and found the place where she had stopped reading. The page overleaf was titled 'Tannie Rachel' in Gisela's neat handwriting.

My father told me stories about Tannie Rachel's baking. When he was a small boy, she lived in the Ou Huis and cooked for the family. She baked bread every morning and he would wake to that warm yeasty smell wafting through the house. She made special treats for him, ginger bread men with currants for eyes, syrupy koeksisters, and sweet biscuits which she cut into stars. He would sneak into the Ou Huis and sit with her while she told him stories about his father as a little boy on the farm. His mother didn't like it, so they kept these times secret.

My father said Tannie Rachel laughed a lot. She was not a maid or just a cook. He told me she was part of the family because she had come to Silwerfontein as a little girl, an inboekseling child. I did not know that word and it is only recently, when I started this research, that I found out.

In the middle of the nineteenth century, there was a Boer practice of taking African children into their households as servants, or perhaps more accurately, slaves. Most often, children were kidnapped and sold to Boer families, though it grew into a process of exchange with African tribes, particularly in the Northern Transvaal. Children were exchanged for goods and then taken away to the farms and registered as 'inboekseling' with the local magistrate. They were tied to the family until they came of age at twenty-five years old, though often, as the family was all they knew, they would remain in the household. The practice had largely stopped by the end of the 1800s, but in parts of the country, like the Zoutpansberg, it still occurred from time to time. From what I can gather, my great-great-grandfather, Jakob Badenhorst, brought home a little girl called Rachel. I do not know why or how he came by her, but she was registered in 1890 in the Bethlehem magistrate court as 'inboekseling'. Perhaps I am not cynical enough, but I would like to believe she was loved by the family. The fact that she stayed on the farm as an adult and lived in the Ou Huis rather than with the servants tells me she was different. The letters from Rachel to Wolf, which I found only recently, reveal so much more. I grieve for the pain this country has caused and endured. Love fractured and broken. People torn apart by fear. I only pray that South Africa's future is different, that it can move beyond the barriers which Wolf couldn't bring himself to confront.

My father took me to visit Tannie Rachel once. I was a little girl of perhaps seven or eight, but I remember it clearly. She lived in the township outside Bethlehem called Bohlokong. Her little block house was painted yellow with a bright blue door, and she had planted tubs of flowers under the windows. It stood out on a dry, colourless street. She was a tall woman, beautifully dressed with smart shoes and stockings, her hair coiled into a scarf that looked so elegant to me. She pulled my father into her arms and I remember him lifting her feet off the floor and she laughed. She must have been in her fifties then. She had made soetkoekies for me, just like she had for my father when he was little. They were cut into stars and hearts and flowers, and dusted with castor sugar. When we left, she handed my father a letter and, as we drove away, I looked back at her standing in the street. Tears were running down her cheeks, but she did not wipe them away. My father said that 'Bohlokong' means 'the Place of Pain'.

Hannah felt she was going to burst into tears. She turned the page. Pasted alongside was another photocopied letter. Rachel's writing had aged, and tremored a little. The letter was dated May 1942.

Dearest Wolf,

Life has been cruel to both of us, but we are alive and healthy. We have food in our bellies and houses to call our own. We have lived through worse times.

I am not going to beg; I know it must distress you and I wish you no further pain. I accept you will not fetch me home and, as much as that hurts me, I want you to be happy above all else. I have always loved you, and I now wrestle with the thought that you never did love me in return. Perhaps you did once. Perhaps that idyllic time on Silwerfontein was a desperate dream born of the horror of war. Perhaps the state of our country is too heavy for you; perhaps being together would cause untold grief for you and your family. Your silence keeps me in the dark, Wolf. I can but guess.

I will not write again but, Wolf, I am still here. You hold my heart and that is the way I want it to be.

Always yours,
Rachel

Below the letter, Gisela had added a post script:

I heard Rachel passed away in 1952, eight years after my grandfather, Wolf. They were never reconciled.

CHAPTER TWENTY-SIX

Hannah sat on her bed, her leg straight in front of her, and laptop balanced on her thighs. She was looking for cemeteries in Bohlokong. Maybe she could find Rachel's grave at last.

A soft knock had her looking up to see Alistair in the doorway.

'You have a visitor,' he said, standing back for Joseph to come into the room.

Joseph perched at the end of her bed. 'How are things? You feeling stronger?'

'Every day a little bit stronger, though I'm wiped out after today. I had an interesting afternoon, which we need to talk about.' She smiled at him, and gestured for Alistair to come in too. Alistair settled into a chair under the window and Hannah then noticed Joseph's face, a bit awkward, like he needed to tell her something but didn't know how to go about it. 'What is it, Jose?'

'You know we've been chugging away at the site while you've been' – he waved a hand over her leg – 'you know.' Hannah nodded, puzzled at his tone.

'Remember, up on the site, I told you there was something strange about the camp? That we weren't finding things we expected to find?' Hannah nodded again and he continued, 'The penny dropped for me today that perhaps we were coming to the site with one big wrong assumption, based on who we think Rachel is.'

Hannah let him continue, though she knew now where this was going.

'If we compile what we have found so far, the lack of ration tins, the lack of military buckles, shells, saddlery, the seeming absence of tent encampment, the absence of grave markers, and then the remains of a farming operation, we end up with a very different picture to the Boer camps we know about. Hannah …' He paused. 'This wasn't a Boer camp.'

'I know,' she said, 'it was a black camp.'

Joseph gaped at her. 'How did you know?'

'I was at Silwerfontein today and I found a picture of Rachel. She was a black woman.'

'But,' said Alistair, stunned, 'I thought you had seen a picture of her as a child with the Badenhorsts.'

'So did I, but then looking back I can see now that the child was Paul, the second son. They dressed their toddlers in white smocks, boys and girls. I saw a curly-haired blonde toddler in a white dress and assumed it was Rachel.'

Joseph was looking out the window, the back of his hand drumming on his thigh. 'This changes everything. The old concentration camp narrative is all about the terrible suffering of the Boers. And it is true – they did suffer horribly, but I don't think people understand how much worse it was in the black camps. They weren't fed or given shelter. They had to work or starve. They died like flies up there, Hannah. We're looking at a crazy-high mortality rate if our estimate is correct.'

'And it wasn't even their war,' said Alistair.

'I didn't even know there were black camps,' said Hannah. 'I just assumed that black people living locally would have been left to get on with their lives while the Boers and British fought it out. And instead they were herded into camps to work or die. It's just too ghastly …' She shook her head.

'I'm going to get on the phone,' said Joseph, standing. 'This opens a completely new angle on the project which some key people will be interested in. We might find a lot more funding heading our way.'

When he had gone, Hannah turned to look at Alistair, and found him watching her. 'Would you be able to drive me to Bethlehem tomorrow?'

'Do you have a physio appointment?'

'No, but there's something I really want to do.'

'Of course,' he said, getting to his feet and heading for the door, 'I'll come by around nine.'

'Thanks ... Alistair?' He turned and she changed her mind, shaking her head. 'Never mind, we can talk tomorrow.'

The following day, Alistair helped her into the front of his Toyota Hilux and put her crutches in the back. He drove as carefully as he could until she smiled at him. 'I'm fine, Alistair. You don't have to drive at forty the whole way there.'

She had printed a map of Bohlokong, which she pulled from her bag as they approached Bethlehem. She had marked where the cemetery should be and she directed Alistair away from the town centre towards the sprawling township. Beyond the rows of small houses, grassland stretched away to the horizon with great electricity pylons standing like giants against the blue sky. A short distance from the road, she could see gravestones peering out of the grass. A dirt track wound off the road, and Alistair followed it, driving as carefully as he could over the bumpy tussocks of grass. He pulled to a stop close to the cemetery and helped Hannah out the car, holding her steady while she slid her arms into the crutches.

They made their way slowly through the cemetery, stopping to read what they could on the markers, though many had been weathered smooth. At the far end, they found it. A slab of stone which had been hewn into a smooth square and engraved with her name.

> Rachel Badenhorst,
> Died 10 August 1952.
> At peace with Him who loves her.

Hannah reached into her bag and drew out a copy of the photo she had found in the Ou Huis. She bent and placed it at the foot of the stone, tucking it under a pebble to secure it. Rachel and Wolf. He had come to her at last. A breeze picked up a sigh in the grass.

'He wasn't strong enough,' Hannah said to Alistair, who was standing a few feet away, watching her. 'Wolf couldn't bring himself to fetch her, to choose her, even though she waited for him. Rachel was his one big chance at happiness and he missed it.' She turned towards Alistair and he reached out a hand to steady her. 'Alistair, I don't want to be Wolf in the story. I want to be strong and courageous and sure of what I want. I want to be like her, not him. She had every possible hardship thrown at her, and still she hung on to life, pursued love with a tenacity that shames me.'

Hannah stepped close to him and looked up into his face, which was intent on her, his eyes fearful. 'That's not all.' Her eyes filled and tears burnt the back of her throat. 'I didn't realise until I came to Leliehoek that I have always felt alone. I didn't miss what I didn't know.' She wrestled for words. 'People here ... they ... you ... really see me. You tell me that I'm beautiful. That I can do anything. That you love me. Nobody has ever said that to me before, not even my parents.' She drew a breath, wiping her eyes. 'It sounds ridiculous but it's the truth. Rachel was the same. Nobody told her, even though she was this amazing, strong, resilient, beautiful woman. Alistair, I don't want to turn my back on the only place, the only person who tells me he loves me.' She took his hands in hers, heard a sob catch in his throat, and she could feel the shake in his hands.

'But, Hannah ... do you love me?'

She reached up a hand to stroke his cheek.

He took a breath and continued, 'You see, I did that before ... I always felt like I was loving the back of Marilie. That she never had her face turned to me. I was forever trying to catch her attention from her horses, her love from them ... but I couldn't. Do you understand? I can't do that again.'

'Shh.' She put a finger to his scarred lips. 'You ... the bravest, most beautiful man I have ever met. You ... I love that you care about an old lady on a farm. I love that you love your dogs. I love that you are so proud of your parents. I love that you want to shield your sisters. I love that you want to restore your land. I love that your hair sticks up in the front and you don't notice. I love that your truck is a mess. I love that you are so careful with me, but still turn my knees to jelly when you kiss me ... Alistair, should I go on? I love you. I love you. I love you—'

Alistair pulled her tightly to him. 'Hannah.' His voice choked into her neck. Her crutches collapsed into the grass, and he buried his face in her hair, his body shaking as he wept. Hannah held him tightly, her hands rubbing circles of comfort on his back as she lifted her face into the sun and closed her eyes. Behind them, the breeze pulled at the sepia photograph, tugging. It twitched under its pebble but remained lodged there.

On Goshen, Kobie straightened up from the water trough. The float repair was holding. He pushed his hands into the small of his back and arched, feeling the stiffness in his spine loosen slightly. The sudden sound of a hollow step on the ground jumped his heart up a pace. His skin shivered with the awareness that he was being watched. He spun around. On the edge of the plateau, for the first time, the large male blesbok had moved over the ridge. It watched him and then snorted a warning. Kobie held his hand to his chest, willing his heart to slow. He began to back away slowly towards the gate.

The afternoon light stretched the shadow of the wind pump long across the plateau. The site was quiet. The herd picked their way through Joseph's equipment and mounds of earth until they reached the reservoir. The big male bent his head to drink there. The rest of the herd gathered around the reservoir, nibbling at the clumps of grass and taking their turns to drink. The air was sweet with the scent of summer and, when the gum trees picked up their rattle in the evening breeze, it was soft and peaceful.

Author's Note

This novel is based partly in the time of the South African War, fought between October 1899 and May 1902. Apart from a few historical figures mentioned in the text, all characters are fictional and bear no resemblance to any person living or dead. My intention while writing was to create people and places that are not real, but could have been. There was no camp called Goshen, nor is there a town called Leliehoek, though people might find some similarities to Clarens in the Free State. In fact, Leliehoek is the name of one of the original farms where the town of Clarens came to be founded. Wanting some freedom to build up a town to my liking, I confess to borrowing the name. The Goshen camp is based on archaeological evidence found at other sites across South Africa, some only recently excavated. The extent of camps like Goshen, the horrific treatment of black inmates, and the resultant loss of life haven't even begun to be realised. They are stories blatantly missing from our understanding of the South African War.

There are no written accounts by women like Rachel, but plenty of photographs documenting their presence in various camps. It might be unlikely that a girl like Rachel be as well educated as she was, but not impossible, as many Boer households were highly literate.

The inboekseling system is a part of South African history not widely known. The slave trade finally came to an official end in 1838 after a mandatory four-year period of 'apprenticeship' to acclimatise slaves to being free. It is clear that slavery or 'apprenticeship' practices continued beyond this date, because in 1851 the British government sent commissioners to negotiate with the Voortrekkers the terms by which they could govern themselves. Part of the provisions of this Sand River Convention agreement was that the Voortrekkers desist from their inboek-seling practice. Nevertheless, there are records of magistrates registering children as 'apprenticed' to households beyond this date.

Acknowledgements

Thank you so much to everyone at Penguin Random House South Africa for publishing this novel, but especially to Fourie Botha and Beth Lindop for taking a risk on this first-time author, for your gentle accommodations and encouragement. To Claire Strombeck, editor whizz, for making double quick time and turning a manuscript into a real novel. Your humour and warm engagement with the text gave me a (usually impossible) insight into a reader's thoughts. To Dr Garth Benneyworth who, in the early days of this story, allowed me a fascinating peek into concentration-camp archaeology, giving me thoughtful answers to foolish questions and actually making my plot credible. To Prof. Fransjohan Pretorius for generously answering a series of emails about life on commando. To David and Heather Doull, for a grippingly macabre discussion over lunch about paramedic protocol and fatal injuries. To my hosts at De Molen Farm near Clarens, for telling me stories of the valley, showing me the site of the old house destroyed by the British, and letting me find pieces of broken, charred china in the sheep pen. Nothing could have inspired me more to finish my manuscript than your cottage. To Bridget Latter, Lin Visser, and Phil Murray, my readers – your willingness to read and give honest feedback is testament to a long friendship. To Diane Stewart, thank you for walking beside me through the first two years of writing, for your encouragement and wisdom in a foreign world. To my family, who have shown all the excitement and pride about this process that I've been too scared to feel. And to Peter, my rock, who encouraged me to give myself permission to dream and then chase those dreams.

Suggested Reading

Boje, J & Pretorius, F. 'Black Resistance in the Orange Free State During the Anglo–Boer War.' *Historia* 58.1 (2013): 1–17.

Delius, P. *The Land Belongs to Us: The Pedi Polity, the Boers and the British in the Nineteenth Century.* Berkeley: UC Press, 1984.

Grobler, JEH. *The War Reporter. The Anglo–Boer War Through the Eyes of the Burghers.* Cape Town: Jonathan Ball Publishers, 2004.

Hall, D. *The Hall Handbook of the Anglo–Boer War.* Pietermaritzburg: University of Natal Press, 1999.

Kinsey, HW. 'The Brandwater Basin and Golden Gate Surrenders, 1900.' *Military History Journal* 11.3/4 (1999).

Pakenham, T. *The Boer War.* London: Futura, 1982.

Pretorius, F. *Life on Commando During the Anglo–Boer War 1899–1902.* Cape Town: Human & Rousseau, 1999.

Nasson, B. *The War for South Africa.* Cape Town: Tafelberg, 2010.

Nasson, B & Grundlingh, A. (eds). *The War at Home.* Cape Town: Tafelberg, 2013.

Roberts, B. *Those Bloody Women. Three Heroines of the Boer War.* London: John Murray Publishers, 1991.

Van Heyningen, E. *The Concentration Camps of the Anglo–Boer War.* Johannesburg: Jacana, 2013.

Von der Hyde, N. *Field Guide to the Battlefields of South Africa.* Cape Town: Random House Struik, 2013.